A SNOWY SEASIDE CHRISTMAS

ELIZA J SCOTT

Storm
PUBLISHING

This is a work of fiction. Names, characters, businesses, places, events and incidents are either the products of the author's imagination or used in a fictitious manner. Any resemblance to actual persons, living or dead, or actual events is purely coincidental.

Copyright © Eliza J Scott, 2025

The moral right of the author has been asserted.

All rights reserved. No part of this book may be reproduced or used in any manner without the prior written permission of the copyright owner. This prohibition includes, but is not limited to, any reproduction or use for the purpose of training artificial intelligence technologies or systems.

To request permissions, contact the publisher at rights@stormpublishing.co

Ebook ISBN: 978-1-83700-029-6
Paperback ISBN: 978-1-83700-030-2

Cover design: Rose Cooper
Cover images: Shutterstock

Published by Storm Publishing.
For further information, visit:
www.stormpublishing.co

ALSO BY ELIZA J SCOTT

Welcome to Micklewick Bay Series
The Little Bookshop by the Sea
Summer Days at Clifftop Cottage
Finding Love in Micklewick Bay
Christmas at the Little Bookshop by the Sea
Cupcakes and Kisses in Micklewick Bay
A Wedding at the Little Bookshop by the Sea

Life on the Moors Series
The Letter – Kitty's Story
The Talisman – Molly's Story
The Secret – Violet's Story
A Christmas Kiss
A Christmas Wedding at the Castle
A Cosy Countryside Christmas
Sunny Skies and Summer Kisses
A Cosy Christmas with the Village Vet

Heartshaped Series
Tell That to My Heart

*To my little brother. Thank you for your wise words.
Much love, big sis xxx*

ONE
SUNDAY 30TH NOVEMBER

Lark crunched her way over the newly fallen snow that covered the ancient, cobbled pathways of Old Micklewick, her head bowed against the swirling snowflakes as she clutched tightly onto the old leather suitcase. Her cheeks and nose were pinched red from the cold, her fingers and toes numb. The scent of woodsmoke, whipped from the squat chimney pots, permeated the air, mingling with the ever-present tang of seaweed.

'Brr!' she exclaimed, as a bone-chilling wind swept in from the North Sea and stole its way around the old part of town, biting mercilessly at any exposed bits of skin. Though she was wrapped up well in her heavy wool coat and brightly coloured tracker hat and scarf, the wind still managed to sneak its way in. It didn't help that she was already shivering before they'd even left Crayke's Cottage.

Tucked away in Micklemackle Yard, the place had stood unoccupied for years, its walls and furnishings absorbing winter's icy chill. The fridge-like cold had seeped into her bones during the time she'd been there, and at this very minute she couldn't imagine ever feeling warm again.

Walking alongside her was Nate, his chin tucked into his scarf, eyes scrunched against the driving snow. He'd been at the cottage, too, and was carrying the larger of the two old leather suitcases they'd found that afternoon. Despite the inclement weather, he still strode along with his familiar, easy lope.

Dusk had fallen early in Micklewick Bay on the North Yorkshire Coast thanks to the dark, brooding clouds that had gathered over the quaint Victorian seaside town. It was what had forced them to leave the cottage when they did, the electricity supply being switched off years ago. The batteries in their torches had started to fade, making moving around the place treacherous, so they'd called it a day. Lark hadn't been sorry about that, and not just because of the permeating cold.

Now, the vintage-style streetlamps cast their golden glow on the newly fallen carpet of snow, while fairy lights from the Christmas trees in the windows of the higgledy-piggledy cottages that huddled together limpet-like on the steep cliffside twinkled cheerfully. If it hadn't been so bitterly cold, Lark would have taken delight in the jolly, festive atmosphere, but right now her focus was on getting home and into the warm as quickly as possible.

They continued on their way, hurrying past the entrance to Blatherin Alley, as much as the slippery, snow-covered pathways would allow, rounding the corner onto Gabblewick Gate where they walked head-on into a ferocious gust of wind. It hurled yet more snow at them, making Lark's pale green eyes water. She gasped, blinking quickly. 'Argh! Could it get any more Arctic?'

'Aye, the weather sure has taken a turn for the worse,' said Nate, swiping a gloved hand over his face, his dark fringe that peered from beneath his woollen beanie hat now soaked.

The freezing temperature and wind-chill factor made the distance from Crayke's Cottage, where they'd spent the last few hours, seem twice as long. Lark couldn't wait to get back to Seashell Cottage, glad she'd had the foresight to light the log burner before she left. It was much more efficient than the decrepit combi-boiler that had previously fuelled the central heating Elfie, her godmother – whose house it actually was – had installed years earlier, and the compact cottage was now toasty warm. Lark loved her little home and regularly felt the word "cosy" could've been coined for it.

They eventually came to a halt before the characterful cottage painted a soft shade of sugared-almond pink. Lark had swapped the wreath of seashells that usually adorned the old oak door for an oversized festive version. A window box, jam-packed with winter-flowering plants, sat beneath a wonky sash window to the left of the door. Like the wreath, it was threaded with fairy lights.

'Oh, thank goodness we're here! I can't wait to get out of these icy temperatures,' she said through chattering teeth, her frozen fingers fumbling to push the key into the lock. She couldn't recall the last time she'd felt so glad to see her home.

'Aye, me too,' agreed Nate. 'That wind's what I'd call savage.'

The door, which had swollen in the damp weather, was reluctant to open, but after giving it a hefty nudge with her shoulder, Lark stumbled into the tiny vestibule, the warm air instantly wrapping itself around her along with the fragrance of the lavender and rose geranium aromatherapy oils; a scent which anyone who knew her would say was unmistakably Lark Harker. Nate stepped in after her, quickly closing the door on the freezing night air that seemed eager to push its way in like an unwelcome guest.

Once they'd divested themselves of their snowy coats and boots – which wasn't easy in such a confined space and with the two suitcases to negotiate – the pair headed into the small living room. Lark flicked on the light, pleased to see the stove was still glowing and chucking out a welcoming warmth. Luna, her fluffy grey and white cat, leapt down from one of the armchairs leaving a gentle dip in the squishy cushion, and sauntered over, purring as she rubbed herself against Lark's legs. The cat pulled back in an instant as she came into contact with the cold air that still clung to her owner's thick, patchwork trousers in shades of purple and blue, making Lark chuckle.

'Hello there, Luna.' She bent to give her pet a scratch between her ears, the metal bangles she always wore jangling around the cuff of her purple woolly jumper, her blonde mermaid plait falling over her shoulder. 'Ooh, you're lovely and toasty.' Beneath her chilly fingers, Luna's soft fur felt blissfully warm from the heat of the stove.

Apparently unimpressed, the feline slinked her way back to the seat where she made herself comfortable once more, watching them with knowing, soft green eyes.

'By, it's nice and warm in here,' said Nate, rubbing his hands together. 'You're in the best place there, Luna.'

'She is,' Lark said with a laugh. Luna had only resided at Seashell Cottage for a couple of months, but she'd settled so quickly anyone would think she'd lived there for years. Lark's friends suggested it must be something to do with the calm atmosphere of the place, since whenever any of them visited Seashell Cottage they'd instantly succumbed to the wave of relaxation that washed over them.

Lark had returned home from work one evening early last October to find the cat on the doorstep, looking up at her with enquiring eyes, mewing gently. It was as if she'd been waiting for her. On opening the door, the cat had sauntered in and proceeded to give the downstairs rooms of the cottage a thorough appraisal which had tickled Lark. Apparently satisfied that the place passed muster, she'd curled up on the armchair and made herself at home. She'd been a permanent fixture at Seashell Cottage since that day, with Lark naming her Luna.

A week after Luna had turned up, and concerned that such an adorable creature was more than likely a much-loved pet whose owner would be frantic with worry as to her whereabouts, Lark asked around Old Micklewick, placing notices on lampposts, as well as in shop windows and on the town's noticeboard, enquiring if anyone had lost a cat. But, despite her efforts, no one had come forward to claim her houseguest. Lark had found herself secretly hoping no one would; she'd grown fond of Luna's gentle presence, not to mention the warm welcome she received as soon as she stepped through the door, the cat weaving through her legs, purring happily, as pleased to see Lark as she was to see her.

Luna was shamelessly fond of her creature comforts and regularly bagged herself the toastiest spot in the armchair by the inglenook fireplace, just as she had that evening. 'Luna and I are both pleased you encouraged me to get the wood burner fitted,' Lark said as she headed to the window where a stout Christmas tree sat, its bushy boughs bedecked with a multitude of colourful baubles. She pushed a plug into the nearby socket and in an instant, the Christmas tree was aglow, its twinkling fairy lights adding to the cosiness of the room with its low beamed ceiling and uneven chunky walls. 'I'd say it's the best investment that's been made on the cottage in a long time; works well alongside the new combi-boiler.'

'Glad you think so.' Nate beamed at her, his kind brown eyes crinkling at the corners. At over six feet tall, he seemed even taller in the snug proportions of the living room. 'Shall I grab the suitcases? Might be a good idea to put them by the wood burner for a bit.'

'Good point, they could do with drying off,' she said, flicking her plait over her shoulder. Though she was excited to find out what was inside the old pieces of luggage, Lark preferred to wait until she was alone. That way she could take her time to examine the contents and give herself the chance to get a proper feel for them, just as she did when considering items to sell in Lark's Vintage Bazaar, her shop that sold a variety of vintage clothing and accessories in the town's Victoria Square. Being highly sensitive to not only atmospheres, but also the energy of people, places and even inanimate things, meant Lark could detect the slightest trace of negativity. Anything that triggered a feeling of unease, was instantly discarded; there was no way such an item would find its way into her shop for her to pass its negative energy onto someone else.

'Righto.' Suitcases in hand, Nate skirted around the small sofa and armchair and placed them either side of the hearth. While he was there, he threw a log onto the stove which immediately sprang to life, flames dancing merrily behind the glass.

The compact room looked achingly cosy. A squishy sofa covered in a vintage quilt sat in front of the wood burner. It was flanked by a couple of mismatched armchairs set with plump, colourful cushions. Underfoot was a sisal carpet that had seen slightly better days, the worst of its wear and tear hidden beneath strategically placed Persian rugs, while a basket filled with logs sat to the right of the fireplace. An old Victorian pine sideboard that belonged to her godmother, and had come with the cottage, was set against the wall on the right. Its surface was arranged with an array of Lark's treasures, including a selection of books on crystal healing and aromatherapy that were wedged together by a couple of angel wing bookends carved from rose quartz. It was a favourite crystal of hers thanks to its soothing, calming qualities, amongst many others. In fact, she had several pieces of rose quartz dotted about her home and always kept a piece in a pocket or about her person on a daily basis.

'You're welcome to stay for your tea, if you fancy.' Lark thought it was the least she could do after Nate had generously said she could have the suitcases and their contents from the house clearance. Plus, it would give him a proper chance to dry off and thaw out after their icy stint at Crayke's Cottage before he had to head off home. 'I've got some homemade soup ready to heat up – it's tomato – and there's a chunky loaf of basil bread from the deli to go with it.'

'Mmm. Can't think of owt better for a snowy, winter's evening. And since your tomato soup's a favourite of mine, I'd love to, thanks.' He grinned at her, ducking to avoid the low beams as he stood up straight.

'Fab, you can give me a hand getting it ready, if you like? Maybe slice the bread.'

'Aye, happy to.'

Lark could feel the familiar warmth of his presence behind her as he followed her through to the kitchen. He was easy company; good to be around and someone who brought an element of contentedness to her life, almost like a favourite snuggly jumper.

She regularly found herself thinking how glad she was he'd chosen to settle in Micklewick Bay after moving to the town from the small village of Beckinthwaite on the North Yorkshire Moors where he'd grown up.

Lark had first encountered Nate some four or five years ago. She'd popped into his newly opened upcycling shop on Endeavour Road to enquire about a vintage dressing table in the window that had caught her eye. She'd been looking for something to display the range of homemade aromatherapy products she sold in Lark's Vintage Bazaar and thought it would do perfectly. She and Nate had hit it off straightaway, both thrilled to have found someone who shared their love of all things vintage, chatting away with great enthusiasm. And though an unmistakable frisson of attraction had sparked between them, and their friendship had deepened over the years, their relationship had never developed into anything more, much to the chagrin of her group of best friends.

That aside, Lark would even go as far as to say she'd come to value Nate's friendship and opinion as much as she did the four women she'd known since childhood. They regularly teased her for keeping him in the "friend zone". None of them could understand why her relationship with Nate hadn't blossomed romantically, especially given how well suited they appeared to be, sharing a laid-back, easy-going nature and happy outlook on life. Lark repeatedly told them – with much eye rolling on their part – that she didn't want to lose his friendship if things didn't work out. On top of that, at just approaching twenty-eight, making him seven years her junior, she also said she considered Nate too young for her. She chose to ignore her friends' playful comments declaring she'd make a fabulous "cougar", letting them fall on stony ground as she smiled serenely. But, in truth, these weren't the only reasons. There was something else holding her back. Something she'd never shared with anyone. Something she preferred to keep to herself.

TWO

Lark was glad to have finally warmed through, the feeling returning to her fingertips as she pulled off a chunk of bread and dipped it into her soup, festive folk music playing softly in the background. 'So, what d'you know of Crayke's Cottage?' She popped the bread into her mouth, glancing across at Nate who was sitting opposite her at the table in her compact kitchen. The sunny yellow walls of the room were a stark contrast to the hailstones that were currently drumming hard at the windows where a small festive arrangement twinkled as if oblivious to the wintry weather raging behind it.

It had been far too cold at the uninhabited cottage to have much of a conversation; they'd just been focused on the task at hand, intent on getting done as quickly as possible and heading back to Lark's home.

Of course, she'd always been aware of Crayke's Cottage, just as she had the other cottages that snuggled together in the various yards and winding alleyways in the old part of town, but she hadn't paid it much attention before now. And she couldn't remember the last time she'd needed to venture to that particular part of Old Micklewick. Being tucked away in the town's historic Micklemackle Yard meant you had to go out of your way to get to the property, and those who had reason to be there simply walked by en route to one of the inhabited cottages in the yard. Crayke's Cottage stood silently in the shadows, barely warranting a second glance. Lark hoped old Mr Thurston – the now joint owner of the property, and who'd tasked Nate with removing the contents – had shared some juicy snippets of information about its past.

'Hmm.' Nate looked thoughtful as he chewed. It was only recently that Mr Thurston had approached him about emptying the cottage of its contents which meant he hadn't had the chance to share much more than scant details with her. But now, after seeing it for herself, Lark couldn't shake the delicious feeling of intrigue that had struck her as soon as she'd turned into the ancient yard paved with centuries-old uneven cobbles. Her finely tuned senses had heightened further once she'd arrived at the cottage's creaky old door.

He swallowed his mouthful. 'I doubt I know much more than you, really. I mean, I was aware that no one seemed to know who owned it, and that it had been unoccupied for donkey's years.'

'As the dusty spiders' webs proved! I reckon my hair's still full of them.' Though Lark giggled, she hadn't liked to give it much thought at the time. The cottage had been festooned with the lacy arachnid creations, thick with dust, and she'd imagined huge spiders lowering themselves onto her head every time she ventured into a room. She couldn't believe she hadn't thought to leave her hat on – it wasn't as if the place hadn't been cold enough to warrant it.

Nate narrowed his eyes, looking intently at the top of her head. 'Aye, now you come to mention it...'

Lark's stomach lurched. 'What?'

'I'm sure I just saw one running over the top of your head. You know, the massive sort with the thick, hairy legs. Here, let me get it for y...' He went to reach across the table, struggling to bite down on a smile.

'Warghh! Please tell me you're joking.' She pushed her chair back, hurriedly swiping her hands over her hair, Nate's shoulders shaking with mirth. 'Quick! Put a glass over it! Don't kill it, whatever you do!'

'What are you like? "Put a glass over it",' he said, through his guffaws. 'I'm just joshing, there's no spider.'

'Not funny!' She shot him a mock-stern look, running her hands over her hair one last time. Lark didn't mind creepy-crawlies but she'd rather not have them running amok all over her.

'I promise you, we left all the spiders and the dust behind at Crayke's Cottage.'

'Can't say I'm sorry to hear that.' She gave an exaggerated shudder, tucking her chair back in, her heart rate slowly returning to normal.

'To be honest, it was that cold there, I'm surprised they hadn't packed their bags and left,' he said. 'Rodents an' all.'

Lark groaned. 'Ugh! Can we please change the subject from spiders and rodents before you put me off my soup? Let's get back onto what Mr Thurston told you about Crayke's Cottage, that's far more palatable.'

'Aye, well, he didn't say much other than it had stood empty for ages which, from what we saw today, was pretty obvious. The place looked like it had been frozen in time. Don't know about you, but I thought it felt more like walking into a museum exhibition than a home.'

'Mm.' Lark nodded. 'That'd crossed my mind, too.'

The cottage was brimming with character and had many of its original features intact, from the age-worn Yorkshire flagstone floor to the dark oak beams. The date carved into the sandstone lintel above the low front door said 1725, with the initials JC and AC below. They matched those in the door of the spice cupboard to the left of the inglenook fireplace. Even the furniture seemed centuries old, amongst which was a settle by the fire, an old carved oak coffer and a dark wood dresser, the shelves of which had been lined with pewter plates. And though Seashell Cottage was of a similar age and just as characterful, it couldn't have been more different. Stepping into Lark's home, visitors regularly declared that they felt instantly at ease. It was as if the happy atmosphere wrapped its arms around them, welcoming them in. The cottage was bright and cheerful, vintage items mixed with new, showcasing her eclectic taste perfectly. Evidence of her "boho, hippy vibe", as her friends referred to it, was everywhere from the brightly coloured soft furnishings to the embroidered wall hangings to the carved Buddha head on the shelf in the living room. There, in the kitchen was a classic example of her style, in the wooden dresser she'd picked up from Nate's shop and painted a bright sky blue. The shelves that she'd trimmed with fairy lights were crammed with a variety of mismatched knick-knacks, while the small window that looked out onto her tiny back yard was hung with a pair of patchwork curtains she'd made herself. It filled Lark with happiness that she was regularly told there was something about her home that made visitors not want to leave. Nate being one of them.

'Spiders and rodents aside, I thought it was fascinating,' said Lark. 'But did Mr Thurston hint at its past, or give any clues as to why the cottage had been left like that?' She loved Nate to bits but his habit of going around the houses when explaining or asking about something meant he occasionally needed a gentle nudge to get back on track, particularly when she was trying to get to the bottom of something, the history of Crayke's Cottage being a prime example!

He set his spoon down in the bowl, looking thoughtful once more. 'Well, I'd heard of it, knew it had a smuggling connection like a lot of the houses round here, but I'd never given it much thought till old Mr Thurston popped into my workshop on Friday morning. He told me the property had belonged to his uncle who'd died. Apparently, this uncle had never married or had children of his own, so had left everything to Mr Thurston and his brother who lives down south somewhere. He never mentioned owt about its history though. To be honest, he didn't seem that interested. Seemed more bothered about getting it emptied before Christmas so they could put it on the market in the New Year.'

'Wow, if that was me, I'd be itching to find out as much as I could about its past, especially with all the rumours attached to it.' In truth, as soon as they'd set foot in the dusty house, Lark had been bombarded with voices from the past, whipping around her, all scrabbling to be heard. The place was thrumming with energy, alive with spirits all vying for her attention, desperate to share their decades'-worth of pent-up frustration. There'd been such a cacophony, it had been impossible for her to home in on a single voice.

'Aye, me too.' Nate nodded. 'Plus, I'd be wanting to go through all the cupboards and sideboards, see if there was owt of interest in there before I even considered selling anything. There could be valuable heirlooms tucked away, but going from what we saw today, it looks like he hasn't so much as opened a drawer. I did mention if I found owt valuable, I'd be sure to pass it on to him, but you should've seen the way he shook his head and told me I could keep everything. It was as if I'd said summat unpalatable.'

'Hmm. That does seem odd.' Lark could understand such a stance if there'd been any sinister rumours attached to the property, like the one further up the coast in Skelby-by-the-Sea where a brutal murder was supposed to have taken place in the seventeenth century. Rumours of poltergeist activity meant no one had lived there for long, and the cottage had been boarded up for years, its roof tiles gradually sliding off and leaving the building open to the elements. But Lark couldn't recall hearing anything of the sort about Crayke's Cottage.

A small frown drew Nate's eyebrows together. 'Now I come to think of it, he did a lot of muttering under his breath whenever I asked him about the place, and I'd swear he said summat about the house being cursed with bad luck and how it'd be a relief when they were shot of it. When I asked him what he meant, he just shook his head and said to ignore him, that it was nothing.'

'Really?' Lark's eyes widened, as her heart gave a little leap, her interest well and truly piqued. *Why didn't you mention this before, Nate?* She let his words percolate around her mind for a few moments. Being highly sensitive to the atmosphere buildings generated, she hadn't detected any overly unpleasant vibes while she'd been at Crayke's Cottage, more a sense of intrigue and adventure, that the walls were groaning with past memories. Granted, she wasn't sure she'd fancy spending much time there on her own, especially at night, but she assumed that was probably more to do with the giant spiders or owners of the scurrying, clawed feet that lurked in the dark shadows, all of which were in plentiful supply there.

'Aye. I tried to subtly bring it up in conversation a couple of times after that, but he was having none of it. Just waved it off, saying summat about resurrecting things from the past and that there was no need to trouble me with it.'

'Blimey, I wonder what he could've meant. I've heard people talk of it being haunted, but I've never heard anyone mention it being cursed with bad luck before.'

'Well, whatever it was, it clearly bothered him a fair bit. Made me wonder if it's why no one's lived there for so long.' Nate dipped his spoon into his soup. 'Maybe we'll find something stashed away in one of the drawers or cupboards that'll give us a clue as to what it could be.'

'Ooh, let's hope so.' Lark's thoughts went back to the old leather suitcases currently drying by the wood burner; she couldn't wait to see what the contents would reveal. 'I wonder if there's any truth in the stories about the cottage having smuggling connections and a secret tunnel to The Jolly Sailors.'

'If rumours are to be believed, *every* house in Old Micklewick has a secret tunnel leading to the Jolly,' he chuckled. 'Mind, after what we've seen this afternoon, I wouldn't be surprised if it had a tunnel leading somewhere; I've heard there's a cottage or two round here that have tunnels leading to the cave on Contraband Cove yon side of Thorncliffe, where smugglers hid goods before they were distributed.'

'Yeah, I'd heard that, too.'

Old Micklewick abounded with swashbuckling tales of pirates and smuggling that had been particularly prevalent there during the seventeen-hundreds. Indeed, a local gentleman by the name of Benjamin Fitzgilbert, whose grand home purportedly had a tunnel that led straight to The Jolly Sailors pub on the seafront of Old Micklewick, had become legendary for his connection to a local band of smugglers, particularly so his friendship with the most notorious smuggler of them all: the dark-eyed and dark-hearted Jacob Crayke. Despite his reputation for being cruel and ruthless, the smuggler's image had altered considerably down the centuries and he was now spoken of as some sort of romantic figure who'd had women swooning and men filled with admiration for his daring deeds and fearless missions. Adding to his notoriety, his decommissioned pistol was on permanent display in a glass case on the wall of The Jolly Sailors which was only a stone's throw away from Lark's cottage.

Momentarily lost in her thoughts, something told Lark that Crayke's Cottage had more than a few interesting stories to tell, that its walls were imbued with memories of scandal and intrigue. The place had practically vibrated with energy while they were there. And now she felt a sudden eagerness to dig into its history, especially after what Nate had just imparted about Mr Thurston believing it to be cursed.

'I don't know about you, but I reckon it's no coincidence it's called Crayke's Cottage, that it has a connection to Jacob Crayke rather than being a whimsical name given by someone who simply knows the history of Old Micklewick,' she said.

'Aye, I reckon you're right. So, am I right in thinking you sensed summat while we were there?' Nate asked, his chocolate-brown eyes peering enquiringly at her from beneath his fringe. 'Or did the freezing cold stop you from being able to focus on anything other than shivering and desperately trying to keep hypothermia at bay?'

Lark flashed him a grin then leant back in her seat. 'Well—'

It wasn't always easy to articulate the feelings she'd picked up in places or from people, and it hadn't helped that the vibrations she'd detected at Crayke's Cottage had become tangled with the voices of previous tenants who'd whispered with great urgency in her ears, creating an almost overwhelming cacophony. Not that she liked to make a big thing of that. Lark didn't mind admitting to being sensitive to the vibes of a place or an item, or even a person, but she preferred to keep to herself, or at least play down, the fact that "spirits" seemed to fly at her as soon as she entered a room. It was as if they'd sensed she was tuned into them. Though she was comfortable with her sixth sense in the main, this was the part of it she wasn't so keen on, and she'd done all she could to shut out the scrabbling voices. She'd found them distracting, and because she hadn't found a way to be selective with the spirits she could hear and filter out those that were unfriendly or had a sinister edge, it hadn't always been a pleasant experience. Her gentle, sensitive nature had been at odds with the hostility of some of the voices she'd encountered, which was why she'd done all she could to close herself off to them. Unfortunately, recent years had proved it wasn't the only part of her sixth sense she was keen to turn her back on.

'You're right about the cold,' she continued. 'It always interferes with me picking up vibes or sensations, but the overwhelming feeling I got was that the cottage had witnessed so much, was keeping so many secrets – and this is going to sound totally bonkers – I had the weirdest notion that the place itself didn't want to share any of them. I've never experienced that before. It wasn't a *bad* feeling, I didn't pick up on any negative energy per se, though I did detect the presence of several spirits – for want of a better description – but overall, I just got a sense of—' She sighed, her eyes roving the room as she searched for the right word. Nate, her parents and her group of best friends were the only people Lark was comfortable speaking freely like this with. 'I got a sense that you were better off not knowing what the house was hiding. My head started reeling with it all as soon as I began to thaw out here, actually.' In fact, the feelings it had stirred inside her were still crowding into her mind and pushing their way to the forefront of her thoughts, desperate to be heard.

'Blimey,' he said, his eyes wide. 'You sensed all that?'

'Yep, I did.' As she met Nate's gaze, she was suddenly conscious that what she'd picked up at the house wasn't the only thing making itself known to her. Her brow crumpled as an unwelcome sensation started to creep in. In the next moment, a pulse of alarm shot through her, making her heart jolt. 'Ohh!' Startled, she dropped her spoon and it fell to the table with a clatter. Her eyes darted away from Nate as she hurriedly tried to marshal her thoughts. She fought against the squeeze of anxiety in her chest and the notion that whatever was causing it was somehow connected to Nate. *Oh, my God! No! Please, not this!*

She swallowed and quickly composed herself before pushing her mouth into a smile; she didn't want to arouse his suspicions, especially if her change in demeanour had something to do with him. She'd give it more thought later when she was on her own and had time to give whatever it was her full attention. She hoped she was mistaken, that the horrible feeling of foreboding was simply linked to Crayke's Cottage. The alternative didn't bear thinking about. After the last time, it didn't take much for her fears to leap to attention and set her emotions swirling. She often found herself wondering if this part of her extra sense would ever go away. And right now, she wished more than ever that it would.

'You okay?' asked Nate.

'Oof! Yes, yes, I'm absolutely fine. Sorry about that.' She gave a small laugh and shook her head as if shaking the feeling away, regretting that she'd caused him concern. 'It'll be because the cottage has been locked up for so long; the atmosphere will have been building, kind of like a pressure cooker, hence all the powerful feelings. Like I said, it's all a bit bonkers.' Lark forced what she hoped sounded like a casual tone into her voice, relieved that Nate appeared none the wiser that he was potentially the cause of her sudden strange reaction. She picked up her spoon and dipped it into her soup, telling herself she'd overreacted. That the alarm she'd felt was simply down to her being bombarded by so many pent-up forces and spirits at Crayke's Cottage. *You've been overloaded by the place's energy, that's all. It's completely understandable.*

Lark was relieved to find her internal pep talk had the desired result and she felt her heart rate begin to settle.

'It's not bonkers. I kind of know what you mean, but it was that cold there, my brain was too frozen to work out whether I couldn't wait to leave because I was so nithered, or because summat or *something* didn't want us there.' Nate rubbed his hand over his chin. 'S'pose it might explain why Bear didn't seem too keen to hang around.' He smiled, giving an amused hitch of his eyebrows.

Lark laughed, recalling how their friend, who'd offered to help transport the contents, had lingered outside the cottage despite the biting wind and icy sleet, only venturing over the threshold when he was needed to give them a hand lifting something heavy or awkward. 'Yeah, he was definitely in a bit of a hurry to get done. Like me, he's Micklewick Bay born and bred, so I daresay he'll have heard the rumours about it being haunted and wasn't too eager to find out if they were true. He's such a big softy,' she said fondly.

Bear Marsay was married to Maggie, who was one of Lark's best friends, and was a familiar sight around Micklewick Bay. Though his height and broad shoulders, not to mention his dark bushy beard and wild, chin-length mop of hair, lent him a decidedly Viking air, it belied the gentle-natured man who wouldn't hurt a fly that lurked beneath. He worked part-time for his parents at Clifftop Farm as well as being a local odd job man whose services were always much in demand. And when Bear had offered to give a hand helping shift furniture from Crayke's Cottage to Nate's van, Nate had bitten his hand off. The historic roads in Old Micklewick were too narrow to allow vehicular access and meant he'd have to park his van a good distance away from the property. Lugging heavy bits of furniture wouldn't be an easy task, particularly with the uneven, icy cobbles to negotiate. But, with Bear's help, they'd made short work of it, especially since their friend had been so eager to get it over and done with!

'Anyroad, at least we got most of the stuff out before the snow started coming down too heavily.' Nate blew on his spoon, sending ripples over the soup. 'This is delicious, by the way, it's warmed me right through.'

'Glad to hear it. I was beginning to think we'd never thaw out.' Lark smiled over at him, relieved to find the unsettling feeling had leached away, leaving just a faint shadow lingering in the background. 'I'm happy to help shift the rest of the stuff with you, by the way, especially if Mr Thurston's in a hurry to get the cottage emptied.'

'Thanks, I'll probably take you up on that. Might be a good idea to tackle it first thing tomorrow before the snow gets any worse.'

'True. I can give you a hand before I open the shop.' Lark's Vintage Bazaar didn't open its doors until ten a.m., though Lark very much doubted she'd have many customers with the weather being the way it was. Folk tended not to venture into town when it was snowing, though she'd recently seen an increase in footfall with people looking for something unique to wear for their office Christmas parties.

'Thanks, Lark. And since it's just small stuff that's left, I won't trouble Bear – and not just cos he thinks the place is haunted,' Nate said with a chuckle. 'He was telling me he's got a busy few weeks with customers wanting things doing before Christmas; last-minute rush kind of thing.'

'Yeah, Maggie was saying he's been working late most nights, trying to get jobs finished.'

'Which makes it really decent of him to help shift the stuff from the cottage. I told him I owe him a couple of pints at the Jolly.'

'Bet that went down well.' Bear was known for enjoying a pint or two with his mates at the pub.

'Aye, it did. And getting back to the subject of the cottage, I reckon there'll be more clothing which you're welcome to.'

A flurry of excitement rippled through Lark at the prospect of more items all with their own stories to tell. 'Ooh! Let's hope so, mind, you've got to let me give you something for them.'

'Don't be so daft! I got a decent rate for the clearance, plus, you're doing me a favour by taking them; I've got no use for clothes so you might as well have them. Plus, you've fed and watered me which is payment enough.' He gestured to the now empty bowl in front of him.

'In that case, I don't want any money for the ticket to Jack and Jenna's Christmas reading at the bookshop next week.' Though Lark spoke in her usual soft tone, the look in her eyes told Nate she'd brook no argument.

'Aye, fair enough,' he said reluctantly.

Jack Playforth and Jenna Johnstone were well-loved, nationally famous authors who shared a cottage not far from Lark's home. The couple regularly gave readings at The Happy Hartes Bookshop in the town. Their self-deprecating sense of humour and gift for storytelling meant their events were always popular and sold out quickly. Luckily for Lark, she was best friends with Florrie Appleton who co-owned the bookshop with her boyfriend, Ed Harte, and she, together with the rest of their group of friends, always had first refusal on tickets for the events held there. Lark was looking forward to the latest reading, especially since it was to have a Christmas slant.

'In the meantime, how d'you fancy a warmed mince pie? They're from the deli; I popped some in my basket when I was buying the bread.'

'Are they the ones with the chunks of crystallised ginger?' he asked, a hopeful gleam in his eye. She'd picked up a couple earlier in the week and he'd raved about them then.

'They are indeedy. I can heat up some custard to go with them, if you fancy?'

'You really need to ask?' Nate grinned, rubbing his hand over his stomach as she got to her feet and reached for the tin containing the mince pies.

Much as she was itching to delve inside the suitcases – after her conversation with Nate regarding the rumours about Crayke's Cottage, it was almost beginning to feel like the items locked within were calling to her, pleading for her to listen to their stories – Lark's conscience wouldn't let him leave without at least offering him a mince pie, especially considering how much he liked them. She'd bought another two before he'd even mentioned the clearance of Crayke's Cottage, knowing he'd call round at some point over the weekend; he usually did, unless they were off on one of their sourcing trips.

Sliding the festive pastries into the oven, it wasn't long before the spicy aroma of Christmas filled the air, making her mouth water in anticipation.

THREE

Nate didn't hang around for long once they'd devoured the mince pies and custard. After scraping his bowl clean, he helped with the small pile of washing-up – as he always did – then gathered up his coat, declaring it was time he headed home.

With his woolly hat pulled over his ears, he delivered a gentle kiss to Lark's cheek, his eyes soft with affection. 'Thanks for feeding me and for your help with Crayke's Cottage.'

'You're welcome.' Lark smiled up at him, thoughts of how handsome he was crossing her mind. 'Thanks for the suitcases. I'll let you know if I find anything exciting.'

'I hope you do – find summat exciting, that is.' He lingered a moment as if contemplating saying something. 'Right then, I'll be in touch about tomorrow.' He opened the door and stepped out into the elements. Despite the shockingly cold wind howling around the huddle of houses and sucking the warmth from Seashell Cottage, Lark found herself rooted to the spot. She was unable to tear her eyes away from her friend, watching as he disappeared into the night, his head bent against the swirling snow. She pressed her hand to her mouth as the unwelcome sense of foreboding crept over her once more.

Closing the door, she headed back into the cosiness of the

living room, her unease building and her stomach churning as she flopped onto the sofa. 'Why am I feeling like this?' She scrubbed her face with her hands. 'I wish it would stop!'

Today wasn't the first time her senses had alerted her to something inexplicable about Nate, but the sensation had never been as intense as this, never been as disconcerting. Perplexing as it was, she'd always known instinctively it wasn't simply a warning telling her to avoid him, that he was a "wrong 'un" intent on causing her hurt or heartache. There was no escaping he was a genuinely kind and decent man who had the biggest heart. And it wasn't just Lark who held him in such high regard; all who knew him thought so, too. He was well liked and well respected by the locals of Micklewick Bay. Her instincts had always been quick to detect those with dubious intentions who should be treated with caution. Local "businessman" Dick Swales – or Dodgy Dick as locals referred to him – with his increasingly unscrupulous dealings, was such a person. He tried to pass himself off as some sort of respectable gentleman, but he fooled no one. He was the polar opposite of Nate who, like Lark, had a gentle nature and saw the good in everyone. From their first meeting, her gut had told her that he was as honest as the day was long, that he didn't have a bad bone in his body. She trusted that feeling implicitly and he'd never given her cause to doubt it. Despite this, the puzzling background feelings he aroused held her back from taking their relationship to the next level. She just wished she could fathom out what the heck they were all about, gain some understanding of them. It didn't help that the sensations or, rather, "premonitions" she regularly experienced with other people usually presented themselves more clearly – she'd known that her friend, the relationship phobic Stella would find love with Alex, and determinedly single Jasmine would fall head over heels for Max. Those feelings had been clear and strong. But the fuzzy "image", for want of a better word, that filled her mind whenever she thought about Nate was too vague for her to decipher. Yet it was still enough for her to take it as a sign that she should steer clear of becoming romantically involved with him. In fact, she'd grown so used to its presence over the years, she barely noticed it now, which she assumed was owing to her acceptance that she and Nate were destined never to be more than friends.

She gave a sigh, recalling the look in his eyes when he'd kissed her cheek just before he left. It had been enough to send a warm glow spreading through her. How could such a pleasant sensation have dissipated so quickly? Talk about frustrating! And what had caused such an unsettling feeling to leap into its place and snuff out the positive vibes of mere moments before? But much as she'd like to know the answer, she was afraid to search her mind too deeply, fearful of what she might find.

Not for the first time did she regret that she'd inherited her mother Serena's ability to read auras and her gift of precognition. Having a sense or an awareness of something that was going to happen in the future wasn't always a good thing. At times, it had the power to make Lark's skin prickle with unease, and she'd wish the ability away. Which was what she'd done just now after the unsettling vibes she'd picked up from Nate.

She swallowed the lump of stress that had lodged itself in her throat. Lark knew exactly why this feeling was causing her such concern, making her afraid to search her mind too deeply for answers. The last time she'd been overwhelmed by a premonition with such a sense of foreboding, it hadn't turned out well, and had resulted in her being distraught and desperate to distance herself from her psychic abilities. Being in possession of such knowledge had become too stressful for her. Become a burden rather than a gift. So much so, that it had resulted in her making a concerted effort to keep her attention away from reading auras and doing all she could to block any sense of precognition that presented itself to her. It hadn't been easy, especially since she'd taken the time over the years to hone her skills.

Lark had first become aware she could read auras when she was a young child, seeing what she'd described to her mum as "glowy colours" around people and even animals. She'd soon learnt that different coloured auras signified different things – a blue aura meant a person was calm, while a yellow aura usually signified someone was full of energy. And sometimes a person's aura could change. It had taken her a while to learn how to concentrate sufficiently such that she could not only read an individual's aura, but also understand the different colours that made up their "auric field", as it was known. This had eventually become something she did automatically, without giving it a second thought. But after what had happened just over three years ago, Lark had become almost resentful of her ability and deliberately avoided the temptation to read anyone's aura, consciously blocking her mind to it. It still sneaked in from time to time and her skin would prickle as an unexpected sense of whatever it was came over her, but it wasn't anywhere near as heightened as it had been. It was the same with moments of precognition, though that hadn't been so easy to ignore. Despite this, she'd managed to reduce her psychic moments to a manageable level, consciously pushing away anything that aroused a feeling of unease and not engaging with it. It could be draining at times, which was why she was vigilant in her distribution of crystals around her home and her person in a bid to add a layer of protection and support.

Lark was glad, and not a little relieved, that her endeavours hadn't stripped away all of her psychic abilities, and she was still able to pick up on the vibrations of people and places. They still came through loud and clear. She valued this aspect of her extrasensory ability for when she was selecting vintage garments and items to sell in Lark's Vintage Bazaar. Since that didn't involve anyone or anything personal to her or those she loved, she was happy to put it to good use for such purposes. That way, only things with a good energy would make it to her shop; she didn't want to risk anything that was hanging on to negative vibes sneaking in. Other than that, Lark decided to also focus her attention on her aromatherapy range and crystal healing which had become a passion of hers and which she hoped would engender a more positive and less stressful existence for her. She'd been pleased to find her new strategy had worked. Until now, with Nate.

The reminder sent a wave of disquiet washing over her. She tipped her head back and released an exasperated gasp, causing Luna to jump down from her spot on the armchair where she'd been quietly observing her and leap up onto Lark's lap, mewing as if sensing her owner's thoughts.

'Oh, Luna, you can tell something's not right, too, can't you?' She smoothed her hand over the cat's silky fur, Luna purring loudly as she made herself comfortable. 'I wish I could understand what it is.' *Please be okay, Nate.*

If she was being honest, Lark would admit that the feelings she had for Nate ran deep. Deeper than she dared admit to herself, never mind anyone else – and definitely not her best friends! If only she had the courage to face how she felt. The emotions he stirred inside her were more than those of simply friendship and there'd been times when she'd struggled to keep a lid on them. But the inexplicable warnings that something wasn't right, meant that she'd quashed her feelings, telling herself she and Nate were only meant to be friends. Nothing more. But now, with this dark sense of foreboding shrouding Nate, there was a whole maelstrom of emotions raging around inside her, sending her mind into turmoil.

But one thing stood out loud and clear: she felt scared. Scared of whatever it was that was generating this new level of warning regarding Nate. And scared that she didn't know what to do about it.

What she did know, however, was that she needed to rein in her anxiety before it spilled over and alerted him, and others, that something was wrong.

FOUR

Though Lark had been itching to find out what was inside the suitcases, her unease about Nate had taken the edge off her enthusiasm. She couldn't seem to shake him from her mind. It wasn't like her to allow negative thoughts to take over, her naturally positive disposition meant she could usually contain them or beat them back. She'd tried telling herself that she was overreacting, that some obvious explanation would eventually reveal itself, but there was no denying her disquiet had knocked her off kilter.

Given her current state of mind, she reluctantly decided it would be best to save the suitcases for later, when her thoughts and worries about Nate would, hopefully, be more settled and her usual sense of calm restored. That way, she'd be able to get a better sense of the items, get a proper *feel* for the energy they'd clung onto. Instead, she decided to make a start on making Christmas decorations from what was left of the bolt of ticking fabric she'd picked up at a market in Carcassonne when she and Nate had ventured there on a sourcing trip earlier that year. She'd already sketched out a few ideas, namely stars, Christmas stockings and Christmas trees, to which she'd add little tinkly bells and shiny buttons and beads and finish with a loop of twine to hang them from the tree. The idea was to sell them in her shop as well as give some as gifts to her friends. Lark always found absorbing herself in a small, creative task helped soothe her mind, which was something she was in need of right now.

Unfortunately, she'd only got as far as cutting out a few shapes at the kitchen table when she was forced to admit defeat and accept that her mind just couldn't settle to it. Her concern about Nate wasn't showing any signs of going away. If anything, it had been building. It was stifling her creativity and, worse, she wasn't enjoying making the decorations, which was something she usually looked forward to with relish. Moreover, the last thing Lark wanted was to imbue her creations with negative energy, especially when the items were intended for other people's homes at such a happy, family time of year. It went against everything she believed in and aimed for in her business.

She glanced across at Luna who'd been observing her progress from the doorway. From the expression in the cat's knowing, green eyes, it was as if she could read her owner's thoughts.

'Oh, Luna, why can't I shake this feeling? Please tell me I've got it wrong.'

Luna continued to gaze at her.

'Looking at me like that really isn't helping, you know.' With a defeated sigh, Lark finished snipping out the star shape she was halfway through and set her dress-making shears down. She'd pack everything away and hope she'd wake up with a clear mind so she could pick up where she left off tomorrow. But now, all she was good for was a soothing soak in the bath. Hopefully, she'd get some clarity there.

Lark padded upstairs and headed into the tiny bathroom where she lit a cluster of lavender scented tea lights, setting them on the small windowsill amongst an arrangement of amethyst and rose quartz crystals, where they flickered in the draught. The old brass taps squeaked as she twisted them open, water gushing into the original cast iron slipper bath. She added a generous dash of homemade aromatherapy oil and it wasn't long before clouds of lavender-scented steam filled the air. That done, she searched the playlist on her phone and selected the latest sent by her yogi mum. A moment later, calming zen music with background waterfall sounds poured from the speaker on the shelf above the sink, adding to the already soothing ambience. That done, she placed her pyjamas on the little wooden seat by the heated towel rail, piled her hair on top of her head, then shrugged off her dressing gown and climbed into the bath, allowing the soothing warmth of the water to envelop her. Resting her head back, Lark closed her eyes and slipped into a session of meditation as the aromatherapy oil began to work its magic. By the time she was done, she hoped her worries had been sent packing.

Even with her reluctance to engage in aura reading or be drawn into any psychic messages, she was still sensitive to the energy generated by people or places. For Lark, at times, it could mean that her mind was always buzzing, especially when she ventured somewhere new, with the energy of so many individuals and experiences absorbed into the walls or space. It was the reason she practiced the ritual of meditation on a regular basis, allowing herself to "zone out" when things got too frenetic.

An hour later, Lark heaved herself from the now-lukewarm bath, her fingers and toes wrinkly after their long soak. She was beyond relieved to find her anxiety had eased and she was feeling so much lighter. Meditation always helped soothe her mind, especially if it was combined with a calming aromatherapy oil and one of her mum's zen playlists.

During her soak, she'd analysed the various explanations that had been circulating around her thoughts that could offer an explanation for her discomfort about Nate. She'd slowly turned them over, examining each one from every angle and scrutinising them closely, when realisation struck her unexpectedly. It had made her sit up straight, sending soapy water sloshing over the edge of the bath.

'Of course! It makes perfect sense!' she'd said, bumping her forehead with the heel of her hand. It was a real light-bulb moment, and such a logical explanation she couldn't believe it hadn't crossed her mind years ago when she'd first met Nate. The reason he generated these inexplicable feelings was very probably linked to one of two things – or even both. The first explanation was the clothes he wore. Being a keen recycler like Lark, he regularly bought second-hand or vintage clothing, the heavy wool coat and Arran jumper he'd been wearing earlier being a perfect example; he'd told her he'd bought them from the charity shop in Middleton-le-Moors on a recent visit. And knowing him as she did, she very much doubted he'd given them a wash before he'd worn them! Another equally valid explanation could be the vibes he'd picked up from the furniture he restored. That had just as much of a chance of absorbing negative energy as the clothing had.

The more she'd thought about it, the more it had made sense. There was a definite chance that he'd picked up some of the energy from close contact with these items which was skewing the vibes she got from him.

The realisation had come as a massive relief.

Adding weight to her theory, was her earlier conversation with Nate about Crayke's Cottage. If old Mr Thurston was so convinced there was something negative about the property, then it wasn't surprising that something was lingering on Nate – herself, too, no doubt. After all, he'd spent the whole day there, way longer than she had, and he'd been lugging items of furniture around. It was a valid explanation as far as she was concerned. She only wished this understanding had come to her sooner.

Another wave of relief swept through her as she towelled herself dry and pulled on her pyjamas. Unable to stop the smile that was tugging at her mouth, she brushed out her hair and re-tied her plait, her sense of calm restored once more. Now that she'd got herself grounded, she had a clear mind to tackle the suitcases; a blank slate ready to give their contents her full attention. The prospect sent a shimmer of anticipation rushing over her skin.

FIVE

It was just gone seven o'clock by the time Lark hauled the largest of the old suitcases in front of the wood burner. She knelt before it, her insides dancing with anticipation as she ran her fingers over the battered leather. It was decorated with a variety of faded liner labels, all haphazardly plastered over it: a log of the owner's travels. Unfastening the leather buckles, she pushed on the age-dulled brass clasps beneath. It took a few moments' coaxing but they eventually opened with a satisfying click. Slowly, she eased the lid up, her pulse rate gathering speed as the treasures within were revealed in a waft of fusty air.

'Oh, wow!' She gasped as her breath was whipped from her mouth, every fibre of her body fizzing.

Sitting back on her haunches, Lark took a moment to steady herself. She pushed her plait over her shoulder as her gaze swept over the neatly folded contents looking back at her. If the vibrations that were emanating from the clothing were anything to go by, the previous owner of these clothes had enjoyed a happy and fulfilled life.

A thrill scurried up her spine as she reached for the garment that was begging for her attention. It was made of rose-pink fabric dotted with ditsy white flowers. As soon as her fingers made contact with it, she sensed its positive energy just as she hoped she would. With great care, she lifted it out of the case, the fine cotton unfurling as she held up what revealed itself to be a tea dress in classic nineteen-forties style.

'So beautiful,' Lark said in a whisper.

Closer inspection revealed the dress was exquisitely made, with a run of fabric-covered buttons that stretched from the dainty, round collar, down to the waistband that was edged in pale-green ribbon.

'Oh!' A vivid image flashed through her mind like a bolt of lightning, leaving behind it the imprint of a vibrant young woman with a happy face and dancing eyes, her hair set in victory rolls. Music from the nineteen forties floated at the back of Lark's consciousness, an intense feeling of happiness flooding her chest. The young woman was smiling, her full lips painted with a matt lipstick in a deep shade of red and her eyes were sparkling with vivacity. On her feet were mid-heeled sandals in braided leather. They had an almond-shaped toe and fastened at the ankle, the seam of her stockings running up the back of her legs. The skirt of the tea dress swished as she was swept around the room in the arms of a man wearing a soldier's uniform and slicked back hair. He was saying something that was making the young woman laugh. From their body language and the way they were gazing at one another, there was no mistaking the young couple were head over heels in love.

Slowly, the image faded, leaving Lark filled with a warm sensation and wishing she could've had longer to enjoy such a joy-filled moment.

'Wow!' she gasped, thrilled to have got off to such a good start. She'd had her doubts after what Nate had mentioned about Crayke's Cottage being cursed. She gave the fabric of the dress a quick appraisal, checking for marks and evidence of moth damage. All but for a few dots of mildew, it was in excellent condition.

'That's perfect for the shop, don't you think, Luna?' She beamed across at the cat who had joined her on the mat in front of the fire and was watching her with interest. Lark had just the customer in mind, one who had a particular interest in tea dresses from that time. She carefully folded the garment and set it down on the floor before reaching in and lifting out a square of scarlet silk, covered in white polka dots and trimmed with a striped border. It triggered the same reaction as the dress which suggested to Lark it had been owned by the same young woman. More happy, positive vibes! Oh, boy! She was in her element right now!

Her luck continued as she sorted through the rest of the items, including several cotton skirts in a mix of floral fabrics, a couple of shirtwaister dresses and what she recognised as a jitterbug dress, with its full skirt and soft fabric designed to allow maximum freedom to the wearer while she danced the jitterbug – what else? *How wonderful!* There was also a cardigan with a small hole near the cuff which Lark felt could be fixed easily. All of the items were bouncing with the young woman's energy, and Lark was delighted when a lemon-coloured blouse with a dainty collar evoked an image of the same young couple. They were smiling as they walked along, a blaze of sunshine around them, the sound of the sea in the distance. The young woman – the name Betty slipped into Lark's mind, though the young man's was proving elusive – had her arm linked through his, her gaze drawn to the engagement ring that was glinting on her finger. A wave of happiness rushed through Lark, and she was overcome with the feeling she'd just been treated to a glimpse of the moments immediately after the young soldier had proposed. It was times like this she felt glad to be sensitive to moments from the past. She only wished that was all she was able to pick up.

The last item remaining in the case appeared to be an old, cotton bedsheet with stripes in vintage shades. From the thin feel of it, it had been laundered many, many times. She wondered why it had been included with the items of clothing. But as Lark lifted it out, she noticed an edge of white, silk-like fabric peering from within the folds. Carefully, she opened the bedsheet out and was thrilled to reveal what could only be a wedding dress.

'Oh, how exquisite!' Lark gently took the fine fabric between her fingers, her gaze running over the round neckline edged with shimmering mother-of-pearl beads. She was instantly struck by a feeling of pure joy as images of the day filled her mind. She closed her eyes, keeping hold of the fabric. She could sense the warmth of sunshine on her face, hear the birds twittering merrily in the background as Betty, with her hair set in soft waves and wearing what appeared to be the gown from the suitcase, walked to the local church on the arm of a man Lark assumed was Betty's father. Her cut-glass, drop earrings glinted in the sunlight – something told Lark they'd been borrowed. The pair were chatting and laughing, the bride's short veil – not yet over her face for fear of getting it marked with lipstick stains – catching in the summer breeze, as she clutched a bouquet billowing with carnations in a joyful shade of yellow and trimmed with white gypsophila. The young woman exuded an air of pure happiness as she stepped through the great oak door of the church, the light fabric of her dress fluttering around her ankles. She paused, taking a deep breath as she awaited her cue from the organ. A moment later, the organ wheezed into life as the opening notes of "The Wedding March" bounced off the walls, reaching all the way up to the rafters.

Lark's heart began to beat faster as the image showed Betty making her way down the aisle, the eyes of the congregation on the radiant young bride. And even though Betty's veil was now covering her face, Lark could sense her smile widening as she approached her groom. He was looking smart in his army uniform as he fidgeted nervously at the altar. Lark could feel the anticipation in the air as it mingled with the joy of the occasion. A pocket of happiness in such a worrying time.

The image quickly moved to the young couple sharing their first dance at their wedding reception held in the local community centre – it had barely changed! – Betty's new husband holding her close as the band played "At Last", a song made popular at the time by Glenn Miller and his Orchestra. Her heart swelled as the groom gazed deeply into his new bride's eyes and said, 'Have I told you how much I love you, Mrs Roberts?'

Lark was disappointed when the image started fading, scrabbling to hang on to it just a little bit longer. Once it had completely disappeared, she opened her eyes, blinking before her gaze landed back on the beautiful wedding gown. 'Wow!' she whispered. Holding it up before her, she could see it was a simple design, with the skirt part being made up of panels of silk skilfully stitched together, allowing it to hang in elegant, fluid lines. There were more mother-of-pearl buttons around the cuffs, and fabric-covered buttons ran down the back to the waist.

As her eyes roved over the bodice, taking in the carefully placed darts, she was taken aback by the briefest flash of an image, so fleeting, it was barely enough to make sense of. She hurriedly tried to grapple with it before it disappeared, but all she got was an image of a blue sky punctuated by clouds and the sound of what she assumed was an aeroplane engine. A pulse of adrenalin raced through her. *What was that all about?* Lark couldn't begin to fathom why Betty's dress was giving out this kind of vibration. It made no sense. No sense at all. She waited, the dress in her hands, to see if anything else came to her. Disappointingly, her mind remained clear.

'Hmm. Curious.' Telling herself she'd probably picked up on energy left behind from something else that had been in the suitcase at one time, she carefully folded the dress and packed it away in the sheet, noting the specks of mildew that peppered the hem and part of a sleeve. Other than that, the garment was in perfect condition.

It had been a joy getting a sense of Betty from her suitcase of beautiful clothes, though Lark couldn't help but wonder what the connection to Crayke's Cottage could possibly be. Had it been Betty's home? If so, Lark hoped she hadn't been affected by the curse or bad luck Mr Thurston had referred to, that she'd had a happy and fulfilled life within its walls. She told herself that if the vibes of the young woman's clothes were anything to go by, it seems she hadn't been tainted or troubled by any of the negativity at Crayke's Cottage, which she found hugely reassuring. There was joy and positivity woven into every fibre.

Lark couldn't wait to share what she'd found with Nate – her dad, too; he was as much of a fan of local history and all things vintage as they were. She knew they'd both be fascinated by it all. A thought flittered through her mind, wondering how her dad was doing; she hadn't heard from him in a while and she hoped he was okay. She glanced over at the clock; she'd give him a call once she'd looked through the smaller case. News of what she'd found in the suitcase was bound to give him a boost, start the cogs of his mind whirring. Something new to occupy his thoughts and stop him from dwelling on the past would do him good, Lark thought.

SIX

With all of Betty's garments examined, Lark placed them back in the suitcase. She set it to one side before reaching over to retrieve the smaller one, wondering how it could possibly be filled with anything as exciting.

By comparison, this one was plain in appearance, with no luggage labels adorning it. It had suffered a few nasty bumps and knocks along the way, too. A bitter, acrid smell clung to the leather, and there was something about it that didn't generate the same sense of excitement or anticipation as the first one. On closer inspection, Lark spotted a couple of embossed initials that she hadn't noticed when she'd first found it at Crayke's Cottage. She ran her fingers over them. Though they were somewhat scuffed, she managed to make out the letters: "AC". Could the "C" stand for Crayke? she wondered, as a ripple of intrigue ran over her. Or was it just wishful thinking and nothing more than a simple coincidence?

'Let's see what secrets you're keeping inside,' she murmured.

Luna started mewing and Lark looked up to see she'd jumped onto the armchair opposite. She assumed the cat had become too warm sitting in front of the wood burner. She had to concede, it was pretty toasty, but after how cold she'd been earlier, unlike Luna, Lark wasn't in a hurry to relinquish the heat just yet.

The clasps on this case were more reluctant to open and, after several attempts, she was forced to admit defeat and dig out a flat-headed screwdriver and a can of WD-40 from the cupboard under the sink in the kitchen. It took a few minutes of careful jiggling around before the first clasp popped open, but the other was stuck fast. After struggling with it for over half an hour, Lark sat back, her face flushed pink from bending forward for so long – not to mention the heat from the wood burner. 'Crikey me, Luna, it doesn't want to budge.'

Luna mewed loudly in response.

Maybe there's a reason it doesn't want to open. Maybe I should leave it, Lark thought fleetingly. She huffed out a sigh and sat back, wondering whether to push on or leave it for now, to-ing and fro-ing between her reasons for and against. She was surprised to find she was veering in favour of leaving it; she didn't want to cause any permanent damage to the suitcase, it being a vintage item, especially when she'd planned on selling it in her shop. But it wasn't just that. A peculiar feeling had gradually crept over her as she'd been working on the clasps. Something that told her the contents were best left undisturbed.

She rubbed her chin, looking at it thoughtfully. She could hardly offer it for sale if she didn't know what was inside – it could be chockablock with spiders, and no one would want that! Not only did the case look shabbier than the one that contained Betty's clothes, but from what Lark could detect, it wasn't emanating the same warm and friendly vibes. It made her wonder if it was an item she'd want to have in her shop anyway, never mind sell on to someone else.

She took a moment while her mind did battle, but in the end her curiosity got the better of her and she told herself if the items inside didn't feel right, she could get rid of them and the case. Decision made, she added another squirt of WD-40 and went to make a cup of tea, hoping the time would give the oil a chance to work its way into the nooks and crannies of the clasp and loosen it.

Back in the living room, Lark placed her mug on the coffee table, picked up the screwdriver and set about tackling the stubborn clasps. To her surprise, it only took a few wiggles and pushes before the first opened with a begrudging "clunk". It would seem the oil had worked a treat.

'Oh!'

With the second clasp opened, it took a couple of attempts, but she eventually managed to slacken the lid – she was beginning to think the suitcase was determined she wouldn't find out what it had been keeping hidden inside for so many years.

As she went to ease the top back Luna started yowling loudly in a way she'd never done before.

'What a racket, Luna! What's it all about? Anyone would think you don't want me to open it.' But there was something about the suitcase that made her understand why Luna was suddenly behaving in such an agitated way. The moment the last clasp had clicked open Lark had felt something indefinable shiver through her. It bore no resemblance to the feelings the first suitcase had stirred, and she wasn't at all sure it was good.

Luna continued to yowl.

Lark took a deep, slow breath and braced herself before carefully easing the lid back, trepidation making her heart thump hard in her chest, the acrid smell of the case intensifying.

She sat back on her haunches, taking a moment as her eyes ran over the clutter of contents, tension prickling its way up her spine as she tried to make sense of what she'd just unearthed. She had the overwhelming feeling that this suitcase hadn't been opened for decades. That it had been the keeper of intrigue and secrets, all biding their time, just waiting to be found.

A clutch of nerves jangled in her stomach. She only hoped she wouldn't regret being the person to find them.

Pushing back her concern, and trying to ignore Luna's growing protestations, Lark peered into the case, looking more closely at the contents. She was reluctant to handle them just yet. The suitcase being compact meant everything was packed tightly together. Her first glance told her there was a leather-bound book, tied around the middle with a leather thong. Placed on top of it was an ancient-looking wrought-iron padlock, and a handful of waxy stumps that she assumed were candles. Beside the book lay a battered pewter tankard, a small wodge of blue cloth separating it from a stoneware bottle that had a cork stopper and a small chip in its neck. Beside that was a bulky item wrapped in what appeared to be a piece of old eiderdown. Lark got the feeling that there was nothing haphazard or random about the items' inclusion in the case. Though they were strange – almost sinister – it was as if each one served a specific purpose.

Lark found herself being drawn to the bulky item first, wondering what was hidden beneath the piece of eiderdown. She lifted it out, half aware of Luna's objections increasing in volume, noting it was heavy, and judging by the rattling sound, it and several of the items inside were made of metal.

Her suspicions were confirmed when she unwrapped the eiderdown, revealing a rusty tin battle-scarred with dents. 'Ooh, what have we here?' It evidently had quite a story to tell.

She set the tin down on the floor and went to remove the lid, a feeling of uncertainty creeping over her, so different from the emotions Betty's belongings evoked. She paused a moment, hoping she hadn't unearthed something that would make her regret ever bringing the suitcase into her home.

Pushing her doubts aside, she leant forward and gripped the lid firmly, ready to prise it off, when Luna started hissing alarmingly.

'Oh my days!' A spike of alarm shot through Lark. Pressing her hand to her chest, she glanced over to see the cat crouching down in the chair, her ears and whiskers flattened to her head and her tail tucked under her. It was completely out of character, she'd never seen her usually tranquil feline behave in such a defensive way.

'Luna, what is it?' she asked, concerned. She went to give her a reassuring stroke, but Luna continued to hiss and spit, making Lark withdraw her hand; she didn't want to risk the cat lashing out at her.

'It's okay, Luna, it's just a tin. It can't hurt you,' she said soothingly.

But despite her words of comfort, Lark had already got a sense of something unusual about the tin. Something she couldn't quite put her finger on. It wasn't what she'd call sinister, but neither was it what she could describe as innocent and friendly. It had a story behind it, and instead of making her reluctant to open it, she found herself intrigued to know what was inside.

She turned back to Luna, whose yowling and hissing had subsided.

'S'okay, sweetheart. Everything's fine. If I find anything unpleasant, I'll put it outside. Promise.' This time, the cat allowed her owner to smooth a hand over her head.

Lark was relieved to see her words seemed to pacify Luna who sat watching quietly, though her ears were still flat to her head.

Turning her attention back to the tin, Lark went to remove the lid, but it would appear to be as reluctant to budge as the clasps of the case had been. It evidently wasn't eager to share its secrets.

After a brief struggle, the lid surrendered, but before Lark had a chance to think, it was as if the energy of the contents rushed at her. 'Oh!' She was no stranger to picking up unusual sensations from the items she was considering for her shop, but this was something else.

Luna gave one final hiss of alarm, before leaping down from the armchair and darting out of the room and racing upstairs.

Lark steadied herself, wishing she'd asked Nate to stay; she could do with his level-headed, calming influence right now. She set the lid down, her nose twitching at the bitter smell that rose from the tin, a discombobulating energy loitering around her. A frown crumpled her brow as she tried to make sense of the odd cluster of items arranged within.

Taking up most of the room in the tin was something large wrapped in a piece of heavily stained cloth. Tucked beside it was a container made of dulled copper, alongside a worse-for-wear leather pouch, several pieces of torn cloth and what appeared to be small round balls of lead. There were also several coins, the sort of which Lark had never seen before. But what she found most intriguing was the rusty metal key. It was huge, the type she could imagine for the door to a castle or a dungeon.

She reached in and lifted out the item wrapped in the stained cloth. It was a solid weight in her hand and she had a sickening feeling she knew what it was. Unfurling the fabric, her fears were confirmed, sending nausea swirling in her stomach.

Looking back at her was an old-fashioned pistol.

SEVEN

Her stomach clenched and her pulse started to race. In an instant her mind was flooded with an image of moonlight shimmering on a dark sea, clouds scudding over a troubled sky. The silhouette of a sailing ship, its sails billowing, cries carried on the wind mingling with the sound of gunshot. A sense of fear and danger permeating the misty air.

Lark gasped. 'Oh my God!' She was overwhelmed by the urgent need to get the pistol out of her hands. With her heart pounding, she hurriedly wrapped it in the cloth and set it back in the tin so quickly anyone would think it was burning hot, almost dropping it as she did so. She sat back, putting some distance between herself and the tin when a crumpled piece of paper with writing in an elaborate cursive hand caught her eye. Tentatively, she reached for it.

'"William's pig is farrowing"? *What?*' She turned the paper over but other than a smattering of oily stains, the underside was blank. '"William's pig is farrowing"?' she said again. 'What on earth could that mean?'

Once more, a sense of danger crawled over her as she became aware of the sound of shoes scraping over stone, urgent voices giving orders, the crack of a cannon firing in the distance, the smell of smoke swirling under her nose, the thundering crash of waves as they lashed against the shore. An image of shadowy figures hurriedly moving items – barrels, sacks, packages – from the beach before being swallowed by an ink-dark cave played out in her mind. In the next moment, a gunshot sliced through the air, the whiff of gun smoke, figures dashing about, voices raised in alarm. Lark gasped, her heart racing even faster. She dropped the paper into the tin, snatching her hand away. This was too much. She needed to break free of this unpalatable mix of distress and agitation, it was so at odds with her naturally peaceful and calm disposition.

When her heart rate had finally settled, Lark puffed out her cheeks and released a slow breath, trying to make sense of it all. Still feeling slightly punch-drunk, she felt her eyes being drawn, magnet-like, back to the tin. The small rounds of lead must surely be ammunition and very likely linked to the pistol, though she wasn't so sure what the pouches contained. Maybe the leather one was for coins? As for the key, she couldn't even begin to imagine what that unlocked, though her gut told her it was something at Crayke's Cottage. A secret room or passageway? Or an old coffer, even? As for the piece of paper with the odd mix of words in cursive writing, she wondered if it could have been code for some illicit dealings, and if so, why have it written down? The thought of it sent a shiver running through her. There was no wonder poor old Luna reacted the way she had. Lark had an overwhelming urge to get as far away from the suitcase as possible too.

With dregs of adrenalin still lingering in her bloodstream, she secured the lid back onto the tin, then returned it to the case, making sure to fasten the clasps securely. She didn't want it, and more particularly, the pistol in her home for a moment longer. She needed to get it outside, and get the usual calm ambience restored to Seashell Cottage. Nate may have said she was welcome to anything else that caught her eye at Crayke's Cottage but, right now, she didn't want another thing from there getting over her doorstep. After what she'd just experienced, it didn't bear thinking about what kind of energy it might unleash. There was no way she was going to risk it. She was thrilled with Betty's case and was now wishing she hadn't clapped eyes on the smaller one.

Thinking of Nate, much as she was keen to tell him what she'd found in the suitcases, getting the smaller one out of her house and into the shed in the backyard was a priority, snow or no snow.

Lark hefted it up from the floor and hurried through to the kitchen. She slipped her feet into her wellies and pulled on the raincoat she kept on a peg by the back door. That done, she flicked the switch for the outside light, grabbed the shed key and braced herself for what the weather had in store for her.

Outside, the icy air took her breath away. The snow was considerably deeper than when she'd waved Nate off earlier, and flakes were still tumbling from the sky, settling on her head and shoulders. Lark hurried to the shed, wintry air nipping at her face and hands, making her eyes water. In her haste, she fumbled with the key, pushing the suitcase inside when she'd finally unlocked the door. A sense of relief followed her all the way back to the warmth of the cottage.

Back inside, she gave a shiver. What a day it had been. She couldn't remember one where she'd been bombarded with such an array of emotions. It had left her feeling quite exhausted. On top of that, she wouldn't feel settled until she'd cleansed the atmosphere of her home and made sure she'd ridded it of any lingering negativity. Hopefully, that would tempt poor Luna to venture back downstairs.

Lark busied herself, gathering all she needed to begin her cleansing ritual. It was one she carried out on a regular basis there at the cottage and also at Lark's Vintage Bazaar.

To start, she retrieved her bundle of dried herbs from the sideboard. It was one she'd made herself and consisted of sage, lavender and a sprig of eucalyptus, all bound tightly together with twine.

The sage and eucalyptus she'd added for their powerful cleansing properties while the lavender was included simply because it was one of her favourite herbs and she valued its calming qualities – something she felt in great need of right now! All three were known to be attributed with the power of protection, too, which Lark considered a formidable combination.

Though the wintry weather made it less than ideal, it was necessary for her to open the windows before commencing the cleansing ritual, the reason being twofold: not only did the smoke need to escape, but she also needed to create an outlet for any negative energy. As soon as Lark cranked open the horizontal sliding sash window (a style typical of the vernacular cottages in the area), the freezing air didn't waste a moment and rushed in, diving into every corner of the room. Lark methodically went around the rest of the cottage, opening the windows in each room and temporarily disabling the smoke alarms so the smouldering herbs wouldn't set them off and startle her neighbours – they were well used to the smell of burning herbs emanating from her home and wafting into theirs. That done, she lit the top end of the herb stick and allowed it to catch fire before blowing it out with a gentle puff of breath, then carefully leant it against a terracotta bowl set on the sideboard.

While the fragrant smoke filled the air, Lark picked up the chunk of green, polished malachite crystal she'd prepared in anticipation of any negative energy brought into her home from Crayke's Cottage. That morning she'd rinsed the crystal under running water and left it to air dry in the living room. That way, she felt happy that she'd washed away any traces of negative energy it could be holding on to; she was keen for its properties to be at the optimum level.

Clutching her crystal in one hand, she took the herb bundle in the other and walked slowly around the room, the scented smoke drifting all around her and filling the tiny space. She stretched out her arm, ensuring the smoke reached right into the corners. Lark repeated this action in every room of the house – even the bathroom – until she was satisfied the cottage was adequately cleansed, and every trace of negative energy had been eradicated.

In the living room, she set the herb bundle back down, fragrant smoke still drifting from it. She placed the piece of malachite beside it while she went around closing all the windows. She was just about to hunt for Luna, who was still making herself scarce, when she heard a gentle mewing from her bedroom. The sound appeared to be coming from under her bed. Heading over to it, Lark lifted the edge of the patchwork quilt and peered beneath to see two eyes blinking back at her.

'Oh, Luna,' she said softly. 'You can come out now, sweetheart, everywhere's back to normal. There's nothing left to upset you. Come on.'

The cat gave another plaintive miaow before tentatively inching her way out, letting Lark scoop her up and carry her downstairs. 'I'm so sorry, Luna, I should've taken notice of your warning and not touched the case.' *I should've taken notice of my own warning, too.*

With tranquillity restored at Seashell Cottage and Luna watching from the doorway, Lark set about making herself a soothing mug of camomile tea. Her mind was turning over the items in the second suitcase. As thrilled as she'd been about Betty's clothes in the larger case, the contents had been overshadowed by the smaller one. Could the items inside have anything to do with why Mr Thurston had said Crayke's Cottage was cursed with bad luck? And, if so, did he know anything about that particular suitcase? Was that why he was so determined to not keep any of the items? So many questions!

Lark had decided against texting or calling Nate about it, deciding, instead, to tell him tomorrow. She was at a loss at what to do with the smaller suitcase. She was reluctant for Nate to have it with all its weird energy; she didn't want even the tiniest hint of it to rub off onto him, especially after the weird feelings she'd detected on him earlier. It made her wonder as to the vibes in the furniture currently stored in his van. In fairness, there hadn't been much. The place had been sparsely furnished, though what there was had been heavy, it being made of aged oak. If he was okay with it, she'd treat the van to a spot of sage burning before he moved it, and its contents, to his workshop, hang up a couple of the malachite crystals she had on chains.

As she poured hot water over the teabag, the more she thought about it, the more she wondered if the small suitcase and its contents should be handed over to the local heritage centre – she didn't want it, and she wasn't so sure Nate would either. At least, she hoped he wouldn't. The centre would be the best place for it. Surely it couldn't cause any distress to anyone there?

The Old Micklewick Heritage Centre was dedicated to the unlikely partnership of the town's notorious smuggler, Jacob Crayke and Benjamin Fitzgilbert. Though it was only small, it had an interesting collection of exhibits. Situated in the converted chandlery building, facing out to sea in the old part of town, it had become a popular visitor attraction. It had been a while since she'd looked round the place, but Lark was confident the curator and her staff would be thrilled to receive the items and have them on display amongst the other artefacts. A wisp of a memory flickered in her mind. She felt sure she'd heard something about it being awarded some investment or a grant. And now she thought about it, something told her Florrie was on first name terms with the curator; something to do with the out-of-print books the bookshop stocked.

Another thought popped into her mind. She wondered if there would be anything in the museum's archives concerning the history of Crayke's Cottage. She made a mental note to contact the visitor centre tomorrow, it suddenly dawning on her that it was closed on Mondays except for Bank Holidays. *Drat!* Not only was Lark impatient to dig into the history of Crayke's Cottage, but, more pressingly, she was also impatient to get the small suitcase out of her shed and into the hands of someone who would know what to do with it.

Checking the time on her phone, she saw it was almost nine o'clock. With the usual calm and positive air restored to not only herself, but the cottage too, Lark decided it would be a good time to call her dad, see how he was doing. She couldn't wait to hear what he'd have to say about the case, hoping it would pique his interest. He needed something after the last three years he'd had.

EIGHT

Armed with her mug of camomile tea, Lark headed into the living room, savouring the cosy warmth and the twinkling lights of the Christmas tree. Her nose twitched at the scent of the recent herb burning that still lingered and had joined the scent of pine. Luna stalked behind her, leaping up onto the armchair and tucking her paws beneath her.

She set her mug down on the coffee table and reached over to Luna, treating her to a quick scratch between her ears. The cat rewarded her with a deep, contented purr. It was a sound Lark had grown to love.

As she went to retrieve her phone, Lark found her gaze being drawn to the photo of her with her father next to it on the sideboard. A favourite of hers, it had been taken at the end of the pier on a bright and blustery day in June when she was fifteen. She could remember it as if it was yesterday, the sound of the waves crashing below, the smell of fish and chips from the kiosk on the bottom prom whipping around them and the salty tang of the sea air on her lips. Both Lark and her father were wearing wide smiles, eyes dancing with happiness, enormous ice creams in hand. She'd taken the photo on her phone, and despite the grainy image, there was no getting away from the striking resemblance she bore to her dad, with their matching golden-blond hair that was being roughed up by the wind, and clear green eyes. She'd inherited his straight nose, too. She smiled as she recalled how they'd roared with laughter as they'd battled to eat such mountainous ice creams, Lark's hair getting stuck to hers, which was a mix of raspberry ripple and summer fruits.

She'd be the first to admit she was a daddy's girl. Always had been. It was Silas who'd come up with her nickname: Lark. The name on her birth certificate was Lauren Harker – she had her mother's surname – but since she'd always been an early riser, he'd combined the two names and come up with Lark, which he'd thought most appropriate since he'd said she was always "up with the larks". It had stuck and she'd been Lark ever since.

Lark adored him, and, despite his journey to fatherhood being a little unusual, he adored her in return. There was no escaping the fact that her parents' relationship had been unconventional, which was something they'd never made a secret of. They'd never actually been an item, and Lark was conceived after Silas – who was the brother of Serena's best friend Elfie – real name, Delphine – and four years older than them – had agreed to "help out" when Serena had announced she wanted to become a mother. Though she was only twenty-one at the time, early menopause was rife in her family – her own mother Clarinda had gone through it by the time she was in her late thirties – and Serena didn't want to just get on with her life, indulging in her love of travel, and leaving it too late to conceive. Silas had been understandably shocked and outraged when Serena and his sister first broached him with their request. But he'd eventually backed down after listening to the reasons behind it, accepting that it wasn't just some half-baked whim.

Not long after Lark was born, Serena and Elfie became an item and set up home together, and though Elfie was technically Lark's aunt, the two women thought the title of "godmother" worked better for her.

Despite Lark not growing up in the same household as her dad, she'd stolen his heart the moment he'd first set eyes on her and he'd vowed to be a regular presence in her life. He'd been true to his word, and she'd always looked forward to his visits.

Her heart squeezed at the thought of him and the tough few years he'd had since losing his wife of twenty-six years. It had hit him hard, his grief sitting like a heavy cloak on his shoulders, dragging him down. Lark was beginning to think he was never going to shake it off and it worried her.

The weeks prior to Greer's diagnosis had been one of the most distressing times Lark could ever recall. Never before had she wished so hard that she could be rid of her "gift", as her mum and grandma referred to it. It didn't feel anything like a gift. A curse, more like.

For weeks she'd been overwhelmed by a dreadful sense of foreboding. It had gnawed away in the pit of her stomach, leaving her with the unshakeable feeling that something wasn't right with her stepmother. It had been agonising, occupying all her waking thoughts. Her concerns had been compounded the day Greer called in at Seashell Cottage. It had been a few months since Lark had last seen her and she'd been shocked to find her stepmother's aura so dramatically transformed. The usually smooth, turquoise glow around her had dimmed and become black and faint. Lark had realised in that instant her stepmother was ill. She'd scrubbed her eyes with her fists, doing all she could to unsee it. Even without her gut feelings and hunches, the black circles that sat under Greer's eyes and her pasty pallor was enough to suggest she wasn't well.

It had knocked Lark for six, her thoughts going to her father, wondering how he'd respond once he knew.

Much as she'd been aware she needed to act on it quickly, Lark had been unsure how. It wasn't an easy thing to put into words without sounding melodramatic or bonkers – *I hate to have to tell you this, Greer, but I think you're seriously ill and you need to see a doctor urgently*. It didn't help that Greer had chosen not to hide her scepticism about her stepdaughter's sixth sense. She'd even gone so far as to suggest that it was merely something that had been made up or embellished upon by Serena and Clarinda – Lark's maternal grandmother. 'We can all get a hunch about something, doesn't mean we've got extrasensory perception. It's all about evolution, when you think about it. I mean, there was a time when early humans needed such instincts to keep them safe from sabre-toothed tigers and the like. But we don't need them now, and while some of us have evolved such that it's been erased from our DNA, it's still present in others, like wisdom teeth; some of us have them, some of us don't. That's all this "extra sense" is about,' she'd said on a number of occasions, by way of what she called a "logical explanation".

Lark had lost count of the number of times she'd wished her stepmum was right.

Putting this to one side, all Lark knew was that her stepmum needed to get herself checked over. She'd made up her mind to speak to Greer, and had spent an age working out what to say. She was inordinately relieved to have had the problem taken out of her hands when, at a routine cervical screening appointment at her GP's surgery, Greer had mentioned to the nurse that she'd been experiencing a handful of uncomfortable symptoms including bloating and abdominal pain, joking that it was probably down to eating too much bread. When the nurse had questioned her further, she'd been sufficiently concerned such that she'd booked Greer an appointment to see the doctor straight away. The GP had shared the nurse's concerns and arranged for his patient to have a scan. The results had confirmed their worst fears: Greer had ovarian cancer. Despite surgery and chemotherapy, it had been too late. She died less than six months later owing to the complications of an infection.

Since then, Lark had done all she could to disengage herself from her intuition and premonitions. What had happened with Greer had been traumatic, she'd even blamed herself for not acting on her instincts and speaking to Greer sooner. She didn't want to experience anything like it again, so she closed her mind, and set about breaking the habit of aura reading. If she sensed anything negative in the future, she was determined to ignore it. After all, her intuition hadn't helped Greer. And now her dad was heartbroken. Instead, Lark decided she was going to focus her attentions on something positive that gave her enormous pleasure: crystal healing and aromatherapy. She'd still used her intuition when selecting the items for Lark's Vintage Bazaar, but that was as far as it would go.

Until the dratted warnings about Nate had started to push their way into her mind. She was just thankful she'd worked out what was behind that.

Lark was pulled out of her thoughts by the tinkling ring of her phone in her hand. Glancing at the number that lit up the screen, a rush of love filled her chest.

NINE

'Hey, Dad.' She couldn't keep the smile from her voice. 'I was just about to call you.' It was always good to hear from her father; it had been a while since they'd last spoken so his call was more than welcome. Not only did she want to hear how he'd been doing, but she was also eager to tell him about Crayke's Cottage and the suitcases.

'Hello, sweetheart, I must've picked up on your thoughts,' he said with an affectionate chuckle.

'You must've.' Lark laughed, too. Unlike her and her mother, her father didn't possess their extrasensory gift, so she knew he thought it highly unlikely.

'So, how's things with you?'

'Good, thanks. Actually, Dad, I'm glad you called, I've got something I want to run by you.' Lark made her way over to the sofa, dropping onto it and curling her feet beneath her.

'Oh, aye, and what's that, then?'

'I'll tell you all about it in a minute, but first of all, how're you doing? What have you been up to?' She'd heard so little from him since he'd lost Greer, she sensed he'd called for a reason, that he had something to tell her.

'I'm fine.' He paused, and she could sense his anticipation travelling down the phone line. Lark was just about to say something to fill the gap, when he spoke, stopping her in her tracks. 'I've put the house on the market.'

Her breath caught in her throat, and she took a moment to absorb the implications of his words. *I've put the house on the market.* This was a big step for him. *Huge.*

'And how do you feel about that? Are you okay with it?' Myriad thoughts tumbled into her mind. Was he really ready to leave the place he'd spent so many happy years with Greer?

Denley House had passed to Greer on her mother's death some six years before she and Silas had become an item. It was where she'd lived with Mick, her partner, for two of the four years they were together. A great, rambling Edwardian property, Lark had always been aware her dad had never felt completely comfortable living there, not least because Mick liked to pay them drunken visits, accusing Greer of diddling him out of what he believed should have been his "rightful share" in the house when they'd broken up. He'd stagger about in the front garden and yell that he was going to haul her to court and sue her for what was owed to him, claiming it was what he deserved for putting up with "a stuck-up cow" like her for so long. Greer and Silas had been forced to call the police on a number of occasions when Mick's ranting and thumping at the door had begun to disturb the neighbours. He'd only gone quiet once a restraining order had been slapped on him.

'I feel surprisingly calm about it, and actually quite positive, if I'm being honest,' her dad said.

Was that a tiny hint of optimism she detected in his voice?

'That's good to hear.'

'And I've had an offer – it's from the first couple who viewed it actually, a Mr and Mrs Seaton.' From his tone, Lark thought it sounded almost as if he couldn't quite believe it. 'They've got four lads – all under the age of ten, full of beans and bounce – and they're chain-free. They told me they're renting somewhere at the moment, which is a bit of a squash by all accounts, so they're keen to get the ball rolling as soon as possible.'

'That's fantastic news! You always said it would make a wonderful family home.'

'I did, yeah.' She heard him draw in a deep breath. 'I know Greer loved it, but in all honesty, it was wasted on us. We should've moved somewhere smaller years ago, let a family have the chance to enjoy it. I'm just rattling around it here on my own; seems such a waste.' He paused again and Lark could almost hear the cogs of his mind grinding away. 'You don't... you don't think I'm being disrespectful to Greer's memory, do you? It doesn't look like I'm getting rid of her house as soon as I can, does it? I'd hate to give anyone the wrong impression.'

'Oh, Dad, of course it doesn't! I promise you, no one will think either of those things. You really mustn't torture yourself with stuff like this.' She wished he was here with her so she could throw her arms around him and squeeze him tight, reassure him. He had the biggest heart, was always kind and considerate and put the feelings of others before his own, at times, too much so. They were qualities he'd passed to his daughter. 'It's been almost three years. Greer wouldn't want you to be rattling round the place on your own. She'd be thrilled to think it was going to be filled with a family, especially four boisterous lads.'

Her mum's comment a couple of months ago drifted into her mind, how she'd said he needed to "let go and move on". Though Lark knew it hadn't been meant as cold and heartless as it had sounded – her mum was worried for him and how his usually sunny disposition had all but extinguished since Greer had passed away – Lark still felt her mum's words seemed too harsh to use on her dad, especially when he'd only just started to take tentative steps away from his grief. She'd made a note to remind her mum not to use such expressions the next time she spoke to him. She didn't want anything to set him back.

Her father's voice broke into her thoughts. 'Aye, you're right, Greer would love to think of a family enjoying this place, 'specially the garden. Imagine the games of football that'll be played in it when the Seaton lads move in. She always said it was the perfect house for kids, was desperate for us to have some of our own, till we realised it was never going to happen,' he said wistfully. 'Mind, she used to love it when you came round with your friends.'

Oh, Dad. Lark felt a lump forming in her throat, the sting of tears in her eyes. In her last days, Greer had told Lark she loved her as if she'd been her own flesh and blood. It was a feeling Lark had reciprocated. 'And I loved coming to stay with you both; my friends did, too.' Though her visits to Denley House had been very different to the time she spent with her mum, she'd still loved going. Denley House was always neat and tidy, but not obsessively so, unlike her mum's which was messy to the point of being chaotic, with the heady scent of incense permeating every inch of the place. Despite this, the cottage had been imbued with a strong sense of love and kindness, as had Denley House. And where her mum's parenting style was laid-back, with any boundaries in place being best described as loose, there were rules to abide by at her dad and Greer's home, the boundaries a little tighter, which was hardly surprising since both Silas and Greer were teachers at the local secondary school. Lark hadn't minded adhering to their boundaries at all; if anything, she'd preferred it, it had made her feel somehow safer. Though both environments were dramatically different, Lark had felt equally at home in both. And though Greer may not have been a biological mother herself, it didn't mean she wasn't tuned in to what made children tick or how to entertain them. She may have been strict at times, but she'd had a great sense of fun.

Denley House itself had a generous-sized garden at the back with a spacious summerhouse that always smelt of warmth and dust. It was a space where Lark and her friends, Florrie, Jasmine and Stella, used to enjoy hanging out, chatting and laughing away. And when they weren't in the summerhouse, they were eating ice lollies on the padded swing seats or tearing around the lawns or making dens under the branches of the trees using old blankets and towels. They were the best of times.

A thought popped into Lark's mind. 'So, have you found anywhere suitable to move to? I assume you've been looking.'

'Aye, well, that's the thing...' The pause made Lark sit up straight. 'I was thinking of moving back to Micklewick Bay. It's been on my mind for a few months, actually, but I wanted to let the idea percolate a bit, see if I could really see myself living there again before I mentioned anything.'

'Oh, Dad, that would be wonderful! I'd love having you here in the town, and be able to see you more often.' A feeling of joy filled her chest. 'And is there a particular property that's taken your eye?'

'Hmm, well, there's a couple of houses in the new part of town, but they're not ideal. I quite fancy somewhere with a garden and a bit of character; something I can spend some time doing up.' She could read the subtext: keep his mind occupied, keep his grief at bay.

'And what about your job? Has a vacancy come up at the school here or one of the others nearby?' Her father taught history at High Nedderton Secondary School, which was where he'd first met Greer. He'd been instantly attracted to the bubbly, no-nonsense drama/English teacher.

'Not quite.' Silas cleared his throat. 'I've actually decided to retire.'

Retire? Had she heard right? 'Oh, right.' She didn't want to ask what he'd do once he retired. Her dad wasn't one for sitting around doing nothing.

'As you know, it was always the plan for Greer and I to retire once we hit the big six-o, and since I'll be sixty next June, I'm going to stick to that plan, well, the retirement part of it, at least.' He didn't need to mention his wife would've been sixty in August. The pair had big plans for how they were going to spend their retirement. They'd had a pot of money saved for the trips on their bucket list which included the Galapagos Islands, an exciting journey to Italy on the Orient Express, and a luxury safari in Africa. They'd even talked about a less extravagant holiday experience which involved backpacking around the Greek islands. It was something Greer had done in her gap year with friends, and she had fond memories. Sadly, cancer stole her before they'd had a chance to tick a single thing off their list.

'That's good to hear, Dad.' His news may have struck like a bolt out of the blue, but Lark was thrilled to hear of her father's decision.

'I'm glad you think so, sweetheart. I've decided it's time for a completely fresh start. Thought I'd get a little part-time job, nothing too taxing.' He chuckled at that. 'And I quite fancy doing a few stints as a volunteer somewhere. I'm financially secure, so I'm hoping that should all work out quite nicely. I've got my savings, and with what I get for this place, on top of the... um... I should be able to manage quite nicely.'

Lark knew the "um" was about the life insurance cover her dad and Greer had taken out years ago. It had paid out on Greer's death, which Lark knew had tortured her father, him saying it was no better than "blood money". She'd had to sit him down and explain it was anything but, asking him to think about Greer being in his position. 'You both took it out to make life easier for the one left behind. It offered you reassurance that Greer would be taken care of and have no financial worries if anything happened to you. It would've been the same for her. You know it would, Dad.' He'd reluctantly agreed with his daughter's logic.

'Well, if I know you, Dad, you'll have given this a huge amount of thought and I'm chuffed to bits you've decided to come home.' It felt like a step in the right direction, rather than him being over in High Nedderton, where his memories still had the power to drag him under. Even the school where he worked reminded him of Greer.

Lark found herself bouncing with happiness at the prospect of having her dad live close by again. 'Well, don't feel you need to rush in and buy something that isn't exactly what you want. You're welcome to stay here with me till a decent property turns up. I know it'll be a bit of a commute from here to work, but it's doable and would give you a good idea of what it'd be like if you did move here permanently.'

'I couldn't impose on you like that, Lark. What if I don't find anything suitable for months?'

'I don't care how long it takes, I'd love to have you here. I miss you, Dad,' she said softly.

'I miss you, too, sweetheart,' he said, his voice gruff with emotion.

It had been over six months since she'd last seen him, and any contact with him prior to that had been sporadic to say the least. Lark knew he'd been avoiding her so she wouldn't see the battle he was having with his grief, but the dark circles beneath his eyes had been a dead giveaway. He'd thrown himself into doing up the house, making the changes he and Greer had talked about but had never actually got round to, doing all he could to keep busy. But he was in danger of running himself into the ground. If he moved in with her at Seashell Cottage for a while she'd be able to keep an eye on him, feed him up and get him out and about again. He'd stopped socialising and hidden himself away, and if the amount of weight he'd lost was anything to go by, he'd been barely eating. He was in danger of becoming an old man before his time if he wasn't careful, which Lark thought would be a tragedy, especially since he was only fifty-nine.

She swallowed down the lump of emotion that had lodged itself in her throat. 'And it's been an age since you last sampled the Jolly's fish and chips,' she said, forcing a laugh into her voice. 'And I can assure you, they're as yummy as ever.'

'That's good to hear.' He laughed too, the sound sending a wave of warmth washing over Lark. 'Looks like I'd better take you up on your offer, then.'

'Fab! And how about in the meantime, you come for Sunday dinner next week and stay over for the weekend? We could do some house-hunting for you. It's a shame school hasn't broken up for the Christmas holidays already, Jack Playforth and Jenna Johnstone are giving an author reading at the bookshop on Thursday evening and I know for a fact there's a ticket going spare. You could come for that.'

The enthusiasm in her voice made Silas laugh. 'I've heard so much about these author readings, and as you know, I'm a huge fan of Jack Playforth, which means it's just as well we've got a training day booked for Friday so school's actually closed – Hilary, the head, lets us do the training online. I could set off straight from school on Thursday afternoon and get to you in plenty of time, provided the weather behaves itself, of course.'

'Fab! I'll text Florrie straight away, ask her to keep the spare ticket for you. I promise you'll have a great time, Dad.' A year ago he'd have turned the offer down immediately, not wanting to be around people, but his acceptance and the prospect of him moving back to Micklewick Bay was a positive sign as far as Lark was concerned.

'I daresay I will, flower.'

'There's going to be nibbles on afterwards, in the bookshop's new tearoom.'

'I was sold at the mention of fish and chips, but nibbles at the new tearoom has just confirmed my decision.' He chuckled some more. 'Anyroad, you said you had something to run by me.'

'Ooh, yes. Well, do you remember Crayke's Cottage? It's tucked away down in Micklemackle Yard here in the old part of town, been empty for as long as I've been aware of it.'

'I do, yes. Hasn't crossed my mind for years. Why? You're not thinking of moving there, are you?'

'No, nothing like that – though it is going on the market soon.' Was that a hint of concern she detected in her father's voice? 'Long story short, the two brothers who inherited it want to sell it ASAP and booked Nate to take all the contents off their hands.'

'I thought Nate didn't do house clearances.'

'He doesn't usually; this was a one-off. Anyroad, I went to give him a hand and... Oof! What a place! Honestly, Dad, you'd love it. It was fascinating, just like it'd been frozen in time.'

'And how did you feel when you were there? I expect you'll have picked up all sorts of vibes.'

'I did, though because it was so bone-numbingly cold there, it interfered with it a bit. You'll know it's supposed to be haunted – definitely looks and feels the part. And there's all sorts of rumours linked to it.' She went on to share what Nate had told her of Mr Thurston describing it as being cursed.

'Yeah, from what I can remember, it has a colourful past,' Silas said, sounding thoughtful. 'I'm sure it features in some of the books I have on the houses of Old Micklewick. I'll dig them out and bring them with me.'

'That would be great.' Her stomach gave a flutter at the prospect of delving deeper into the history of the place.

'How's Nate doing, by the way?'

A shadow momentarily crossed her face as she recalled the feelings she'd been getting about her friend. It disappeared quickly once she reminded herself of her theory of him picking up negative vibes from the vintage clothing he wore and the furniture he worked on.

Her dad had always been fond of Nate and the feeling was mutual. Lark assumed it was because they shared a good-natured temperament, a mischievous sense of humour not to mention an interest in old furniture. Lark knew her dad would not-so-secretly be thrilled if she and Nate became an item. He'd dropped it into conversation enough times, but she'd just laughed it off.

'He's fine; he'll be chuffed to bits when I tell him you're coming to stay.'

'It'll be good to see him, too, he's a grand lad.'

Here we go! He was as bad as her friends at times, teasing her about Nate. It was time to steer the conversation in a different direction.

'Don't suppose you've heard from Elfie or Mum recently, have you?' she asked.

Lark's mother and godmother lived on Koh Samui in Thailand where they ran a successful yoga and well-being retreat. They'd been working on Lark over recent months, trying to tempt her to join them without success, thus far.

'Not for a while, no. How about you?'

'Same here. From the way they were talking last time I spoke to them, I'm not sure they'll be coming over for Christmas.'

'Oh, right...' Silas hesitated. 'Listen, if you'd rather head over to them for the festive break, don't let me stop you. I can—'

'Dad,' Lark said, cutting him off. 'There's no way I'll be doing that. I want to spend Christmas here in Micklewick Bay with you.'

'But—'

'No buts and no argument, okay?'

'No argument,' he replied, an unmistakable smile in his voice.

'And besides, I love the snow at Christmas time.'

'Yeah, same here,' he said. 'So, you've had all my news, sweetheart. How've things been with you?'

'Oh, where to start!' Lark launched into telling her father about the suitcases and the contents, to which he'd listened intently, his interest and enthusiasm almost bouncing down the phone line.

Once the call ended, Lark fired off a quick text to Florrie, asking her to reserve the ticket for the bookshop's author event while it was still fresh in her mind. Much as she kept her hunches at arm's length these days, she had a good feeling about her father's return to Micklewick Bay, and she couldn't stop the smile that pushed its way over her face.

It didn't take long for a reply to land from her friend.

> Hi Lark, hope all went well at Crayke's Cottage and the spiders left you alone!! It's great to hear your dad's doing okay. I've kept the book event ticket for him. Don't forget it's the window reveal beforehand. See you then – if the snow doesn't put folk off! Fxx

Lark smiled at the smattering of emojis including a spiders' web and a snowman. She tapped out a quick reply.

> Thanks flower! We're both looking forward to it. And plse don't mention spiders!!! There were hundreds!!! Don't fret about the weather, a bit of snow won't put folk off being there for Ed's window reveal or one of the bookshop's events xxx

Lark added a slew of spider, snow and shock-faced emojis before pressing send. A heart-shaped tapback followed a couple of seconds later.

Ed was Florrie's fiancé as well as her business partner, and his window displays had become a huge attraction in Micklewick Bay, particularly those he created for Christmas. They were kept hidden behind thick curtains until the grand reveal which always generated a buzz of excitement in the town. His displays had set the bar high for the rest of the tradespeople and as a result the festive window displays in particular were stunning.

TEN

MONDAY 1ST DECEMBER

Lark peered through the curtains of the small, low window of her bedroom that looked out over Smugglers Row, straggles of mussed-up hair framing her face. It had just gone seven a.m. and the cove was still cloaked in darkness. Old Micklewick was starting to shake off its slumber, lights flickering on in the cosy-looking cottages while frost glittered in the glow of the streetlamps. Even in the dim light it was easy to see there'd been no let up with the snow overnight, leaving the cobbles and steeply pitched rooftops hidden under a thick blanket of white.

If the weather forecast was to be believed, they were due another load of the white stuff later that morning and it was set to continue on and off through to the evening. Lugging what was left at Crayke's Cottage wasn't going to be an easy task in such weather. Lark wasn't sure Nate would even be able to get his van down Skitey Bank, never mind to the end of the road. This part of town was never a priority when it came to gritters and snowploughs making an appearance, not that one would fit down Smugglers Row nor the surrounding equally narrow streets, but the wider roads that led to the cluster of houses was usually an afterthought to the local council. It was invariably left to the residents and local shopkeepers to keep the pathways clear and scatter rock salt they'd bought themselves. She'd send him a text, let him know how bad it was here.

Luna stretched from her place at the foot of Lark's bed, where she usually slept. She purred contentedly, her distress of the previous evening all but forgotten.

'Morning, Luna,' Lark said through a stifled yawn as she lifted her dressing gown off the hook on the back of the door and shrugged it on over her brushed cotton pyjamas. She normally slept like a log, falling asleep as soon as her head touched the pillow, but last night her mind had been full of so many different things all vying for her attention it had taken her brain an age to wind down. Her dad had occupied a huge chunk of her headspace as she'd gone over the plans he'd shared. It gladdened her that he seemed to be breaking free of his shackles of grief, he was too young to lock himself away. A smile spread across her face at the prospect of seeing him this week; she was looking forward to it.

Of course, she'd found her thoughts being drawn to the small suitcase and its strange clutter of contents too, not to mention the energy it had hung on to. Getting to the bottom of that was going to be interesting.

But it hadn't been her dad nor the suitcase that had been her waking thought. It had been Nate.

As she'd blinked sleep from her eyes, her mind had taken a couple of moments, going over his face, his gentle, dark brown eyes and his easy smile. His presence in her home felt natural and comfortable, as if it was where he was meant to be.

She hadn't been prepared for her mind to wander further, how it would be to have him in this bed, feel the warmth of his lips on hers... Her eyes had pinged open at that point, the thoughts practically propelling her out of bed. *Don't even go there!*

Downstairs, she was pleased to see there was still a glow from the embers in the base of the wood burner. She'd added extra logs before she'd gone to bed and turned the spin wheels right down which meant the place felt warm and cosy. Just as soon as she'd had a cup of tea, she'd empty the ashpan and relight the fire. Lark was also pleased to feel the presence of the familiar soothing energy she associated with Seashell Cottage was still there. The sage burning ritual had clearly done its job.

She was standing at the kitchen sink, filling the kettle, when a text landed. She scooped up her phone expecting to see a text from Nate and was surprised when she saw Florrie's name on the screen.

> Morning Lark, just wanted to warn you the snow's really bad in this part of town. No sign of any snowploughs or gritters. Doubt your little car would make it up Skitey Bank! Fxx

It was unusual for the little seaside town to get such a covering of snow, and what it did get, didn't usually hang around long owing to the salty air.

The message served as a reminder; she was going to ask her friend about the curator of the local heritage centre and see if she had her contact details. Lark was keen to get the ball rolling with the suitcase. After that, she was going to contact Nate and see what his plans were for the day. Her shop wasn't due to open until ten o'clock and she could help him remove the rest of the stuff from Crayke's Cottage before then if that was what he still planned to do.

> Hi Florrie, thanks for the warning. It's pretty bad here too. No way I'd risk tackling Skitey Bank in my old banger! I'll walk to the shop instead. Was going to pop in and see you at some point today, I need to pick your brains xx

Lark had just dropped a clutch of teabags in the pot when another text came through. It was from Florrie again.

> Ooh, sounds intriguing! Looking forward to seeing you! How about a cuppa & some cake in the tearoom here? Fxx

Lark couldn't resist a visit to the newly created tearoom in the bookshop, especially since Jasmine supplied many of their cakes.

> Sounds perfect! Text me whenever's good for you xx

Cradling her mug of tea, she peered out of the kitchen window, her gaze drawn to the shed that was playing host to the small suitcase. There was no trace of her footsteps from last night, the snow had completely covered them, leaving no evidence of her quick dash to the shed. Her mind went back to the feelings that had bombarded her body when she'd lifted the lid of the case, not to mention the tin. She still didn't know what to make of it all, but the reminder made her more determined to dig into the reasons for them being placed together in the case.

She was pulled from her thoughts by the ping of two texts landing simultaneously. The first was from Maggie saying that Bear was heading into town later that morning and wondered if she'd like him to scoop her up in his Land Rover en route. Maggie and Bear lived at Clifftop Cottage within the curtilage of his parents' farm above Thorncliffe which sat on the opposite side of the cove to the new part of town, and he'd pass by the cottages of Old Micklewick on his way.

Lark took a moment to consider the offer. The first thing that sprang to mind was that Bear must be feeling optimistic about Skitey Bank getting cleared by the plough at some point that morning. Just looking at the depth of the snow from her window, she reckoned even a Land Rover would struggle to tackle the bank's notoriously steep incline without the plough and gritters attending to it first. She rubbed her hand across her chin. There was also her offer to help Nate to factor into her plans for the morning. She'd see what he had to say before she replied to Maggie.

She tapped onto the next message while she thought about it. This one was from Nate in his familiar cheery style.

> Hi Lark, have you seen the snow!? Think we'd be better off going sledging rather than heading back to the fridge that is Crayke's Cottage! Not sure my van would manage the roads anyway. Maybe we should take a rain check – or should that be "snow" check?! – see how things go with the weather? BTW did the cases have owt worth putting in the shop? x

His text brought a smile to her face. He was spot on about Crayke's Cottage being like a fridge. She wasn't looking forward to facing the cold there, nor the spiders, for that matter.

She took a moment to consider how to reply, particularly about the small suitcase. She wasn't really sure how to condense her thoughts on it into a text.

> The bigger case was full of fabulous clothes that are perfect for the shop. The other one contained some "interesting" things, including an old key…
> L xx

Lark smiled as she tapped the send arrow, knowing he'd be itching to know more. He proved her right when, seconds later, a reply landed.

> Wow! "Interesting" things? A key? Any idea where it's for? And what made the "interesting" things so "interesting"?

Lark puffed out her cheeks. That was the million-dollar question. She didn't know where to begin answering about the "interesting" things.

> I think you need to see for yourself. Put it this way, the small suitcase spent the night in the shed.

She watched the bubble on the screen indicating that he was typing a response.

> Jeepers! How come it ended up there?

Her eyebrows hitched. 'Good question,' she muttered to herself.

> For starters, Luna went crazy when I opened it!!

As if on cue, Luna arrived in the kitchen, gently butting her head up against Lark's legs and purring loudly. Lark reached down and gave her a scratch between the ears just as a reply from Nate arrived.

> Yikes!!!

Lark couldn't help but laugh at his choice of words and the accompanying shocked face emojis.

> Yikes? Jeepers? Have you been watching a lot of episodes of Scooby Doo recently, Nate?

She chuckled, awaiting his response.

> Is it that obvious? "Those pesky kids..." Am I okay to pop in this morning and if so what time's good for you?

> Yes, it def is that obvious!! And of course. Is 8-ish okay? I'll do us some breakfast xx

She watched the screen anticipating his reply.

> Jeepers! Yikes! Yep, 8-ish is cool with me x

Laughing at his playful response, she found herself looking forward to his visit.

ELEVEN

Lark was feeling calm and relaxed after her thirty-minute yoga session, just as she did each morning. It set her up well for the day ahead, clearing her mind and leaving her feeling energised. Wearing a pair of lined dungarees in shades of plum and green, with a thick purple sweatshirt beneath, she'd made sure to dress warmly for the visit to Crayke's Cottage. She'd fastened her hair into two plaits and arranged them on top of her head in a bid to keep any spiders from finding their way into her waves. She'd be sure to keep her hat pulled firmly over her head this time.

Once she'd finished texting Nate, Lark turned her attention to Maggie's message. She replied, telling her of her plans to help Nate and how she wasn't sure what time they'd get finished so didn't want to keep Bear waiting. Maggie's reply had come through five minutes later, saying Bear didn't mind hanging back and that Lark was to give them a shout when she was ready to leave.

'Ahh, thank you, Maggie and Bear,' she said to herself as she sent a heart tapback. She felt blessed to have such good friends.

She was sitting at the kitchen table sewing beads onto the Christmas decorations she'd made the previous night, the sweet tones of The Mediaeval Babes Christmas compilation playing in the background, when a knock at the door pulled her out of her thoughts.

She opened it to find Nate filling the frame, a broad smile on his face. 'Morning,' he said in his usual cheery tone, his breath curling out around him as he briskly rubbed his gloved hands together. 'By 'eck, it's parky out here.' From her quick appraisal Lark noted his nose and the apples of his cheeks were bright red, suggesting he'd been out in the freezing seaside air for some time. His eyes, however, betrayed that he was a little sleep-deprived.

'Ooh, come in, you look absolutely nithered.'

'Thanks. You're not wrong. That wind's savage, but at least it's stopped snowing.' He kicked the snow off his wellies and stepped into the tiny vestibule where he heeled them off. Lark brushed past him as she closed the door, shutting out the cold, noting the smell of frosty air that clung to him. Before she knew what was happening, her wayward mind leapt unexpectedly to her waking thoughts that morning, imagining the feel of Nate's lips on hers. *Oh!* A flurry of butterflies jumped to attention in her stomach and her cheeks flamed. *Calm your jets, missus!*

'I'll just go and clear the table – I was working on the fabric Christmas decorations. I've got stuff everywhere.' Her words came out in a gabble and she hurried off in the direction of the kitchen, willing her insides time to calm down and hoping Nate hadn't noticed her blushes.

'Aye, righto.' He hung up his coat and woolly hat and followed her through the living room and into the kitchen at the back, ducking to avoid the beams as he went.

'You sure you don't mind giving me a hand at Crayke's Cottage?' he asked, taking in the sewing clutter piled on the small table and nearby worktop. 'I'll totally understand if you're too busy. There's not that much to clear, so I could manage it myself.'

'No, not at all. I'm expecting the shop to be quiet so I'll take this lot to work with me. What I don't get done there, I'll finish here tonight.' She kept her head down, pushing everything into a fabric bag, as if she was focusing intently on clearing the table. She hoped the lack of eye contact and her still-warm cheeks wouldn't make him think there was anything wrong. 'And besides, it shouldn't take us long to get the rest of the stuff out of Crayke's Cottage. It's pretty much ready for us to just lift out.'

When it had become obvious that they were running out of time and light, not to mention being so cold it had become difficult to actually do anything, they'd made the decision to stack the remainder of the items in the living room. It would save them from having to hunt around the cottage for the rest of the stuff, or lug things downstairs.

'True,' he said, bending to stroke Luna who'd followed him into the kitchen and was brushing up against his long legs, purring loudly. 'Now then, miss, what's this I've been hearing about you?' He scooped the cat up in his arms, cradling her like a baby. She lay there, gazing up at him, her purring going into overdrive.

Lark giggled. 'What are you like, Luna?' She'd noticed Nate had a way with animals. Her friends' dogs all loved him. Being an animal lover herself, it was a trait she found appealing, though he was more of a dog person than she, and had mentioned several times of his wish to own one. Lark was fond of dogs too, but she had always been drawn to cats.

'So, tell me about the suitcases,' Nate said. He was now rocking Luna from side to side. 'So many things have been going through my mind after what you said about the smaller one. I assume since Luna seems okay, it's still in the shed.'

Lark nodded. 'Yep, it's still there. I didn't fancy bringing it back into the house, to be honest.' She sat the bag of decorations and fabric out of the way in the corner. 'How about I make us some breakfast first? I can tell you all about it while we're eating. Then I'll show you it afterwards, though I'd rather not bring it back in here. Would you mind if we took it back to Crayke's Cottage, so I can show you the stuff there, rather than opening it up again here?'

''Course, I completely understand. We don't want Luna getting herself all het up again, do we, lass?' Nate said kindly, tickling the cat under the chin.

'Thanks, I appreciate that.' Lark knew he'd be understanding and wouldn't think she was making a fuss over nothing. 'Scrambled eggs on wholemeal toast accompanied by a rasher or two of bacon and an unlimited supply of tea do you?'

'Perfect.' He beamed at her, his dark eyes crinkling at the corners and making her heart perform an unexpected leap. 'What can I do to help?'

What can you do to help? Her wayward mind headed straight back to thoughts of his kisses and she could feel the colour rising in her cheeks once more. She really needed to get this under control before he guessed something was the matter.

'Um, you can set the table, provided Luna doesn't mind you putting an end to your cuddles, of course.' She quickly made for the fridge in yet another bid to hide her blushes.

Soon the kitchen was filled with the aroma of bacon frying and bread toasting. As she stood at the oven, Lark shared what had happened the previous evening, including the feelings the suitcase had triggered in her and how she'd felt compelled to carry out a sage burning ritual.

Nate listened, his eyes growing wide. He knew how seriously she took positive and negative energy, and understanding what it meant to her, realised that it must have been bad if she'd had to resort to a cleansing ritual that late in the evening.

She continued the story as they ate, and when she arrived at the point where she discovered the contents of the tin, he stopped chewing and set his knife and fork down, his expression one of disbelief.

He swallowed his mouthful. 'No way! A *pistol*?'

'Yep, a pistol.' Lark nodded slowly. Annoyingly, she found her attention being pulled away from their conversation and onto his aura, its shades and textures. They seemed so wrong. So unlike Nate.

Her heart juddered as her thoughts flew back in time to the person who'd previously generated this same awful feeling in her gut: Greer.

TWELVE

'Lark? Lark? Lark, are you okay?' said a faint voice at the back of her consciousness. Thoughts barged around her mind, but the thud of her heart galloping and the anxiety whooshing in her ears drowned out all other sounds. Tears started brewing at the back of her eyes.

No! Please, no! Not Nate! I don't want to see this! I don't want to feel it!

The touch of Nate's hand on her forearm yanked Lark back into the room. She blinked and shook her head. 'Huh?' She swallowed, drawing in a slow breath in a bid to calm herself.

'You okay, lass? You look like you've seen a ghost, which I know you probably did, or summat like it last night. I know I'm not sensitive to that sort of stuff like you, but I can honestly say this place still has its familiar calm atmosphere. Still feels warm and welcoming.' He offered a concerned smile and squeezed her arm.

'Sorry, Nate – and thank you, that's reassuring to know.' She arranged her face into a smile. 'My mind just went back to poor old Luna and her reaction to the suitcase. It was quite something and so unlike her.' She hoped her explanation sounded convincing.

'Sounds like the poor lass was terrified.' He moved his hand from her arm and picked up his knife and fork once more. 'I honestly thought it would contain something completely innocent; costume jewellery or accessories like fancy purses or hair slides – the sort of thing you sell in your shop. Never in a million years did I expect you to say a pistol or any of the other stuff you unearthed.'

'Yeah, same here.' With anxiety loosening its grip, Lark was able to think straight once more. She reminded herself of her theory of how Nate had very probably absorbed some of the energy from his vintage clothing and the second-hand furniture he handled on a regular basis. It had very probably interfered with his aura again. The reminder offered instant relief, brightening her mood once more. She told herself to keep it in mind for the next time she found herself focusing on these weird, confusing sensations.

But there was still a part of her that doubted this, still a part of her that wondered about the dramatic change in the energy that emanated from him, the significant change in his aura. Was it too easy to explain it away with her Crayke's Cottage theory? she wondered. There was no getting away from the fact that it didn't rest easy with her. Not that she wanted Nate to know.

Nate looked thoughtful for a moment. 'I s'pose I should let old Mr Thurston know what you found, too. I get that since I've paid him for them, it means the contents technically belong to me – and the cases to you, since I gave you them – but the pistol could have some sort of historic value, might be worth a bit. Wouldn't feel right not mentioning it to him. And the key might be for somewhere in the cottage – he should know about that, too.'

'I agree, that had crossed my mind.'

'Mind, something tells me he won't be interested no matter what it is – well, maybe if it was a chest of gold sovereigns, then I reckon that might make his lugs prick up a bit.' He gave her a wide grin that made her heart melt and sent her worries scurrying away. She felt her gaze drop to his mouth.

Stop that right now!

What the heck was going on? Where were these feelings coming from so out of the blue like this? Not two minutes ago she was worried to death about him. Talk about confusing!

She'd always known Nate was her type, but even despite the strange feelings that had warned her off him, she'd told herself more times than she cared to remember that he was too young for her. It was a fact she'd always accepted. Until now, and her mind had suddenly decided otherwise. Or should she be blaming her heart for steering her mind in the wrong direction?

Was seven years really such a big age gap? she wondered. He was coming up for twenty-eight, so it wasn't as if he was a baby, though admittedly, his boyish sense of humour did sometimes make her think he was younger than his years. His youthful looks didn't exactly help with that either. But he had so much in his favour that made him perfect boyfriend material. He was kind-hearted and considerate, always the first to offer if anyone needed help with anything, and he was rarely without a smile. She found his easy-going, level-headed nature hugely appealing. Like her, he avoided drama and conflict, preferring a quiet life. In fact, in so many ways he put her in mind of her dad – didn't they say girls were always attracted to men like their father? On top of that, there was no getting away from the fact he was really quite attractive. Well, more than "quite" attractive, if Lark was being honest with herself. Looking at him today, his soft, dark eyes that she found so appealing were making her knees go a little weak despite the tiredness that loitered behind them.

It had been a good six months since he'd last tested the water on whether or not there was a chance she'd ever change her mind about them being more than friends. As usual, she'd let him down gently, and, as usual, he'd taken it graciously.

But something had changed for Lark, almost overnight – it was as if realisation had dawned on her that they went well together, that she enjoyed his company on a level that went beyond friendship. And it was in conflict with the ever-present feeling in her gut that was holding her back, warning her that a romantic relationship with Nate was a path she shouldn't walk down. But... 'Ugh!' She huffed out a sigh and brushed the stray curls off her face. She was becoming frustrated with the warning, and couldn't remember a time when her mind had been in such turmoil.

'What's up?' Nate's voice pushed into her thoughts.

'Hm?' She scrabbled around her brain, searching for an answer. 'Oh, I was just thinking about Luna's reaction last night again, poor kitty.' She pulled a suitably sympathetic face.

'I wouldn't worry about her. No permanent harm done there, she seems right as rain to me.' He seemed to have bought her reply – again.

'Yeah, you're right.'

While they finished their breakfast and moved on to the washing up, Lark filled Nate in on her idea of getting in touch with the curator at the local museum, which he agreed would be the best course of action. She also shared the conversation she'd had with her father. Nate seemed genuinely thrilled to hear Silas was thinking of moving back to Micklewick Bay. The way he spoke of her dad, she'd always got the impression he looked upon him as some sort of father figure, which was hardly surprising since he barely saw his own. Ronan Wilkinson had walked out on Nate's mum when Nate was a young boy. The little contact between them had been sporadic over the years, which Nate seemed resigned to.

Lark's heart was beating a tattoo as she and Nate made their way along Smugglers Row on their way to Crayke's Cottage. He had the small suitcase gripped firmly in his hand. The snow-covered lanes were peppered with footprints and despite it being just after nine o'clock, a handful of pavements had already been cleared. Unlike the grey clouds that hung over the town yesterday, today was all bright winter sunshine and clear blue skies. The temperature, however, was a good couple of degrees lower, as the spiteful wind that blew in off the sea reminded them.

Turning into Micklemackle Yard, Lark shivered, and not just because she was cold. Anxiety had started to sneak its way in as she recalled the vibes she'd picked up from the suitcase the night before. She wasn't looking forward to facing them again.

'Right, here we are,' said Nate as they stopped before the old oak door to Crayke's Cottage. It objected with a loud groan as he pushed it open.

Stepping inside, they were met with the same fusty smell that had lingered on the clothes in Betty's suitcase. Lark wondered if the place would feel any different now its peace had been interrupted after so many decades of sitting quiet and undisturbed. Making her way over the flagstones of what would have been the living room, she stood for a moment, letting the atmosphere wash over her. The cottage still wore that indefinable feeling she hadn't been able to fathom yesterday, though today, she detected something extra. It almost felt as if the walls had eyes, all watching her silently. It sent a shiver running up her spine.

She looked on as Nate set the suitcase down on a small oak table. He glanced up at her, his hands poised on the clasps. 'Still want me to do the honours?'

'If you're okay with it.' She'd brought her sage stick, just in case she felt the need to rid them of any negative energy before they left. She'd also dropped a couple of malachite crystals in the pockets of her dungarees as an extra layer of protection. Nate, too, had a couple in the pockets of his overcoat.

'Okay, here goes.'

If she wasn't mistaken, Lark thought Nate looked as apprehensive as she felt.

The WD-40 she'd used last night meant the clasps opened straight away. She watched him slowly ease the lid back until it was wide open, revealing the contents. Her stomach churned in response.

He was just about to reach in for the tin when there was a loud noise that sounded like the slamming of a door. It made the very fibres of the cottage vibrate.

A scream escaped Lark's mouth before she had the chance to stop it, the hairs on her arms standing on end. She caught Nate's eye to see he was wearing a startled expression, his face pale.

He gulped. 'What was that?'

'I have no idea, but it sounded like it came from the back of the house.' Her heart was pounding, her chest heaving and she had the overwhelming urge to run from the cottage as fast as she could.

'It did.' He strode to the door that gave access to the room behind. 'Hello,' he called out.

They stood looking at one another as they listened, but were met with nothing more than an ominous silence.

Nate gave a shrug of his shoulders just as a hushing sound filled the room and an icy breeze rushed in, circling all around them. It lifted the stray strands of hair that peeked from beneath Lark's hat and skimmed over her cheeks, making her gasp and sending a rash of goosebumps prickling over her skin.

As quickly as the breeze arrived, it was gone.

From the baffled expression on Nate's face she could tell he'd felt it, too.

'That was seriously creepy,' she said with a shudder. As used as she was to sensing the atmospheres and energy of a whole host of different places, Lark had never experienced anything like that before.

'I know what you mean.' He circled his shoulders as if shaking the feeling off. 'Surely there must be some explanation for it, like a sudden draught from an ill-fitting window or summat like that. I mean, it was getting pretty blustery out there before we got here.' He disappeared into the back room, the dull thud of his footsteps on the floorboards, Lark hot on his heels. After what had just happened, she didn't fancy being left on her own in the room.

The pair of them took their time to look around, checking for anything that had been knocked over and could explain the loud slamming sound, or any gaps where the wind could have sneaked in. But they found nothing. Yes, the windows were a little old and rattly, but there was nothing that would explain the strength of the gust of air they'd just experienced.

Nate glanced down at his feet, his thick brows drawing together. 'Maybe it's a draught coming up through the floorboards.'

Lark followed his gaze. When they were at Crayke's Cottage yesterday, it had escaped her attention that this floor wasn't flagged like the other downstairs rooms, but that was probably because the cold had stopped her from thinking clearly. She contemplated Nate's suggestion. 'Good point. These little cottages are full of places where draughts can sneak in and make doors slam. I know Seashell Cottage has its fair share, which is why the wood burner's been such a godsend.'

'Aye, my place is the same.' He strode over to the back door that gave out onto the yard and tried the handle, but the door didn't budge. He turned his head to her. 'It's locked.'

'Okay,' Lark said slowly, glancing around her. 'So where did the slamming sound come from?'

'Good question.'

'I don't know about you, but I'm feeling a bit creeped out,' she said.

'Aye, it's a bit odd but I'm sure there's a logical explanation. Maybe it was something blowing over in the yard?' he suggested as he rubbed at the grimy windows with his gloved fingers, peering out through the small circle he'd created.

'I suppose it could've been. Though wouldn't the snow have muffled the sound of anything falling over?'

'S'pose it might've done.'

But they both knew the sound came from inside the cottage and, in particular, this room.

'Why don't you have a look at the stuff in the suitcase, then we can decide what to do with it and leave?' Lark was keen to get done and get out as quickly as possible.

'Yeah, I have to say, things seem to have gone a bit weird here today.' He moved closer, wrapping his arm around her shoulders and giving her a squeeze, the warmth of his body seeping into her.

'We'll get sorted as quick as we can, then we don't have to come back again.'

'I like the sound of that.'

Back in the living room, Nate reached into the case, picking out each item one by one, examining them as closely as he was able in the dim light. 'The stories these things could tell.'

The same thought had crossed Lark's mind when she'd first seen them, and she couldn't shake the feeling these stories wouldn't all be good.

'As sorely tempted as I am to look inside this, I'm going to refrain. The leather looks too fragile and I'm worried it might crumble if I open it.' Nate was turning the leather-bound book over in his hands. 'Best save it for folk who know what they're doing and how to handle such delicate items.'

'That's what I thought, too. The thin piece tied around it looks like it wouldn't take much for it to break into pieces.' Lark watched as he placed it back in the case.

'Right then, what's hiding under here?' he said, lifting out the tin. Anticipation and unease started swirling in Lark's stomach as he carefully unwrapped the piece of eiderdown, lay it on the suitcase and focused his attention on prising open the lid.

'It took a while to loosen it last night,' she said, watching him have the same struggle.

'Aye, it doesn't seem keen to budge.'

The words had just left his mouth when the lid finally conceded defeat and opened with a loud rattle of the metal objects inside. Before Nate could utter another word, the room filled with an icy rush of air followed by an urgent banging at the front door.

The pair froze, eyes locked on each other. Lark could feel her pulse pumping in her ears as fear prickled over her skin.

'What should we do?' she whispered, her teeth chattering from fear as much as the cold.

'I'll take a—'

His words were sliced off as an ethereal cry echoed around the room.

'What the bloody hell was th—'

The thudding at the door resumed, more urgent this time. Another cry filled the room, followed by a second icy gust of air and a crashing sound from the back room.

Lark's heart leapt up to her throat. She'd never been so desperate to leave a place as she was right now.

THIRTEEN

'I really don't like this,' said Lark, trembling.

'I'd suggest it's likely to be Mr Thurston knocking at the door, come to see if we're done,' Nate said. 'But he's got a key, and I got the impression he wouldn't be back here again.'

'I can see why.' Lark wouldn't be sorry if she never set foot in the cottage ever again.

'Lark! Nate!' came a voice from the other side of the door, followed by another round of knocking.

'Jasmine!' Lark couldn't remember feeling so happy to hear the familiar tones of her friend. Tension fell away from her shoulders as she rushed over and flung the door open. 'I can't tell you how glad I am to see you.'

'If that's the case, what the bloomin' 'eck took you so long? It's brass monkey out here! I'm nithered!' Jasmine beamed at her friend before giving a theatrical shiver. She was bundled up well against the wintry weather in a bright green padded jacket, a stripy scarf wrapped several times around her neck and a matching hat pulled over her ears.

'Sorry, Jazz, come in.' Lark couldn't help but laugh at her friend's faux put-out expression.

'Now then, Jazz,' said Nate, smiling at her. 'Mind, I'm not so sure it's much warmer in here.'

After stamping her feet to get the snow off her wellies, Jasmine took a few steps into the living room and shuddered. 'Brr! I see what you mean, it's like a fridge in here. Has a weird atmosphere, too.' She swept her gaze around the room. 'Oh, and I nearly forgot, are you aware there's a peacock on the roof?'

'A *peacock*?' Lark looked at Nate askance. Had she heard right? 'I didn't notice one when we got here, did you?'

He shook his head. 'Can't say I did. And how come it's managed to get onto the roof? I thought they usually had their wings clipped to stop them from flying off.'

'Well, this one's flying feathers are clearly all intact which I reckon is why it's currently perched on the chimney pot to this place.' Jasmine chuckled.

As if on cue, an ethereal cry travelled down the chimney and filled the room.

'It was the peacock!' Lark and Nate said in unison before falling about laughing.

'Have I missed something?' asked Jasmine, glancing between them. The reason for their amusement slowly dawned on her. 'Don't tell me you thought it was a ghost?' she said, her hoots of laughter joining theirs.

After a quick discussion, the three of them managed to ascertain that the bird belonged to a new resident of Old Micklewick who'd brought it with them from their previous home that had benefitted from a much bigger outside space. It had been wreaking havoc in the nearby back yards and gardens ever since.

'They used to eat peacock in Tudor times, didn't they?' said Jasmine.

'I believe they did,' said Lark.

'That bird wants to watch out then. If it ruffles any more feathers – pun intended – it might find itself stuffed and roasted.'

'Don't mess with our Jazz.' Lark chuckled.

Jasmine flashed a jokey grin. 'So, folks, one of the reasons I'm here is to let you know that Skitey Bank's been ploughed and gritted, though I guess you already know that since I spotted Nate's van parked at the end of the lane – unless you stayed over at Lark's, Nate?' Jasmine gave a playful waggle of her eyebrows.

Lark replied with a good-natured roll of her eyes.

'I spent the night in my own home,' said Nate. 'Headed down here as soon as I saw the roads had been cleared.'

'Ah, right, if you say so.' Mischief twinkled in Jasmine's bright green eyes.

'It's true!' said Lark, her non-verbals telling Jasmine to stop this right now! She could feel the heat of a blush rise up her neck and spread over her face.

'It's none of my business, flower.' Jasmine flashed her a cheeky grin. 'Anyroad, the other reason is to have a quick nosy round here. I've always wondered what this place was like. Mags said you were heading here this morning and since I had a birthday cake to drop off, I thought I might as well pop in and say a quick hello.'

Jasmine was a much-in-demand celebration cake maker. Not only did she work freelance, but she was also contracted to make wedding cakes for the Danskelfe Castle wedding packages – a luxury wedding destination near Lytell Stangdale on the North Yorkshire Moors. It was a role she loved.

'I'm glad you did pop in or we'd never have known it was a peacock making the spooky sounds,' Lark said, chuckling. 'I was just about ready to make a run for it.'

The three of them had congregated in the living room after showing Jasmine around the cottage, and were just about to turn their attention to the suitcase when Jasmine's mobile started ringing. She fished it from her jacket pocket and groaned as she looked at the screen.

'Why would school be calling me at half past nine in the morning? The kids have only just got there.'

Lark pressed her mouth into a sympathetic smile. She knew

her friend would be worried about Zak and Chloe after her children had experienced a bout of bullying earlier in the year.

Jasmine took the call, Lark and Nate looking on to see relief washing over their friend's face as she listened.

Ending the call, Jasmine puffed out her cheeks. 'I need to head off. The school's heating's on the blink so they're having to close for the day. Can't imagine how gutted the kids are going to be about that.' She gave a chuckle, pushing her phone back into her pocket.

'Looks like a day of sledging, snowman building and snowball fights is on the cards,' Nate said.

'Hmm. The secretary just told me they'll have to do some lessons online, but I'd like to think they'll get the chance to have a bit of fun outside, like we did when we were kids and had snow days. Remember that dim and distant time before computers took over the world and spoilt everyone's fun?'

'Can't say I do, to be honest,' said Nate.

'Right then, I'd best head off and get the kids. See you later, folks.' Jasmine bid them goodbye and hurried off.

With Jasmine's bubbly personality gone, the room quickly took on its strange air once more. Lark and Nate turned their attention back to the case and, in particular, the tin. Lark looked on, the feeling of unease making itself known once more as Nate reached in and lifted out the pistol she'd wrapped back up in the oily cloth.

'Wow! This is an original, and it's seriously old,' he said. 'I'm certainly no expert, but looking at the elaborate metalwork, I'd say it belonged to someone wealthy. And there's a set of initials here.' He squinted, heading over to the window, examining the firearm more closely in the light. '"J.W.F.".'

'James William Fitzgilbert,' said Lark, excitement suddenly thrumming through her and pushing her disquiet aside. 'He's the wealthy man who was in league with the smugglers. You do realise this is a serious piece of Micklewick Bay history, don't you?'

'I do. And the burning question is, what's it doing here, in what's very possibly Jacob Crayke's cottage?'

'That's a very good question. If I recall from local legend, the two of them had a particularly vicious falling out, though I can't remember the reason.' The detail on the pistol made Lark more determined to speak to the curator of the local heritage centre, see what she could learn from her.

'I remember reading somewhere that there were rumours Fitzgilbert had turned double agent and was accused of tipping off the local excise men when a ship full of contraband was due to land.'

'That does ring a bell actually,' said Lark, the implication of Nate's words swirling around her mind. 'And if it's true, then I wonder what happened to him?'

'Something tells me he disappeared.'

'Disappeared?' Lark echoed his words, catching his eye.

'Aye, in suspicious circumstances.'

A loud clatter of metal hitting stone made them both start and they turned to see the pewter tankard from the case lying on the floor. It had seemingly fallen from where Nate had placed it on the small table.

'How the heck did that happen?' he said, his face paling.

'I don't know about you, but I get the feeling this house is trying to tell us something.' Lark looked around her, uneasy, that same strange feeling from yesterday building in the air around them once more. She pushed her hands into the pockets of her coat and took the pieces of malachite crystal in her hands, squeezing tightly.

'Oh, I'd say it very definitely is.' Nate wrapped the pistol in the stained cloth and placed it back in the suitcase, before reaching for the tankard. 'I reckon we should gather everything together and get done here ASAP.'

'Agreed, but if it's okay with you, I'd feel happier if I did a bit of sage burning before we leave, get rid of as much negative energy as we can, that way it won't cling to us.'

'Suits me. After what's been happening here this morning, I

don't fancy having any of that negative stuff lingering on me.' Though he chuckled, Lark could tell he was serious.

With the last of the items from Crayke's Cottage loaded into Nate's van, he and Lark headed back to her house for her to get changed before she opened the shop. The suitcase would be locked in the shed at Seashell Cottage for the time being; more than ever, she didn't want it in her home. They'd agreed that he should contact Mr Thurston about it and its contents before approaching the curator of the heritage museum, just in case he'd changed his mind about Nate keeping them. They didn't want to risk sharing something Mr Thurston might rather keep private. So, Nate had called the older man and left a message on his answerphone, explaining what they'd found, asking him to call back as soon as possible. While he'd been doing that, Lark had texted Maggie thanking Bear for his offer of a lift and explaining that she wouldn't need it since Nate had offered to drop her off in town on the way to his workshop.

Returning to the warmth – not to mention calm – of Seashell Cottage, Lark wasn't completely surprised to find that Luna kept her distance, observing them with silent interest, as if she knew where they'd been. In a bid to further banish any traces of energy that might be lingering on them from Crayke's Cottage, Lark topped up the aromatherapy diffuser, sending the soothing fragrance of lavender and scented geranium into the air, hoping it would help Luna feel more settled.

While he was waiting for Lark to get changed out of her dusty clothing and gather together the stuff she needed for the shop, Nate made a pot of tea and checked his mobile to see he'd missed a call from Mr Thurston.

In his voicemail message, the older man had sounded more than a little agitated and told Nate very firmly he wanted nothing to do with any of what they'd found, that Nate had paid for all of the contents so was now the legal owner, just as they'd agreed. He could do whatever he wanted with the pistol, etcetera. He'd added, quite snappily, that he didn't want to hear about anything else, and that he and his brother would be glad to have the property off their hands.

After changing into a brightly coloured Scandinavian-style jumper and a pair of dark red trousers, leaving her hair hanging loose over her shoulders, Lark had headed back downstairs. Nate relayed his conversation with Mr Thurston to her. They agreed his response had only added to the intrigue of the old property.

Quickly finishing their mugs of tea, they headed out into the bright winter sunshine.

'Looks like the next plan of action is for us to get in touch with the curator of the heritage museum.' Nate was carefully negotiating one of the many sharp bends of Skitey Bank, snow piled high at the edges of the road where the plough had pushed it back. It took an age for the van to warm up and it was as cold inside the vehicle as it was outside.

'I'll get onto it later today. I've already told Florrie I'll pop over to see her at the bookshop.' Lark was looking out of the passenger window, taking in the view of Old Micklewick below, lifting her gaze and skimming over the snow-covered fields of Thorncliffe Farm that stretched out beneath a vivid blue sky. It looked breathtakingly beautiful.

'Right then, here we are.' Nate pulled the van up outside Lark's Vintage Bazaar in Victoria Square, yanking the handbrake on. 'Everywhere looks pretty quiet. Mind, it's hardly surprising. I should imagine folk'll be waiting for the snow to clear before they head out.'

Lark peered out through the windscreen to see the run of sandstone planters that divided the wide road were completely hidden under a dense blanket of white, and the clock at the bottom, located opposite the station building, was sporting what appeared to be a top hat of snow.

'Hmm. I doubt I'll get much trade today, but that's fine, I've got a load of new stock to get out as well as the Christmas decorations to finish.'

'Aye, I doubt I'll make many sales, but I've got a backlog of restoration to catch up on, so I'll crack on with that.'

'Thanks, Nate.' She leant across and pressed a kiss to his cheek. 'I'll keep you up to speed if I get to speak to the curator.' She grabbed her bag filled with the unfinished Christmas decorations and the one containing her shoes to change into out of her wellies.

'Good stuff. Let me know if you need a lift back home.'

'Thanks, I'm sure I'll be fine.' She didn't like to put on him, or for him to think she expected him to go out of his way on her account. She'd be quite happy to walk back home. She climbed down from the van, her wellies sinking into the snow that was piled against the kerb. 'See you later, hope you have a good day.' Her breath curled into a plume of condensation in the chilly air.

'Aye, you too.' He smiled and gave her a salute as she heaved the door shut.

Lark's Vintage Bazaar was a treasure trove of interesting and intriguing finds, where her loyal customers could lose themselves for hours. Not only did it stock vintage items, but also Lark's own range of homemade aromatherapy products, as well as a range of crystals. No one who entered it ever left empty-handed. The shop was almost directly opposite The Happy Hartes Bookshop which was owned by her friends, Florrie and Ed.

The store, named in honour of Lark, had originally been a joint enterprise opened by her mother, Serena, and godmother, Elfie. By the time she'd reached eighteen, they'd handed Lark the reins while they followed their passion for travelling, knowing it would be left in a safe pair of hands. Lark had been at the helm ever since. Since then, she'd grown the stock, repairing garments where necessary, or tweaking and making alterations in order to increase the item's appeal to a contemporary market – a pair of checked, nineteen-seventies flares had become a neatly tailored pair of ankle-grazers, for example. Now, Lark's Vintage Bazaar did a roaring trade and people came from miles around to have a rummage through the rails.

Standing in front of her shop, Lark took a moment to survey the Christmas display in the large window. It was still a work in progress, but she liked to take her time, make sure she got it just right. Last year's featured a mannequin wearing a white pleated nineteen-seventies maxi dress that she'd styled to look like an angel complete with wings. It managed to look ethereal and bohemian at the same time. This year, she'd opted for two mannequins, each dressed for a Christmas party while building a snowman. They were sporting sparkly vintage dresses, uber-high heels and glittery tights, cocktail glasses in hand. The playful scene was set against an Alpine backdrop with fake snow appearing to tumble from the sky. She'd had fun thinking it up and putting it together.

Her quick appraisal told Lark the mannequins' hair would benefit from a bit of attention. One had a wig of dark waves which she'd brushed back to look as if the wind was blowing it off her face. The other sported a blonde, messy "up-do" from which a few too many tendrils had escaped. A quick spritz of hairspray should fix things. *Small tweaks.*

That morning, the town had been deathly quiet and the time had passed slowly. Only two customers had paid the shop a visit. The first had bought a vintage eighties jumpsuit comprising of satin trousers in a vibrant shade of electric-blue and a sequinned sleeveless top. The other had picked up a selection of aromatherapy products as a Christmas present, along with a shimmering cream blouse.

The quiet shift meant Lark had been able to add some new clothes to the rails and rearrange the display of vintage shoes. That done, she moved on to finishing her Christmas decorations.

She was stitching a hanging loop of twine onto a star-shaped decoration when her mobile pinged. Setting her needle down, she smiled to see a text from Florrie.

> Ready when you are! I've reserved us a table in the teashop as well as a slice each of Jazz's ginger shortbread Fxx

The mere thought of their friend's homemade shortbread was enough to get Lark's mouth watering. Jasmine's baking always went down a storm. She tapped out a quick reply.

> I'll be there in 2 mins xx

FOURTEEN

The old-fashioned bell jangled cheerfully as Lark pushed the bookshop door open, the inimitable smell of books hitting her nostrils.

'Hiya, Lark.' She looked over to the counter to see the bookshop's assistant, Leah, smiling at her. The fresh-faced young woman was dressed in her Happy Hartes Bookshop hoodie, her brunette hair scraped back in a ponytail, festive earrings flashing in her ears.

'Hi, Leah. How're you?' She noted a few customers lingering along the aisles, a couple at the central display where the Christmas tree made of books was set out. The bookshop looked ready for the festive season, with garlands festooned along the top of the bookshelves, trimmed with miniature books and twinkling with fairy lights. She spotted a sign directing customers towards "Santa's Grotto" at the back of the shop where children could see Father Christmas. Florrie embraced the season wholeheartedly and seemed to add more book-themed decorations every year.

'Good, thanks.'

Gerty, the resident black Labrador, whose black leather collar had been switched for one in berry-red fabric printed with holly leaves, heaved herself up from her bed by the counter and trotted over to greet Lark, her tail wagging happily.

'Hello, Gerty, I'm loving that festive collar.' She gave the Labrador a quick scratch between the ears.

'It's been getting lots of compliments,' Leah said, casting a fond look Gerty's way. 'Oh, and Florrie says to tell you she's waiting for you in the tearoom.'

'Thanks, Leah. I'll head up there straight away.'

As she walked across the shop floor, Lark bumped into Jean Davenport whose face broke out into a warm smile. As usual, Jean was looking smart in a hand-knitted cardigan in a flattering shade of lilac that matched her checked skirt, her grey hair trimmed into a neat bob.

'Hello, lovey, what's the weather like out there?' Jean asked, her hands filled with a small selection of books.

'Still bitterly cold, I'm afraid, Jean.'

'I thought as much. Let's hope it warms up a bit for the festive window reveal. We don't want folks to get frozen to the spot,' she said, chuckling.

Jean worked part-time at the bookshop as well as helping out Maggie who owned The Micklewick Bear Company. She was also mum to Jack Davenport, the local author who was officiating at the unveiling of the window displays.

'Well, I'd better dash, lovey, we've got a class from the infant school coming in for a story session this afternoon. We're expecting them to be very excited,' Jean said happily. It was no secret she adored her time at the bookshop, particularly reading stories to the local school children.

'Nice to see you, Jean. Hope it goes well.'

Having a teashop within the bookshop had been a dream come true for Florrie, who'd been keen on the idea ever since her old boss had owned the bookshop. But Mr H, who was also Ed's grandfather, had stubbornly dug his heels in, as he had with all her suggestions; he'd do anything to avoid change. Thankfully, his grandson didn't share Mr H's reluctance to try new ventures, and when Ed had spotted the staircase for sale, he knew it would be perfect for the bookshop, with its dark wood handrail and ornate metal balusters, much to Florrie's delight.

And now it was up and running, it was doing a roaring trade as well as attracting yet more business to the bookshop itself. With Florrie and Ed at the helm, the once flagging fortunes of the Happy Hartes Bookshop had been turned around and now it was thriving.

As she climbed the stairs, she was greeted by the aroma of Jasmine's homemade festive tiffin and freshly ground coffee. Despite her hearty breakfast, Lark's stomach growled; cold weather always gave her a raging appetite. Arriving on the first floor, which had previously been the bookshop's living accommodation, Lark took a left in the newly created open-plan area which was dedicated to vintage and out-of-print books as well as having a separate section for stationery. She made her way towards the front of the shop, floorboards creaking underfoot, as she followed the sound of clinking china and the hiss of the coffee machine.

Arriving in the tearoom, music from the nineteen twenties murmured softly from the vintage-style radio on the old sideboard, both courtesy of Nate's upcycling shop. Flames danced merrily in the faux wood burner tucked inside the fireplace at the far end of the room. A large Christmas tree twinkled away quietly in a corner, while smaller versions occupied the windowsills, continuing the bookshop's festive theme. Lark was surprised to find most of the tables occupied considering how quiet the town had been that morning. After a quick sweep of the room, she spotted Florrie sitting at a window table, poring over a book, glasses perched on the end of her nose. The familiar sight brought a smile to Lark's face. *Florrie Appleton engrossed in a book? No surprises there!*

'Now then, little Miss Bookworm, that looks interesting.' Lark pulled out the chair opposite her friend.

Florrie's head snapped up. Like Leah, she was wearing her Happy Hartes Bookshop hoodie and festive earrings. 'Hiya, Lark,' she said, her startled expression swapped for a smile. She pushed her glasses back up her nose with her finger. 'I didn't see you coming in, I was that engrossed in this.' She held up a dog-eared book, turning the cover to face Lark.

'*A History of Smuggling in and around Micklewick Bay*,' Lark read the title out loud. The slightly faded cover image depicted an old-fashioned sailing ship splicing through a choppy sea, Thorncliffe to the right, and a collection of whisky barrels in one corner and a chest of gold coins in the other. It wasn't the most imaginative of covers and looked a little dated. 'Oh, wow! Where did you find that?'

'I rooted it out after our conversation. I had a feeling we had a book on local smuggling somewhere in our stock. Thought you and Nate might be interested in it.'

'Ooh, definitely.' Lark hung her bag over the back of the chair, unbuttoned her coat and slipped it over the bag. With recent events, she'd found herself eager to learn more about the town's smuggling heritage. 'Does it mention anything about what happened to Benjamin Fitzgilbert?'

'I haven't got that far yet, but he features heavily, as you can imagine. Jacob Crayke, too. As well as the rumour of a missing chest full of gold coins. You never know, they might turn up under the floorboards at Crayke's Cottage. Mr Thurston did say Nate could keep the contents, didn't he?' She gave an impish grin that made Lark laugh.

'He did, but I'm not sure either of us wants to go back and find out. I think we'll leave anything else that's there to the next owners, chest of gold coins or not.'

'I'm guessing the place must've seriously spooked you.'

'You're not wrong.' Lark tucked her hair behind her ears. 'I'm keen to find out why.'

'There you go, it's yours. Let's hope it helps.' Florrie slid the book over the table to Lark.

'But you're still reading it.'

'Not really, I was just interested in a particular chapter and I've finished that.'

'Well, in that case, I have to give you something for it. If it's out of print then it's probably worth quite a bit, you can't just give your stock away,' said Lark. 'You've mentioned plenty of times how there's always a demand for books on local history like this.'

'We've got a few copies actually.'

'Yes, but all the same...'

'Think of it as an early Christmas pressie,' Florrie said jokingly. 'And anyroad, you're always giving me stuff from your shop, like this gorgeous item.' She tapped the silk scarf she was using as a hairband to keep her dark bob off her face. 'It's so versatile, I love it.'

Lark smiled. As soon as she'd spotted the scarf, she'd known it was perfect for her friend. The pattern of vibrant red poppies against the cream silk background hadn't been the only reason; it had oozed positive energy, which Lark had thought would be the perfect boost to her friend, who was finding things tough at the time.

'In that case, thank you.'

'You're welcome.' Florrie leant forward, resting her hands on the table and lacing her fingers together. 'So, come on, tell me everything, I've been dying to hear what you found at Crayke's Cottage, it all sounds so intriguing.'

Lark puffed out her cheeks and was just about to speak when a waitress appeared at the table, tablet in hand. In her early thirties, she was dressed in the tearoom's uniform of black skirt and white blouse with lace collar and white apron tied at the waist. Her shiny auburn hair was fixed into a neat bun.

'Hi, I wondered if you were ready to order?' she asked with a smile.

'Ooh, sorry, Abbie, we've been that busy chatting we haven't even looked at the menu,' said Florrie, hurriedly reaching for a couple of menus, passing one to Lark.

'No worries, I can pop back in a few minutes, if you like?'

'Actually, I think I know what I'd like,' said Lark. 'I've got a real taste for a smoked cheese and chutney toastie on brown bread with chunky sweet potato chips.' She was almost salivating at the thought. 'Ooh, and some of that yummy spiced tomato relish, too, please.'

'Mmm. That does sound good,' said Florrie. 'Can you make it two, please, Abbie, and a large pot of tea, thanks?'

'Of course, no problem.' Abbie tapped the order into her tablet.

Once Abbie had left, Lark launched into an unabridged version of everything that had happened since her first trip to Crayke's Cottage with Nate, finishing off with what had gone on there that morning.

'Wow! That cottage sounds seriously creepy if you ask me. And there's no wonder poor little Luna was terrified of the suitcase. Animals are so tuned in to things like that. Larks, too,' Florrie added with a grin.

'Yeah, I still can't decide whether it's a good thing or not,' Lark said, just as their food arrived.

'So, have you thought about what you're going to do with the pistol and the other things you found?'

'Actually, it's what I wanted to pick your brains about. I know you're friendly with the curator of the heritage museum and wondered if you'd mind giving me her number. Nate and I were going to ask her if she'd be interested in the pistol for the museum, especially with the initials pretty much identifying it as belonging to Benjamin Fitzgilbert. We'd also like to ask if she has any information on him and Jacob Crayke, see if there's any genuine connection to Crayke's Cottage – other than the items in the suitcase.'

'I'm sure she'd be thrilled to hear from you. Her name's Louisa Norton and she's really friendly and hugely enthusiastic about local history. Remind me to text you her number before you leave.'

The conversation moved on to Florrie updating her on the latest with Ed's parents who were moving back to the UK from abroad since his father was diagnosed with heart problems. It hadn't gone down well with Peter and Dawn that Ed had inherited the bookshop along with Florrie after Ed's grandfather, Mr H, had died. They'd caused a shedload of trouble trying to convince Ed to hand his share over to them and convince Florrie to do the same. They'd planned to sell the bookshop and use the proceeds to fund their lifestyle of living overseas in sunnier climes. It had come as a huge relief to the couple when things had calmed down and Ed's parents had finally accepted the bookshop was to stay in Ed and Florrie's hands.

'I'm so glad things have settled down with them,' said Lark, dunking a sweet potato chip into some tangy tomato relish. 'They're a far cry from your parents who have always been loving and supportive.'

'True.' Florrie nodded. 'Talking of parents, how's your dad?'

Lark's mouth curved into a smile as she recalled the recent phone conversation with her father. 'He seems really good actually. I feel he's turned a corner, at long last.' She continued, filling Florrie in on what her dad had told her about his planned retirement and move to Micklewick Bay.

'I'm really chuffed for you both. I know you've been worried about him since Greer passed away.' Florrie reached for her cup of tea. 'But I reckon moving back here'll give him a new lease of life.'

'That's what I'm hoping.' Lark paused for a moment, debating whether to mention the other matter that had been bothering her, buzzing away at the back of her mind like an annoying fly.

Despite convincing herself of her theory about Nate and him absorbing the energy of his vintage clothing and the furniture he worked on, she couldn't shake off the lingering doubt she had about it. The bright sunlight bouncing off the snow earlier that morning when they'd headed off to Crayke's Cottage had been unforgiving and only served to emphasise the dark shadows she'd noticed hanging under his eyes like a couple of purple bruises. He'd looked pale, too. She told herself it was probably due to lack of sleep. After all, he'd mentioned his mind had been too fired up about the furniture from Crayke's Cottage the night before and he hadn't managed to drift off to sleep until the early hours. She was sure she must be overthinking things, and had tried to push it from her mind, but she still hadn't been able to shake the annoying little niggle. It didn't mix well with the way her feelings towards Nate had been changing.

Before she could make up her mind, Abbie arrived at the table. The server cleared their plates, making friendly small talk as she did so, then went to fetch the ginger shortbread Florrie had reserved, along with a fresh pot of tea.

As soon as she was out of earshot, Lark opened her mouth, deciding she'd feel better running it by Florrie. Her friend was calm, level-headed and the soul of discretion. Plus, Lark was confident she'd tell her the truth if she thought there was genuinely something to worry about.

'I wouldn't mind your opinion on s—'

Before the rest of her sentence could pass her lips, a harsh cackling laugh filled the room, causing conversation to halt and heads to turn.

There was only one person in this town who possessed such an ear-splitting laugh: Wendy Swales.

Lark's suspicions were confirmed when her gaze followed the sound to see the very woman. She was accompanied by her husband, Dick. The pair were swanning around the tearoom, making a show of looking down their noses at the décor.

'What the heck are they doing here?' said Florrie, her expression darkening.

'I have no idea, but they seem to want everyone to notice them.'

'Hard not to when they're dressed head-to-toe in black like some sort of caricature mobster and his moll. They clearly don't realise how ridiculous they look. And I don't know how they *dare* come in here after what they did.'

It wasn't like Florrie to be so critical and harsh, but Lark understood where she was coming from. On the run-up to Christmas last year the crooked pair had tried to force Florrie and Ed into selling the bookshop to them so they could fulfil Wendy's plans of turning it into an "exclusive" hair and beauty salon, as she'd called it. When their offer to buy them out had been refused, the duo started a campaign of intimidation until their plans were thwarted by Jean

Davenport and her son, Jack Playforth, who bought into the bookshop in order to galvanise its future. It sent the message loud and clear that the business and the property were not for sale.

Since then, the disreputable pair had given the shop a wide berth. Until today.

'Just stay calm and act as if they're not here. If they see they're getting to you, they'll do it all the more. It's just the sort of people they are,' Lark said, her heart going out to her friend who was now looking agitated as the dodgy businessman and his wife strutted about the place, mocking the tearoom in their loud voices.

Florrie took a fortifying breath. 'I know you're right, but it's bloomin' difficult after what they and their criminal relatives did, hassling us last year. It was awful.'

'Just ignore them, they're not going to do anything in front of all these people. Concentrate on your shortbread instead, which is absolutely sublime, by the way. Our Jazz has excelled herself again.' Lark hoped she could take Florrie's mind off the dodgy duo. But Florrie appeared not to have heard a word she'd said.

'I don't believe it! They're heading over here.' Florrie's shoulders tensed, a look of horror on her face.

'You're kidding me?' said Lark, just as Wendy Swales' familiar harsh perfume grabbed her nostrils as it descended upon them, overpowering the aroma of mince pies and freshly ground coffee. The woman's even harsher cackle grew louder as she drew closer.

'Oh my God! Don't look now, but they've sat down at the table behind you. They clearly know the couple there.'

'What?' Hard as it was, Lark resisted the urge to turn round. 'Do you recognise the other people?' She had a vague memory of a man and a woman in her peripheral vision when she'd first arrived. It had half-registered with her that they seemed overdressed for the teashop. A thought sent a swift spike of panic through her. She hoped they hadn't overheard their conversation about what they'd found at Crayke's Cottage or the rumoured gold coins. She didn't want to be responsible for attracting attention to Crayke's Cottage, especially with it standing empty.

'Never seen them before.' Florrie peered surreptitiously over Lark's shoulder, rubbing her fingers against her chin anxiously. 'They look as if they're from the same ilk as Mr and Mrs Dodgy Dick though.'

Not good. 'Would you prefer it if we left?'

'Much as I'd rather get as far away from them as possible, I'm not going to let them intimidate me in my own shop,' Florrie said, a determined tone in her voice.

'Good for you, flower.'

Florrie pushed her mouth into a smile that didn't quite meet her eyes. 'Anyroad, you were about to tell me something...'

FIFTEEN

In the end, Lark had decided to keep her concerns about Nate to herself since Florrie seemed so unsettled. Despite her protestations about not allowing herself to be intimidated by Mr and Mrs Dodgy Dick, it was obvious she was distracted, and it didn't feel right to trouble her. The two friends hadn't hung around in the tearoom once they'd finished their shortbread and pot of tea. Instead, they'd headed down to the bookshop where they found Leah serving a customer. The expression on the young woman's face said it all.

When the customer had left, Leah's words came out in a torrent. 'Did you get my text, Florrie? I sent it to warn you about Dodgy Dick and his wife. They spent ages down here, swanning around like they owned the place. Her *perfume*, if that's what you can call it! *Omigod*! It was literally burning my eyeballs, it was that strong! It was sickly, too! Bleurgh!' She mimed being sick.

Lark couldn't help but laugh. 'It is a bit overpowering.'

'*A bit?*' said Leah, incredulous, before turning to Florrie. 'Did they say anything to you?'

'No.' Florrie shook her head. 'But they made sure I was aware of their presence. Thanks for the warning, though, Leah. I should've checked my phone, then I would've been prepared for them. Hopefully, they won't hang around for too long.'

'Yeah, let's hope so. Oh, and I'm not a hundred per cent certain, but I could've sworn I saw her take a couple of baubles off the big Christmas tree and slip them into her bag.'

Florrie shook her head wearily. 'Why doesn't that surprise me?'

'Sorry, I didn't know what to say.' Leah pulled an apologetic face.

'Hey, you don't need to apologise, I wouldn't want you to confront either of them. You were right to say nothing. And we can always access the security cameras, see if they captured anything – not that I'd do anything about it anyway; I don't want the hassle.'

Lark watched as Florrie headed over to the Christmas tree, checking for missing decorations. 'Listen, I'd better head back to the shop, but if you need me, you know where I am.' With her friend being so flustered, she didn't like to trouble her for the curator of the heritage centre's number right now, she'd text her about it later when she was sure Florrie's unwelcome customers had gone.

'Thanks, flower. Ed should be back soon. Oh, hang on.' Florrie took out her phone and tapped on the screen. 'There, I've just sent Louisa's number across to you. Let me know how you get on.'

'Thanks, Florrie.' Lark strode over and pulled her friend into a hug, pressing a kiss to her cheek, glad she didn't have to bother her. 'Don't let that pair get to you. They're bullies, full of bluff and bluster.'

They were distracted by the bell above the door jangling loudly as Bear Marsay walked in.

'Now then, lasses,' he said, beaming.

'Talk about perfect timing,' Lark said with a laugh. 'Here's your bodyguard.'

'Why d'you need a bodyguard?' asked Bear, looking between them askance. 'Who's giving you grief?'

'I'll let Florrie explain, but you might find you fancy a cup of tea,' said Lark, patting his arm as she went by. She knew Bear's presence in the tearoom would deter Dodgy Dick and his wife from behaving too badly.

. . .

The shop had been quiet all afternoon, so by half past three, Lark decided it was time to close up and head home. She fixed a note to the door, telling customers if they needed anything to call the number displayed, then hopped on the bus that dropped her off on the bottom prom in Old Micklewick and not far from the cobbled lanes that led to her home.

Arriving at Seashell Cottage, she was treated to a warm welcome from Luna whose loud purring filled the living room as Lark threw a couple of logs on the wood burner. Louisa Norton had been on her mind ever since her number had landed on her mobile earlier that afternoon.

Having changed into a fleecy onesie and with a mug of camomile tea in hand, she curled up on the sofa and called the curator's number, hoping it wouldn't go straight to voicemail.

'Hello, Louisa Norton speaking,' said a friendly voice with a gentle North Yorkshire accent.

'Oh, hi, um... my name's Lark Harker and I've been given your number by my friend Florrie Appleton who has the bookshop in town.'

'Ah, yes, I know Florrie well. How can I help, Lark?'

'Well, I hardly know where to start with this, but...'

Louisa listened, uttering exclamations of interest, as Lark explained about Crayke's Cottage and the suitcases.

'Oh my goodness, Lark, this sounds utterly fascinating, and I'd love to take a look at it all. I'm not sure if you're aware, but I've only been the curator here since the summer – I was at The Museum of Moorland Life over in Beckinthwaite before then – and I've been having a wonderful time going through all the artefacts and archives we have hidden away here. I've come across a whole heap of wonderful information I'm keen to display. I've got big plans for the heritage centre. With it being the winter season, it's closed during the week but I'm still there from nine to five, working behind the scenes, as it were. If you and Nate would like to pop in with the items you mentioned, I'd love to take a look at them. I'm free in the morning, any time after nine a.m., if that's any good? Or I could hang back tomorrow evening if you'd prefer to call after you've shut up shop. Whatever suits best.'

'That's great, Louisa. I'll check with Nate, see when he'd be available, and get back to you as soon as possible, if that's okay?' From their short discussion, Lark had already deduced that Louisa was a warm and friendly person.

'Of course, no problem. And in the meantime, I'll have a rummage through our archives, see what interesting info I can dig out about Jacob Crayke and Benjamin Fitzgilbert.'

'Wonderful, thank you.'

With the call ended, Lark was bouncing with excitement. She'd never given the town's smuggling history much thought before now, but she suddenly found herself intrigued to know more.

She tapped out a quick text to Nate, briefly outlining her conversation with Louisa, hoping he'd be free to call at the heritage centre tomorrow. She'd also quite like to get the suitcase out of the shed and away from Seashell Cottage.

She didn't have long to wait for his reply and was delighted, and relieved, to find he could manage a visit first thing in the morning.

With the visit confirmed with Louisa, Lark sat back and sipped her tea, gazing at the flames dancing behind the glass in the wood burner, her mind filling with the recent happenings at Crayke's Cottage, wondering if Louisa would find any information on its history. Her thoughts drifted to Dodgy Dick and his wife Wendy, wondering what they were up to and why they'd shown their faces in the bookshop. Much as she didn't like to think it, wherever they went, trouble usually followed. She hoped they weren't going to give Florrie and Ed any more grief.

SIXTEEN

TUESDAY 2ND DECEMBER

Lark was making a list of essential oils and crystals she needed to restock, while she waited for Nate to arrive. They were due to meet Louisa at the heritage centre in quarter of an hour. The building was only a five-minute walk from her house, so Lark didn't need to worry that they'd be late.

Her phone started ringing with a FaceTime call. *Uh-oh!* She didn't need to check the ID to know who it would be. She reached for her phone to see her suspicions were confirmed: it was her mum's number. A quick mental calculation told her it would be two o'clock in the afternoon in Thailand, the country being six hours ahead of the UK. Lark had been anticipating a call since a text had landed yesterday morning, asking if they could arrange a FaceTime session.

She quickly accepted the call, smiling to see her mum beaming out at her. Serena was bathed in sunshine, a gloriously blue sky above, views of the clear-blue sea behind.

'Hi, Mum, how are you?' Lark beamed back, taking in her mum's blonde hair, piled on top of her head, the floral sarong worn as a dress that offset her golden, sun-kissed skin to perfection. Silver, beaded earrings dangled from her ears.

'Hello, darling, it's so good to see you,' her mother said warmly, her eyes crinkling as her smile deepened.

'You, too, Mum. Looks lovely and sunny there. I'm *so* jealous! We've had quite a bit of snow and it's been freezing. I've been really glad of the wood burner.'

Serena gave a shiver. 'Brr! You're making me feel cold just thinking about it.' They both laughed at that. Her mum was known for her hatred of cold weather.

'How's Elfie?' Lark asked.

'She's fine, she's busy with a group meditation session at the moment. I've got an Ashtanga yoga class starting in half an hour, which is why I thought I'd take the opportunity to have a chat with you, see if you've had a chance to think about what we suggested about the Reiki course and everything else?' She hitched her eyebrows hopefully.

The yoga and well-being retreat that Serena and Elfie ran had proved to be hugely popular, which had allowed them to expand the services they offered. The pair had got it into their minds that having Lark join them as a Reiki healer – once she'd refreshed her skills – would be an excellent idea. They were both keen for her to embrace her "gift" once more, feeling that to ignore it was a waste.

Lark released a sigh. 'I've thought about it loads, Mum, but the answer's still no, I'm afraid. My life's here, it's where I'm happy. I love living in Micklewick Bay, I've got my business, I've got my friends, and—'

'You've got Nate,' said her mother, her mouth twitching with a smile.

'Yes, my *friend*, Nate, is here, too, but that wasn't what I was going to say.' She fixed her mother with a knowing look.

'Oh, okay. So what else is keeping you in that chilly little spot on the edge of the North Sea?'

Lark gave an affectionate shake of the head at her mum's description. 'It looks like Dad'll be moving here soon.'

Serena's eyes widened in astonishment. 'Your father's moving back to Micklewick Bay?'

'He's seriously considering it. In fact, he's had an offer on Denley House and is coming to stay with me for a few days so he can do a spot of house-hunting.'

'But what about his job? He loves teaching.'

'Ah, well...' Lark continued, filling her mum in on Silas's plans for retiring from teaching and downsizing his home.

When she'd finished her mum said, 'Well, your dad's a genuinely lovely man. He deserves to find happiness again after losing Greer. And you never know, he might even find his way to love again, too.'

Though she didn't say anything, Lark wasn't so sure he was ready for that. 'It was just good to hear him sounding brighter and more like his old self. He's not quite there yet, but he's definitely heading in the right direction.'

'Oh, that is good news. Elfie'll be chuffed to hear it, she worries about her brother – we both do.'

'Yeah, me too.' She hadn't told her mum the half of it, how gaunt he'd looked, how much weight he'd lost. He'd managed to dodge FaceTiming her and Elfie, which meant they hadn't seen him at his lowest ebb. And Lark hadn't wanted to worry them by sharing her concerns. Of course, she'd told them bits – she'd had to, Greer's loss had totally blindsided him – but she'd kept the worst to herself, hoping she could help him through the grieving process, help draw him out of himself. And it would seem they were finally making progress.

'I've never had a moment's regret, choosing him to be your dad. Not one. And not just because he has the most *amazing* genes,' Serena said, having the good grace to laugh at her own comment.

Lark laughed too, adding lightly, 'Yeah, I have to say, I'm kinda chuffed you chose him too. I couldn't have wished for a better dad.'

'He could've fulfilled his end of the deal and just walked away, but he didn't. Says a lot about him, that.'

'*Mum!*' Lark grimaced. 'Talk about TMI! Conversations like this are proof that staying put here in Micklewick Bay is definitely the right thing to do if I'd be exposed to more talk like that!' she said with a giggle.

'Oh, lovey, I promise I wouldn't mention it any more than... ooh, let's see... I reckon I could limit myself to about twenty times a day. That do?' Serena laughed, poking fun at herself.

Lark shook her head fondly. 'Sad thing is, you're not joking.'

It wasn't that Lark minded how unconventional her conception was, it was just that she didn't feel the need to be reminded of it as much as her mum seemed to deem necessary. They were her parents, after all.

SEVENTEEN

The Micklewick Bay Heritage Centre was located in the cove's old chandlery building on the Hedda Staithe – *Staithe* being an old English word for landing – and had recently acquired the tall, thin four-storey-cottage next door with plans to extend into it. With nothing to shield it from the elements, particularly the savage winds that charged in off the sea, the staithe was in one of the coldest spots in the cove.

With the ground still hidden beneath a thick covering of snow, Lark and Nate made their way carefully along the seafront, seagulls braving the elements and shrieking overhead. After almost taking a tumble on a particularly icy patch – Nate had come to the rescue and somehow managed to keep her upright even though he had the small suitcase in his other hand – Lark was now clinging onto his arm and she found herself thinking the close proximity was rather nice, though she told herself it was simply because she was so cold, and he, in contrast, felt nice and warm. That was all. Nothing else. Absolutely not!

She ignored the little voice that said, 'And who are you trying to kid, Lark Harker?'

It had a point if the image that had sprung into her mind of Nate's lips being millimetres away from hers was anything to go by.

The timing couldn't have been much worse. The heat in the blush she felt race over her cheeks was so intense Lark was sure there'd be steam coming off her any minute. She took solace in the thought that she could blame having such a red face on the cold wind.

As if there wasn't enough to think about with the suitcase, and the tin with everything inside it, not to mention these strange vibes she'd been getting about Nate. *Ugh!*

She was glad when they arrived at their destination.

'Come in out of the cold.' Louisa Norton held the entrance door to the heritage centre open, greeting them with a warm smile. Lark would put her in her late forties to early fifties. She had highlighted blonde hair and kind, dark eyes, while her black trousers and fitted beige polo neck jumper lent her a smart but casual air. She was friendly and had an easy manner, and Lark found herself instantly warming to her. She was a far cry from her predecessor who constantly wore a sour expression – or as Jasmine had succinctly put it in her inimitable style, he had a face "like a bag of spanners". His permanent grouchiness had resulted in all but one of the volunteers leaving, and everyone assumed she'd only stayed because she was his wife. Even she had ended up leaving eventually, which said it all, really.

Lark wondered if the new curator knew what a task she had on her hands. Winning round the local community and gaining their support once more wasn't going to be easy.

'I'm Louisa,' she said, holding out her hand to Lark. 'Thank you so much for getting in touch. It's lovely to meet you. I've been like a cat on hot bricks all morning, waiting for your visit.'

'I'm Lark.' Smiling, Lark took the curator's proffered hand. 'Thank you for allowing us to drop in at such short notice. This is Nate, who I told you about. Mr Thurston contacted him about removing the contents.'

'Pleased to meet you, too, Nate.' She held out her hand to him as well.

'Aye, good to meet you, Louisa.' Her small hand was lost in his as he gave it an enthusiastic shake. 'Before we get started, I'd just like to stress that I've contacted Mr Thurston about the items we're about to show you, and he couldn't have put it more clearly that he wants absolutely nowt to do with any of them.'

'Okay, thanks for letting me know.'

'And I've got a receipt as proof, if you need it. It clearly states that it covers all contents.'

Lark noticed Nate looked relieved to have got that off his chest. She knew he liked to be upfront with everything he did as far as his business was concerned.

'I don't doubt that for a second, Nate.' Louisa smiled. 'Come through, I'll make a pot of tea, then we can take a look at the suitcase.'

They followed the curator into the back of the building, Lark's eyes taking in the artfully arranged exhibits. How had it been so long since she'd last paid it a visit? It looked fascinating! She reminded herself of the grouchy former curator, which answered her question perfectly.

'I've dug out a few things that might be of interest to you,' Louisa said as she walked along, a spring in her step. 'I was so excited after your call, I couldn't wait to dive in, and I'm sure there'll be heaps more.'

'It sounds intriguing,' said Lark, instantly struck by Louisa's friendliness and easy manner. But there was something else, too – she sensed that the older woman had suffered enormous sadness in recent years; the loss of someone close. It had affected her deeply, though she was through the worst of it now. *How come I'm sensing all of this when I'm trying to block these feelings?* Lark tried to force her thoughts back to the reason she and Nate were there, but the vibes seemed to have other ideas and kept pushing through. She found herself sensing kindness and compassion as well as a joie de vivre that had been dimmed but was now ready to be reignited.

'Okay, here we are.' Louisa pushed through a door with a sign that indicated it gave access to staff only. She stopped at a large table in the middle of the room. 'If you'd like to pop the suitcase on here, we can take a look inside.' She rubbed her hands together excitedly, catching Lark's eye and giving a wide smile. Though Lark felt anxious about the reopening of the suitcase, she couldn't help but smile back.

Nate lifted the small case, setting it in the middle of the table.

Lark felt her stomach flip over. She drew in a deep breath, gripping the pieces of malachite crystals she'd deliberately left in her coat pockets as Nate pressed his thumbs against the clasps. Louisa looked on, an expression of anticipation on her face.

He lifted the lid, sending the damp, acrid smell rising into the air. Tension made Lark's stomach churn, and she braced herself for the weird energy to show itself once more.

Louisa gasped. 'Oh my goodness!' She slid a pair of tortoiseshell glasses onto her nose, her eyes eagerly roving over the contents. 'I wonder how long the items have been in there?'

Lark's heart was thudding so loudly, she was sure the others would be able to hear it. She wondered if Louisa had sensed the change of energy in the room. Lark certainly had. She took another steadying breath, concentrating on putting up an invisible shield to the sensations that were now rushing over her and vying for her attention. There was an undeniable power in the energy, but it had grown weaker since she and Nate had opened the case yesterday. Had the sage burning helped? Lark felt the pressure lift slightly and heaved an inward sigh of relief. Maybe this wasn't going to be as stressful as she'd feared. Nate's voice drew her back into the conversation as he replied to Louisa.

'I've no idea, but according to Mr Thurston and other locals, the place has stood empty for decades.'

'May I?' Louisa asked, her hand poised above the item wrapped in the piece of eiderdown.

Nate nodded. 'Of course.'

Lark and Nate focused their attention on Louisa, watching as she carefully folded the eiderdown back and lifted the tin out. The lid came off more easily this time, revealing the pistol, the ornate metalwork and the rich patina of its wooden handle glowing under the bright lights. It felt as if the room and everyone in it was collectively holding its breath.

'Oh my days!' Louisa's face was transfixed as she examined the pistol, gingerly turning it over in her hand, her fingers smoothing over the embossed initials. 'J.W.F.,' she said softly. 'James William Fitzgilbert.'

'That's what we thought,' said Nate, excitement in his voice.

'If this is original – which I'm pretty certain it is – then it's of great historical importance to the town. I'm not a fan of guns by any stretch of the imagination, but I can hardly believe I'm looking at the pistol that belonged to and was very likely held in the hand of Benjamin Fitzgilbert,' she said, her voice filled with awe.

'How will we find out if it is genuine?' asked Lark, concentrating her focus on keeping a clear head and not letting the energy that was prodding at her interfere with her thoughts.

'I know an expert who can examine it. He should be able to age it quite precisely.'

'Wow!' The larger-than-life stories of danger, daring and suspicion that had been legend for so many years were suddenly becoming very real. They were talking about actual people who had once walked the very same streets in Old Micklewick that she had. The realisation sent a shudder running through Lark.

'What about the other things in the case?' asked Nate.

'Yes, there's a leather-bound book and a piece of paper with some odd words written on it that I couldn't quite decipher,' added Lark.

'Let's have a look.' With great care, Louisa placed the pistol on the table before lifting the book out of the case. She agreed with them that the leather was too fragile to handle for her to consider looking inside right now, but the curator assured them she had a contact who was an expert in working with such artefacts, and would contact her later that day.

'I expect it's some sort of ledger, keeping records of smuggling activity. I've heard there are other such books in existence. And how thrilling to think there's one for Micklewick Bay.' The prospect sent excitement dancing across Louisa's face.

'Hey, you never know, Lark, you might even find a distant relative listed in there.' Nate chuckled, giving her shoulder a nudge.

'Oh, blimey, can you imagine what my mum would make of that!'

'Pfft! Not so sure she'd be impressed. Your dad would love it though.'

'I reckon you're right on both counts there.' Though she laughed, his comment set her thinking. Could that explain why she'd had such a strong reaction to the small suitcase? Thanks to her dad researching her family tree, she knew her family on both her parents' sides had lived in Micklewick Bay for many generations, since long before the newer Victorian part of town was built. There was every possibility she could have a splash of smuggler's blood in her veins. However, her mother being such a lover of peace and kindness wouldn't be too happy to learn she potentially had cut-throat forebears; if the history books were to be believed, some of the smugglers of Micklewick Bay had a reputation for being ruthless and weren't afraid to use violence. The most infamous of them all being Jacob Crayke. Heaven forbid she turned out to be related to him.

Lark put that thought aside for now. 'I'm interested to hear what you make of the piece of paper, Louisa.'

'Me too, though would smugglers have even used paper?' Nate asked. 'Wasn't it expensive at the time? I never think of smugglers as having loads of money.'

'Yes, good point, paper was an expensive commodity in the eighteenth century, but Benjamin Fitzgilbert's pockets were well-lined so he'd have had the funds to pay for it. And, being a man of great wealth, he very possibly funded the local smuggling ventures, too.'

Nate nodded thoughtfully as he absorbed the information. 'So d'you think the note might have come from him, then?'

'Quite possibly,' Louisa replied. 'As for the ink used to write the note, it was very probably made from iron salts and oak galls – they're funny little growths found on oak trees. The galls were usually soaked in water or vinegar to help release the dark colour. That and the iron salts would then have been mixed in water. Sometimes gum arabic was added to make the ink a bit more durable and long-lasting, though it still didn't stop it from fading. And I'm sure I don't need to tell you, but they wrote using quills dipped into the gall ink.' Louisa laughed. 'Sorry, history lecture over. I can sometimes get a bit carried away, sharing little facts.'

'No need to apologise, it's all so interesting and helps add depth to what we already know,' said Lark, meaning it.

'I agree. Keep the facts coming,' added Nate. 'I never tire of hearing about stuff like this. Lark and me both have businesses in vintage and reclaimed items, so we're already interested in things from the past.'

Lark thought her friend had a good point – their choice of work very probably did mean they shared an interest in local history. Maybe she got it from her dad; he was a history teacher after all.

It suddenly struck her that her father would get on well with Louisa. Maybe she could introduce them while he was here. She stole a quick glance at the curator's wedding finger and found herself being pleased to see it was free of rings. She'd have to handle any potential introductions gently, make sure her dad didn't think she was match-making – which wasn't her intention at all. She knew he'd find that upsetting and she didn't want to set him back now he was taking tentative steps on the road to being his former upbeat self. But making a new friend who had a shared interest in history could surely only be a good thing in her book.

'I don't mind admitting I have been referred to as a bit of an anorak in the past, so it feels rather nice to have people willing to listen to me gabbling away. But please feel free to haul me back if I go off track,' Louisa said good-naturedly.

Her words made Lark smile – she used to tease her dad affectionately about his love of history. She used to call him an anorak, too.

'Right, where were we?' Louisa cut through her thoughts. 'Oh, yes, the note...'

The curator lifted the crumpled piece of paper from the tin, taking a moment to read the faded ink scrawled across it in an elaborate cursive hand. She gave a laugh of delight. 'Oh, this is wonderful!'

'What does it say?' asked Lark. 'I couldn't make any sense of it.'

'It says, "William's pig is farrowing".'

'"William's pig is farrowing"?' Nate repeated the words, his dark brows knitting together in confusion.

'That's what I thought it said, but it didn't make sense.' Lark scrunched up her nose, turning to Louisa askance.

'What the bloomin' 'eck does it mean?' asked Nate.

'I can tell you exactly what it means.' Louisa's dark eyes were shining with intrigue. 'It's smuggler code specific to the smuggling gangs of Micklewick Bay, which included Benjamin Fitzgilbert. Bizarre comments like this were rumoured to have been used to let them know that a ship was nearby and ready to offload its contraband, and this tiny piece of history proves the rumours to be true. This very message would have been repeated verbally in a sort of relay to the members of the smuggling gang, who'd know it was time to get into position.'

Lark's mouth fell open. She glanced over at Nate to see him looking equally in awe.

'Sounds like it was a carefully thought-out operation,' said Nate.

'Oh, it really was – it had to be. And speed was of the essence with so many patrolling officers watching their activities. Most of the residents of Old Micklewick will have been involved in smuggling in one way or another, but the main team was made up of men with specific roles. There'd be the "spotsmen", who'd be responsible for guiding the lugger closer to shore – a lugger was the type of ship they used. Here in Micklewick Bay the landing spot was Contraband Cove – no guesses as to why it's called that! – tucked away at the other side of Thorncliffe where they'd be out of sight. Small boats would be used to transfer the goods from the lugger to the beach where the "landers" would take charge of unloading the contraband. The "tubsmen" – or "tubmen" as they were also known – would be waiting, ready to lug the goods off to their hiding places until it was safe for them to be distributed or carried off inland. Speed really was of the essence if they were to avoid capture by the customs officers.'

'Blimey,' said Lark.

'I've heard all sorts of stories where some of the ships had secret compartments or false bottoms in which illicit goods were hidden. The smugglers were very resourceful in that respect. You're familiar with the expression "bootleg" as referring to something that's sold illegally?'

'Yes,' Lark and Nate said in unison.

'Well, its origins are in smuggling. The legs of the long boots worn by smugglers were ideal for hiding smaller items of contraband, or "bootleg" as it became known.'

'Crikey, I hadn't a clue about all of this.' Lark was in awe of Louisa's local knowledge, especially since she'd only just moved to the area.

'Another interesting fact.' Louisa grinned, clearly in her element. 'You might think of smuggling as being an enterprise based purely by the sea, but a lot of the contraband was actually moved very quickly inland. There's an exhibition at The Museum of Moorland Life dedicated solely to it. A local family there, the Fairfaxes, had smuggling connections with Old Micklewick and a James Fairfax owned a house where contraband was found centuries after it had been secreted in a hidden cellar. It was found during renovation work some ten years ago. I do believe there are still members of the Fairfax family living in the villages nearby. And there have been other cottages on the moors where whisky casks and other items were found tucked away in long-since-forgotten secret compartments.'

'Sounds like we might have to take a trip over there,' Nate said, looking at Lark.

The dark shadows beneath his eyes momentarily distracted her, setting a pang of concern squeezing in her chest. 'Oh, erm... yes, I'd love that. We could take my dad, if it's still open at this time of year, that is.'

'It's open at the weekend, same hours as the heritage centre,' Louisa said.

'So you think this is all genuine smuggler-related stuff?' Nate asked, directing the conversation back to the suitcase.

'I do.' Louisa nodded, picking out one of the small rounds of lead and holding it up. 'These are what we call bullets these days, and the pieces of ripped cloth would've been soaked in grease or oil and packed into the pistol, or even wrapped around the lead balls to keep them in place and stop them rolling back along the barrel of the gun.' She placed it back amongst the others and lifted out the dulled copper pouch, giving it a gentle shake. 'And this was used to store gunpowder – from the sound of it, I'd say there's still some in there. A small amount would've been tipped inside what's called the "pan" of the pistol, and once the trigger was pulled, it would "trigger" a fast-moving sequence of events. A small hammer mechanism would hit the flint and the resultant spark it generated would ignite the gunpowder. The force from this would propel the bullet out of the barrel at great speed.' She gave another laugh. 'I'm so sorry, I did say the history lecture was over, but it would seem I can't stop myself. I've got thoroughly swept away by my enthusiasm for your suitcase.'

'Honestly, Louisa, there's no need to apologise, Lark and me are both fascinated, and it's amazing to learn about the other stuff in the tin.'

'I agree,' said Lark. 'You've been enormously helpful.' She was struck by the curator's passion for her job. She could tell Louisa practically lived and breathed her work. Did it have something to do with the sense of loss she'd picked up on? she wondered. Maybe submerging herself in her job had been a coping mechanism, occupying her mind and keeping sorrow at bay. Or maybe she just simply loved her work.

'There's so much in this case that's offering up clues to an intriguing period of time in Micklewick Bay's history. There's little wonder the eighteenth century was called the "golden age" of smuggling.'

'As for the coins' – Louisa selected three different ones, turning them over in her hand, pointing to the first – 'this is a silver shilling. And this rather battered gold one is a gold guinea, and this one, I think, is a Spanish doubloon. There's no guarantee they'll be genuine since a lot of counterfeit coins were in circulation at the time, particularly so amongst the smuggling community, but it's promising that all three coins tie in perfectly to the dates we're interested in.'

'Cool,' said Nate, as he and Lark peered at the coins in Louisa's hand. Nate picked each one up in turn, looking at it closely. Lark viewed them from a distance, reluctant to touch them and risk absorbing their energy.

The curator slipped the coins back into the case. 'I don't suppose you have any idea where this is for?' She lifted out the large, old key along with the iron padlock. 'There's no way the key fits that lock, so they clearly don't go together.'

'Actually, I wouldn't mind hanging on to the key for a few days, there's something I need to check at Crayke's Cottage,' said Nate. 'It struck me earlier this morning that there was a loose panel near the cupboard where we found the case. I wondered if there might be a door behind it; there could be something else hidden away.'

'Of course, let's hope you find something,' said Louisa.

Though Lark didn't vocalise it, she really didn't fancy going back to Crayke's Cottage. She'd felt an enormous sense of relief bringing the suitcase here and thought that would be the end of it. But it didn't feel right to leave Nate to go on his own. She just hoped he wasn't going to suggest heading there once they'd left here, or worse, after work this evening. The darkness would make it extra spooky.

'Have you any idea why the case might have been put together like this?' Nate's question stopped her from having to worry about another trip to the cottage for the moment.

'Hmm. It does seem very deliberate rather than the items simply being randomly thrown together.' Louisa clasped her chin between her thumb and her forefinger. 'The suitcase postdates the other items by a considerable amount of time. Suitcases weren't introduced until the late nineteenth century – trunks were used before then – so any theory would be purely conjecture. I guess we'll never know for sure, so it'll just have to remain a mystery, and an intriguing one at that.'

She set about putting the items back in place and closing the suitcase. 'Well, thank you so much for letting me see all of these fabulous items. Are you sure you don't mind me hanging on to them until I can get the experts to take a look at them?'

She was beyond thrilled when both Lark and Nate had told her they were donating the suitcase and its contents to the museum, declaring the items would be perfect for a new exhibition they had planned. 'I promise to let you know what the experts have to say about the pistol and the ledger.'

'You said you had a couple of interesting things to show us,' ventured Lark once the suitcase was closed.

'Oh, yes, thank you for reminding me.' Louisa gave a mysterious smile before heading over to her desk.

EIGHTEEN

Louisa returned with a handful of items. The first was a sepia photograph of what was very clearly Crayke's Cottage, the door of which was half open. Leaning against the wall was a young fisherwoman dressed in the typical garb of the period, comprising of an ankle-length skirt, worn with an apron over the top and tied at the waist. She had a shawl fastened crossways over the long-sleeved bodice of her outfit, and a checked scarf of rough-looking fabric covering her head, which suggested the weather was cold the day the photo was taken. The young woman rested a large basket on her hip as she gazed casually at the camera, a riot of wild curls resting on her brow. Lark noted there was a warmth to the picture that suggested the sun was shining, though the cobblestones underfoot glistened with rain.

'Oh my goodness! This is amazing!' Lark instantly recognised it as being the work of George Stainthorpe. The famous Victorian photographer, who hailed from further along the coast at Skelby-by-the-Sea, had set about capturing everyday life in the nearby towns and villages. His sepia prints were always high in demand and were sold in the local art gallery.

As Lark gazed at the photograph, her mind tumbled with an array of senses, the sound of seagulls, the smell of fish mingling in the air with the earthy sent of freshly fallen rain, the warmth of the sun breaking through the clouds. Instinct told her that though the young woman's days were filled with hard work, there was an innate happiness to her. Lark got a powerful image of her singing as she set about her business with her fellow fisherwomen, her sweet voice rising above the sound of the waves and the cries of the herring gulls, her workmates joining in with her song.

'The young woman's identified as Molly Ventriss of Gabblewick Gate, and the basket she's holding was for carrying fish or bait. She'd have carried it on her head, hence its wide shape which helped even out the balance.' Louisa's voice snapped Lark out of her thoughts.

'Ah, right.' She nodded, unable to take her eyes away from Molly's mesmerising gaze that seemed to reach into her soul.

'The cottage has hardly changed,' exclaimed Nate. 'Maybe the windows look a bit different, but nowt else.'

'And there are these.' Louisa handed Lark a couple of pieces of A4 paper that appeared to be photocopies of newspaper reports.

The first was a photocopy of a newspaper article dated September nineteen forty-one and bore the headline LOCAL GIRL STAR OF THE SHOW! Beneath it sat a grainy photograph of a young woman with dark, wavy hair wearing a floral tea dress and a huge smile. In the piece the reporter described how a young woman by the name of Betty Pearson of Crayke's Cottage in Micklewick Bay had stunned locals with her wonderful voice. *Crayke's Cottage?* It would seem a well-known singer from York who'd been booked for a much-anticipated Saturday night event at the town's dance hall the previous weekend had let them down at the last minute. Rather than the organisers having to cancel and refund the ticketholders, Betty had stepped in and taken the microphone, saving the day with her beautiful renditions of popular wartime songs.

A shadowy photograph of Betty in a stunning evening gown featured further down, the article concluding with the reporter predicting a "wonderful future for the young seaside songbird".

Lark could scarcely believe what she was reading.

She moved on to the other sheet of paper which was copy of a different newspaper report. This one, dated June nineteen forty-two, bore the title 'Wedding Belle!" and included another black and white photograph. This time it was of Betty on her wedding day, linking the arm of her new soldier husband, Ralph Roberts. Betty wore a white gown with a round neckline and long sleeves while her hair was set in waves and brushed back off her face. The look was finished with a veil that fell to the waist, a huge, frothy bouquet in her hands. The whole style was so typical of the nineteen forties. Ralph Roberts looked dashing in his uniform, his hair slicked back. And, despite the poor quality of the print, it was still easy to see the young bride and her groom radiated optimism and happiness.

'Oh, wow!' Lark's heart started thudding as she marshalled her thoughts. She could hardly believe it. This was without doubt the couple who'd appeared in her mind when she'd pulled out the clothes of the first suitcase a couple of nights ago. The details were identical, from the wedding dress, right down to Betty's bouquet! And then there was the name: Betty. There was no way this could be a coincidence. No way at all. 'This is incredible! I can hardly believe it!'

'I think that's your Betty,' said Louisa, peering over her shoulder at the report.

'I think it is,' replied Lark, a sense of happiness washing over her. 'From what I can make out in the photo, she's wearing the very same wedding dress as the one I found in the first suitcase which proves it must've belonged to her. Like I mentioned over the phone, it's made of panels of silk.'

'Yes, I was thinking about that. Because rationing was in place for clothing as well as food, it was quite common at the time for brides to make their own wedding dresses out of whatever they could get their hands on. Would you believe that included parachute silk?'

'Parachute silk?' said Lark and Nate in unison.

'Yes. And, interestingly, there was a parachute factory not too far from here over in Lingthorpe. It closed down some ten or so years after the Second World War, but it would've been a handy place for brides-to-be to get their hands on any seconds, or off-cuts of silk, and use the panels to construct their wedding dresses. In fact, some even used silk that had come from actual parachutes that had been used in active service. It was particularly poignant if the 'chute had helped save an airman or soldier's life, or assisted him in making a safe landing.'

'That's fascinating, and I can't help feeling that Betty's dress has a special significance like the sort you've just described.'

'It would be lovely to think so, wouldn't it?' Louisa smiled.

Lark felt almost euphoric to know that Betty had enjoyed a happy life and that Crayke's Cottage wasn't just filled with tension and been witness to whatever it was the items in the second case were trying to warn her about.

'I reckon that's what you'd call a successful visit,' Nate said as they walked away from the heritage centre, the wind whipping in from the sea, skimming over the waves.

'I reckon you're right. Louisa certainly knows her stuff.' Lark blinked, the cold making her eyes water.

'Aye, she does that.'

A thought crossed her mind. 'You know you mentioned about going back to Crayke's Cottage to investigate that loose panel?'

'I do, why?'

'I just wondered if Mr Thurston would mind you going back now we've got all the stuff out.'

'He'll be fine, he actually asked me to have a last check round in his phone message so I was sure I'd got everything out. Come to think of it, I'll need to get the key to the cottage back to him, but he didn't give me his address.' He turned to her, his nose glowing red. 'Don't suppose you know where he lives, do you?'

Lark shook her head. She recalled Nate telling her that Mr

Thurston had told Nate to meet him at Crayke's Cottage to hand over the key. Nate said the older man hadn't even set foot inside and simply handed the key over. 'I don't, now you come to mention it.'

'Looks like I'll have to give him another call. Let's hope he doesn't bite my head off this time!' He caught her eye and chuckled.

A spark of electricity danced between them and Lark's heart skipped a beat. There was that feeling again.

NINETEEN

THURSDAY 4TH DECEMBER

'Dad! It's so good to see you!' Lark's words came out in a plume of condensation. She hadn't been able to wait for her father to arrive and had headed down to the car parking reserved for locals and their guests in anticipation. She'd spotted him climbing out of his grey metallic Range Rover and rushed over, almost losing her footing on the icy ground. She flung her arms around him, absorbing his familiar "Dad" aroma that she'd always found instantly soothing.

'Hello, sweetheart, it's good to see you too,' he said, chuckling affectionately at the enthusiastic greeting.

Lark pressed a kiss to his cheek, which was still warm from the car and was a striking contrast to the chilliness of her own. Releasing him from her hug, she stepped back, her eyes roving his face. Even under the dim glow of the vintage-style streetlamps, she could tell he'd lost weight since she'd last seen him – there was a gauntness to his face, and his cheekbones were more pronounced. It triggered an ache in her heart, and she made a mental note to make sure he had plenty of hot, comforting meals while he was in Micklewick Bay.

'You made good time.' She pushed her concerns away and smiled. Despite his sunken cheeks, it really was good to see him.

'Aye, I put my overnight bag in the car first thing so I could set off straight from school. Mind, the roads weren't as bad as I expected, which helped; we haven't had as much snow as you have here. And it was good of the head to let me leave an hour early.' He closed the car door and made his way round to the boot, his feet crunching over the frozen, churned-up snow. 'What time did you say we need to be at the bookshop?' He heaved his overnight bag out and slung it over his shoulder.

'Five forty-five for the festive window reveal. The reading follows on from that at six o'clock. It should give us enough time to have something to eat before we head up to town. Maggie says she and Bear'll call at around quarter past five; they're scooping us up in the Landie en route.'

'Good stuff.'

'There's a chicken, sage and leek casserole bubbling away in the oven as we speak. And there are some cheeky herby dumplings and mashed potato to go with it.' Knowing this evening was going to be a quick turnaround, Lark had prepared the dish the night before. All that had been left to do today was peel and boil the potatoes, which she'd already done. She'd then added butter and a splash of cream before mashing them until they were smooth and fluffy. They were currently keeping warm in the oven on the shelf below the casserole.

'Mmm. Sounds perfect for a chilly winter's night like tonight.' Her dad smiled over at her.

'Yep, that's what I thought. Should warm us through before we head out.' She beamed back at him, the wind lifting her hair. She'd made the dish knowing it was a favourite of his. She'd got some of his preferred Double Gloucester cheese to grate on top of the dumplings, too. He used to rave about them. 'Can I help carry anything?'

'There's just this.' He handed her a small paper carrier bag before closing the boot and locking the car with a beep of his key fob.

A gust of icy wind appeared as if from nowhere, whipping around them.

'Brr! I'd forgotten how cold it can get down here in Old Micklewick.' Silas shivered.

'At least we don't have far to go.' Lark linked her arm through his and they trundled off through the snow. She didn't like to say his weight loss probably meant he could feel the cold even more.

Arriving at Seashell Cottage, Silas kicked off his boots and hung up his coat, the comforting aroma of the casserole dominating the usual greeting of aromatherapy oils. 'Mmm. That smells *so* good.' He inhaled deeply. 'And it's so toasty in here too.'

'It's the wood burner, Dad. It's made a massive difference. I've been really glad of it this last week.'

'I'm not surprised.' He stepped into the living room, bending his head to avoid the beams. 'And you've got it looking very cosy and inviting, with your Christmas tree and fairy lights dotted about. I can feel myself relaxing by the second! I think I need to steer clear of that sofa for a while or I'll be in serious danger of nodding off,' he said, laughing.

'That's probably best saved for when we get back after the reading, then you can snooze away to your heart's content.' She smiled. It felt good to have her dad back in Micklewick Bay.

A miaowing caught their attention. 'Ah, this must be Luna.' Silas beamed down at the cat who was giving him a thorough check over, nudging against his legs. He bent down to stroke her. 'Hello there, miss. I do hope we can be friends.' Luna responded with a loud purr.

'I think we can safely say that's a given.' Lark chuckled as she watched the cat close her eyes, savouring the attention from Silas. 'Can I get you a cup of tea, Dad?'

'Aye, that'd be grand, thanks, sweetheart.'

Silas straightened and Lark was shocked by the sight of his jumper hanging loose on him. Being so tall only seemed to accentuate how much weight he'd lost. Her stomach twisted and she was overwhelmed by the urge to hug him close, squeeze him tight and tell him he was going to be okay. Which, come to think of it, he was if he was moving back to Micklewick Bay. She was going to make sure of it. She'd cook him chicken casserole and herby dumplings every night if necessary!

Sensing her face had dropped she pushed her mouth into a smile before he noticed.

'Oh, I almost forgot.' Silas reached for the paper bag Lark had carried to the cottage and set down on the sideboard. 'These are for you.' He reached inside the bag and lifted out a pink box trimmed with a gold ribbon and gold writing.

She hadn't noticed the logo on the bag was that of The Chocolate Cherub, the chocolatier in Middleton-le-Moors. 'Ooh! My favourite! Thanks, Dad!' She delivered a grateful kiss to his cheek. 'I'll take them through to the kitchen, keep them away from the heat of the wood burner. Why don't you come through? You can update me on the house sale while I make a pot of tea and grate some cheese on the dumplings.'

'Sounds like a plan. I'll just take my bag up to my room, then you can tell me all about your trip to the heritage centre.'

'Deal.' She flashed him a grin.

Over the course of the meal, she listened as he told her how the sale of Denley House was moving smoothly, and how the couple who were buying it had been round to measure up for curtains and blinds the previous evening. It seemed to please her dad that they were so excited about moving in. She hoped it would make leaving it easier for him.

'I'm happy to come over on completion day, if you like?' She didn't want him to have to face locking up for the last time alone. She couldn't even begin to imagine how hard that would be for him. In fact, she didn't like to think about it.

'I'd like that.' The smile he gave faltered a little and this time Lark couldn't help herself. She set her knife and fork down and rushed over to his side of the table, wrapping her arms around him, burying her face into his neck.

'It's going to be fine, Dad. I promise. I'm here whenever you need me. And there's always Mum and Elfie if you'd rather offload onto them, you know. They just want to make sure you're okay, same as me.' Her voice cracked and she bit down on the tears that were threatening.

Silas sniffed. 'I know that, sweetheart, thank you. You've all been amazing and I'm so grateful.' He pulled back, his pale-green eyes shiny with tears. He took her hand, squeezing it as he gave her a smile. 'I'm sorry I've made you all worry about me over the last few years – particularly you. Losing Greer too soon and so quickly was such a shock, but I've slowly been managing to work my way through it all and I now feel ready to face the world again.'

'That's great, Dad, I'm so pleased.' Lark sat back down in her seat, squeezing his hand before letting go. There was something about him that told her things were going to get brighter for her dad. An unshakeable feeling of positivity washed over her, filling her with a warm glow. He really was going to be okay.

'Which is why I want to move back to Micklewick Bay. The only reason I've stayed at Denley House is because of my loyalty to Greer. I've been clinging on to the memory of her there. It's taken a while, but I've accepted she's not coming back and it's time to move on.'

'It's the right thing for you, Dad, and you had to do it when the time was right for you, never mind anyone else – I'd have had you moving back in a heartbeat, as you know, but it would have been wrong to force you. You had to be ready.'

Her words raised a smile. 'I know you would. And I also think you know that I've never really felt settled at Denley House. I've been fooling myself for these last few years, but I've had to be honest and accept that Micklewick Bay is where I belong. It's where my heart is and it's where my amazing daughter is.'

'Well, you might not think I'm so amazing when I tell you it's your turn to do the washing up!'

His resultant roar of laughter was a joy to hear.

'So, fill me in on what happened at the heritage museum,' said

Silas as they tackled the washing up together – Lark washed while her dad dried. 'Was the curator helpful?'

'Honestly, Dad, it was so interesting, and she had much more information than we expected. She was so full of knowledge. I'll show you the photocopying she did for us.' Lark went on to share details of their meeting, her dad listening, his interest obviously piqued. She hoped she'd have an opportunity to introduce her father to Louisa while he was here.

'It sounds fascinating. I'd love to see the suitcase and the contents. I can't imagine what it must be like to look upon something with such history attached to it.' The drying finished, Silas hung the tea towel on the hook by the Butler sink.

'Tell you what, the heritage centre's open on Saturdays, why don't we pop in? I'm sure Louisa would be okay to show you the case. And I've organised it so Zara's holding the fort at the shop, so I'm free all day. We could have a sniff around a few houses for sale, too.' Zara was the new part-time assistant she'd employed to work at the shop.

'Wonderful!' Her dad's eyes were shining and it felt good to see him so fired up about doing something. She'd call Louisa in the morning, double check it really would be okay for her dad to take a look at the suitcase.

'And how's Nate?' asked Silas.

That was a loaded question if ever there was one. But Lark was saved from answering by the ping of a text landing on her mobile.

'That'll be Mags telling me they're setting off.'

TWENTY

The Land Rover pulled up just as Lark and Silas arrived at the bottom of the row near the seafront. As soon as Silas opened the rear door, he and Lark were treated to a warm greeting from Maggie and Bear.

'Hiya, thanks for this,' said Lark, sliding onto the bench behind Bear while her dad pulled the heavy door shut with a slam. The Landie had a smell to it that was distinctly farm.

'Now then, Silas, it's grand to see you,' said Bear.

'Hi, folks, it's grand to see you, too.' Silas opted for the bench opposite his daughter, clicking his seat belt shut. 'How's motherhood treating you, Maggie?' he asked.

She turned to face Silas from the front seat. 'I have to say, it's treating me very well, thanks. Of course, having the most perfect baby in the world definitely helps.' She gave him a wide grin.

'Aye, she's a little angel,' agreed Bear, a smile in his voice. 'She's slept right through the last couple of nights.'

'She has, bless her, it's been *bliss*. You can't beat a good night's kip.' There was no mistaking the thankful tone in her voice.

Maggie and Bear had waited for an age for baby Lucia to arrive, their hopes dashed month after month, plagued by an agonising mix of miscarriages and false alarms. They could scarcely believe it when Maggie had found herself pregnant and carried the baby full term. And since Lucia's arrival into the world last Christmas, they'd been besotted with their little daughter. 'Granted, I'm exhausted, but she can scream and yell as much as she wants, I wouldn't swap her for the world,' Maggie had told Lark when Lucy – she and Bear used her nickname on a daily basis rather than Lucia which had been chosen to reflect Maggie's Italian heritage – had been suffering from six month colic and screamed at the top of her lungs from six p.m. through to midnight for two weeks solid. Lark had given her friend a selection of rose quartz crystals to dot around Clifftop Cottage, telling Maggie it would instil a sense of calm into their home which baby Lucy would absorb. Though Maggie had been sceptical, she'd accepted the gift and to her surprise, Lucy's colic came to an end.

Arriving in the town, Bear managed to find a parking space at the bottom of Endeavour Road, which was just around the corner from Victoria Square.

Despite the biting cold, they found a substantial crowd had already gathered outside the bookshop and were spilling onto the road, a buzz of anticipation tangible in the air. Everyone was bundled up well and the chill wind didn't appear to be dampening anyone's spirits. Out of nowhere a rich baritone voice struck up with the opening line of "White Christmas". It didn't take long before the rest of the crowd joined in, mumbling along when they didn't know the words.

The square looked impossibly festive with Christmas trees above every shop doorway, their soft white lights twinkling out into the darkness. More white lights were festooned from shop to shop as well as being strung between the vintage lampposts, all adding to the festive vibe. The huge Christmas tree at the top of the square was also bedecked in hundreds of fairy lights, its boughs swaying in the breeze.

And, of course, the shop windows were all decorated for

Christmas. Artist Ed had set the bar high since he'd given his creative skills free rein on the Happy Hartes window displays, and, not to be outdone, the other storekeepers had put extra efforts into their own. The results were stunning.

'Wow! I had no idea the bookshop window displays were so popular.' Silas looked on in amazement. 'And, if I'm not mistaken, I'm sure I've just spotted what looked like a television camera over there.'

'You probably will have, Silas, they were here for last year's unveiling too,' said Bear. 'It used to be that Jack giving a reading was what tempted them over, but Ed's windows are a big enough draw in their own right now, particularly the Christmas ones.'

'And since Jack and Jenna have become an item, it's generated an extra level of interest,' said Lark. 'Jack doing the window reveal and then a reading with Jenna afterwards has become a big event for the town.'

'Well, that's got to be a good thing,' Silas said.

Lark watched as his gaze swept around the dazzling rows of shops where the displays ranged from yet more decorated Christmas trees with fake presents set out beneath, to snowmen, to festive floral arrangements. It was good to see him taking an interest in things again. She slotted her arm through his, hugging it close.

'Ooh, look, there's Jazz with Max and the kids.' Maggie waved enthusiastically at their friends. 'Her mum and dad are with them too.'

'Ah, she looks all loved up. I'm so happy for her.' Lark waved too, smiling at the happy scene.

'I was so pleased when you told me about her and Max, it seems so fitting that they should end up together,' said Silas. 'Do you think we'll be hearing wedding bells in the near future?'

Lark and Maggie exchanged wide-eyed expressions. 'I wouldn't mention that within her earshot unless you fancy having your head bitten off,' said Maggie.

He gave an easy laugh. 'Ah, it's good to know she hasn't changed.'

Jasmine had had a tough few years since the death of Bart, her partner and father to her two children, Zak and Chloe. Her relationship with Bart had been difficult and she'd sworn off getting involved in a relationship until her childhood best friend and neighbour, Max Grainger, had returned to Micklewick Bay after a twenty-five-year absence. It hadn't taken long for the pair to fall for one another. And Jasmine hadn't stopped smiling since. Though never one to talk about her emotions, mention of the "M" word was enough to stir up her quick temper.

'Now then, missus.' The unmistakable tones of her lawyer friend, Stella, behind her made Lark turn.

'Stells! I'm so glad you could make it. You too, Alex.' She nodded to Stella's boyfriend.

Stella worked as a criminal barrister and was based at a set of chambers in York. She'd warned her friends there was a chance she'd be late since she was prosecuting a drugs trial in York Crown Court and had a conference following straight on at four thirty. From the way she was dressed, in her fitted black wool overcoat, black trousers, and her hair tied back in a sleek chignon, Lark guessed she'd come straight from work.

'The con was cancelled at the last minute, so I raced over here and scooped Alex up en route.' The diamond star earrings she always wore glinted under the streetlight. 'Hi, Silas, it's good to see you.'

'Hello there, Stella, it's good to see you, too. Sounds like the criminal fraternity is keeping you as busy as ever.'

'It certainly is.' Stella laughed. 'And you'd be surprised how many are from the same family.'

'That sounds worrying.' Silas switched his gaze to the tall darkhaired man standing beside her. 'And how's work for you, Alex? Have the plans for the new Art Deco themed house you were working on been given the go ahead?'

'I'm very pleased to say they have. In fact, work's already started on it. I'm managing the project too, and I'll be calling in to see how things are progressing tomorrow afternoon. You can join me, if you like?'

'Sounds great, I'd love to.'

It warmed Lark's heart to see how thoughtful her friends were with her father. They were all fond of him, and all aware of what he'd been through over the last few years, that she'd been worried sick about him. She appreciated their kind gestures.

Alex was a self-employed architect who'd made a name for himself with his sympathetic conversions and creative designs. He and Stella had been dating for the last year which was unheard of for lovephobic Stella who'd been scornful of love and relationships. Until Alex Bainbridge had walked into her life and forced her to rethink her stance.

With all the women in her friendship group now being in romantic relationships, it had left Lark wide open for teasing and hinting about moving Nate out of the friend zone. 'If you're not careful, he'll take root there, Lark, and you won't be able to budge him when you finally realise you fancy the pants of him,' Jasmine had said the last time they were at the Jolly and the group were teasing her about him. She knew it was good-natured and kindly meant, and she took it in her stride, but the recent butterflies that had started fluttering in her stomach whenever she caught his eye or even thought of him, were happening more often than she cared to admit. And they were beginning to rock her equilibrium. It didn't help that she wasn't quite sure what to do about it, especially with all the other things she'd sensed recently.

She scanned the gathering for sight of the man in question – being so tall he was usually easy to pick out – but she couldn't see him. The pang of disappointment she felt quickly morphed into unease. She hoped he hadn't decided to go back to Crayke's Cottage tonight. It would be pitch black, not to mention absolutely freezing, and it would be nigh on impossible to search for any hidden cupboards or false panels. But then again, she reminded herself, he'd told her he'd be here, that he was keen to catch up with her dad. It would be most unlike him to forget, especially considering how fond he was of Silas. The thought offered a degree of reassurance.

A flurry of activity behind the glass door of the bookshop sent a ripple of excitement around the crowd. In the next moment, the door to the bookshop opened and Jack Playforth stepped out, a broad smile on his face.

'Good evening, everyone,' he said in his gravelly North Yorkshire accent.

Cheering and clapping rang out, accompanied by whistles and whoops, the sounds bouncing off the buildings and filling the square.

Laughing, Jack raised his palms in a bid for quiet, but it was met with yet more whistles and cheers.

'Sorry I'm late.' Nate's voice in Lark's ear startled her and the feel of his hand on her shoulder set off an unexpected tingle. She turned to see him gazing down at her, making her stomach loop the loop. The shadows under his eyes weren't so pronounced in the half-light and she was glad to see he looked more like his old self.

'Nate!' A wide smile spread across her face. 'No worries, you're here now. Had a busy afternoon?'

'Put it this way, it's been eventful.' He pulled a face for emphasis.

'Oh? Not in a bad way, I hope.' She was half-aware of Jack's voice in the background, asking for the children to be brought to the front of the gathering to ensure they weren't stuck behind the taller grown-ups who would block their view of proceedings.

'I'll explain later. How's your dad?'

'He's good, thanks. Been looking forward to having a catch up with you.'

Nate looked genuinely pleased to hear that. 'The feeling's mutual.'

'So, good people of Micklewick Bay, without further ado, it's time for me to reveal the first of The Happy Hartes Bookshop festive window displays. And what a great honour it is!' Jack's voice brought an end to Lark and Nate's conversation as he drew the crowd into an enthusiastic countdown. 'Please feel free to join in with the countdown. Five! Four! Three! Two! One!'

Magical sounding music filled the air as the curtain eased back, revealing a sparkling winter scene set against a stunning Alpine backdrop complete with bright-blue sky. A collective gasp ran around the crowd as they looked on, enraptured to see miniature hand-crafted rabbits, mice and red squirrels dressed in an array of colourful woollen jumpers, bobble hats, scarves and ski goggles whizz down a faux snow-covered mountain. While above, a cable car transported skiers back up the slope. At the foot of the mountain, woodland creatures skated on a mirror-like frozen pond as glittering fake snowflakes floated down.

More clapping and cheering ensued before a second countdown struck up and the curtains opened on another festive scene. This one was set against a starry, moonlit sky with Santa Claus driving his sleigh, the legs of the reindeer moving as they raced above snow-covered rooftops. Lark noted the miniature town below bore more than a passing resemblance to the huddle of cottages in Old Micklewick, with fake smoke curling from their chimney pots. The stars started twinkling as the moon began to shine. But it was when Rudolph's nose glowed red that the younger members of the audience went into raptures.

'Oh, wow! That's stunning!' Lark clapped her hands excitedly. She knew behind the scenes Ed, who was working the controls, would be enormously relieved it had all gone off without a hitch. He created everything himself and Florrie had told her how he spent hours crafting the various characters and components, working on the moving parts until everything was perfect.

'I think we can all agree Ed's created another couple of festive masterpieces for us to enjoy,' said Jack. Another appreciative round of applause went up. The author waited for it to settle. 'Now, those of you who've come for the reading, if you'd like to form an orderly queue at the right just here, then we'll start taking tickets and you can get in out of the cold before you get frozen to the spot. As soon as everyone's in, those of you who're left can start queuing to take a closer look at the displays. In the meantime, thank you all for coming and supporting The Happy Hartes Bookshop this evening.'

The crowd were clearly in high spirits as yet more cheering and applause followed before they started to slowly disperse, filling the square with the sound of their excited chatter. It mingled easily with the music that floated from the bookshop speakers.

'Nate, lad! It's grand to see you,' said Silas, who'd suddenly clocked the younger man. He went over and gave him an affectionate clap on the back.

'Silas, it's grand to see you too. Feels like ages since you were last here.' Nate's expression said he was genuinely pleased to see Lark's father.

'It has been ages. Lark's been telling me all about Crayke's Cottage and the interesting items you found there.'

'Aye, it's not what we expected at all. Mind, Louisa, the curator at the heritage centre, was really helpful in shedding light on what some of the items were.'

'So Lark was telling me. And I've brought a couple of books from home that have a bit of info about the cottage and some of the other properties in Old Micklewick. It was quite the smugglers' paradise by all accounts, what with all the tunnels and secret cellars.'

'So it would seem.'

A nearby bark drew Silas's eyes downwards. Lark followed her father's line of sight, her gaze settling on a black Labrador with a greying muzzle. She couldn't remember noticing it there before. It took a couple of moments for it to dawn on her that Nate was holding the Labrador's lead.

'Who's this fella, then?' asked Silas, bending down and offering his hand for the dog to sniff. That done, he smoothed his hand over its ears, which if the tail wagging was anything to go by, was gratefully received.

Lark's brow crumpled as she wondered why Nate had a

Labrador with him, and why he would bring it to the reading. Her next thought was that maybe he wasn't going to hang around for that.

But Nate answered her questions before she could vocalise them.

'I don't know who he is or who he belongs to. He just turned up outside the workshop this morning, looking cold and hungry, and wanting to come in. He had no collar on him, so there was no name tag, or owt. I didn't have the heart to leave the poor lad shivering outside so I let him in, gave him a couple of digestive biscuits which he wolfed down then sat himself down by the heater and made himself comfortable.'

Lark bent to give the dog a quick ear tickle as Nate went on to say how he'd spotted the Labrador lingering around Endeavour Road earlier in the week and had assumed it belonged to someone local, but after making enquiries nearby no one seemed to know who the dog belonged to.

'The vets very kindly squeezed him in this afternoon so they could check if he was chipped but that came up blank. He had a quick going over while we were there. From his teeth and grey muzzle, the vet thought he was about eight or nine years old. And other than being a bit underweight, she said he seemed to be in good health and had a gentle nature. Poor lad took all the prodding and poking without grumbling – though he wasn't too happy about having his temperature taken. Looked like he thought that was a step too far.'

'Can't say I blame him.' Bear gave a hearty chuckle. He'd joined the conversation along with Alex.

'He seems a pretty good-natured fella,' said Silas, pulling himself upright.

Nate nodded. 'Aye, from what I've seen of him so far, I'd say he is.'

'And he seems to have taken a real shine to you,' said Alex.

'That's just what I was thinking,' said Lark. The dog hadn't taken his eyes off Nate. 'What are you going to do with him?' She knew her friend had a kind heart, and she couldn't see him taking the dog to a rescue centre, especially this close to Christmas.

Nate crouched down, ruffling the Labrador's ears. He was rewarded with a lick across his cheek.

'Thanks for that, lad,' he said, with a chuckle, before turning his attention back to Lark. 'Well, he's staying with me for the time being. We're going to try to find out who he belongs to – apparently there are databases that have lists of missing dogs. I'll check if anyone's reported him missing on the town's social media pages, and we'll see what happens from there. The vet mentioned a woman who takes in rescue dogs and fosters them out until new owners can be found, but I'm happy to keep him till we know the score.'

'He looks like a grand lad,' said Bear.

'He does, and his coat looks shiny and clean which suggests he's cared for. I reckon someone out there's really missing him.' Maggie crouched down and smoothed her hand over the Labrador's head. 'I'd definitely miss you, lad.'

The dog rested his paw on her lap.

'Ah, well, the reason he's looking all groomed is because he had a bath this afternoon.'

'Oh?' Maggie quirked an eyebrow. 'You don't hang around.'

'Wasn't my suggestion, though it was pretty obvious he was badly in need of grooming and his coat was really grimy to the touch. On top of that he smelt pretty ripe – no offence, fella.'

The Labrador blinked up at him.

'It was so bad, the vet asked if the dog groomer next door could fit him in for a quick spruce up, which she did. He came out all glossy and smelling like a baby.'

'Ahh, bless him.' Maggie gave the Labrador a sympathetic smile and ruffled his ears.

'And the vet let me borrow a collar and lead they had spare, a food bowl, too. And here we are.' Nate shrugged.

'So, what happens if you can't find his owners?' asked Silas.

'Ah, well, I reckon we'll cross that bridge when we come to it, won't we, lad?' Nate gave the Labrador a pat. 'But right now, I'm happy to look after him for as long as necessary. And, since we don't know his name, I've decided to call him Buddy for the time being. Thought it suited him and he seems to respond to it.'

'Buddy does suit him,' said Lark.

The Labrador jerked his head in Lark's direction.

'See what I mean?' Nate said. 'And I'm not saying I've somehow managed to miraculously guess his name, but I reckon it must be something close to Buddy.'

"Buddy" turned his head back to Nate, his tail sweeping back and forth over the floor as he gazed up at his temporary owner, the look in his amber eyes touching Lark's heart.

'Ahh, bless him,' she said. Buddy had the kindest face. And it didn't escape her attention that Nate appeared to be as taken with Buddy, as Buddy was with him. Knowing how much Nate would love to have a dog of his own, she hoped it wasn't going to end in heartache for either of them.

'Oh, my goodness, who's this gorgeous lad?' said Stella, who'd suddenly spied Buddy. Despite her austere appearance, she was tender-hearted and a serious dog lover, having fallen in love with Alex's characterful Labrador Teddy. She was quickly followed by Jasmine and her two children, Zak and Chloe, along with Max and his son, Connor, all fussing over Buddy, who was in raptures with the attention.

The group fell into conversation, chatting away as they headed to join the queue at the bookshop. Nate explained how he'd spoken to Ed earlier and told him about Buddy and how he was reluctant to leave him at home on his own in case he got upset. Both Florrie and Ed were fine with him bringing Buddy along, suggesting he sit at the end of the row in case the Labrador became unsettled, that way they'd be able to make a swift exit with minimal disturbance.

Lark was glad when they finally got inside, the icy air beginning to bite. And though her boots were lined with fleece, it hadn't stopped the cold from seeping in from the pavement, leaving her toes numb.

. . .

'Hello, everyone. Welcome.' Jean Davenport offered a warm greeting at the door to the reading room where she was standing with Florrie's mum, Paula, festive music still playing in the background. They were there to guide people to their seats, which was something they did at all the readings.

'Silas! It's grand to see you.' Paula beamed at him, patting him warmly on his arm. 'Our Florrie said you'd be here tonight.'

'It most certainly is grand to see you, Silas,' said Jean. 'You've been a stranger for too long.' If she wasn't mistaken, Jean seemed extra glowy tonight, as if she'd had some good news. Lark observed her closely for a couple of seconds. *Hmm, there was definitely something...*

'And it's lovely to see you two ladies, too. You're both looking well,' Silas said.

Lark switched her attention to her dad, happy – and relieved – to see he looked pleased by the friendly welcome, his naturally sociable nature gradually emerging from its torpor. It was a good sign.

'Oh, this looks wonderful,' he said, looking around as they stepped into the reading room.

'Florrie and Ed certainly make a good team.' Stella followed Silas's gaze.

The space had been decorated to resemble a Victorian-style living room at Christmastime. A large Christmas tree bedecked in vintage-style baubles twinkled away in the corner, while garlands trimmed with fairy lights were swagged from the picture rail that ran around the room. Remarkably realistic faux candles flickered on the desk that was parked between two high-backed leather chairs, woollen throws that complimented the plump cushions, draped over the back of them. Set against the wall behind, a table was piled high with the two authors' books, while a cash register and card reader were positioned alongside ready for purchases to be made after the reading. A festive aroma of spiced orange and cloves thanks to a strategically placed oil diffuser permeated the air, adding to the seasonal vibe.

Lark spotted Florrie in discussion with Leah. She caught her friend's eye and they exchanged a wave. She knew these events made her friend nervous, especially after the attempted sabotage of the one last Christmas. Luckily the perpetrator had been caught and nothing like it had happened since, but it still didn't stop Florrie from worrying. Dodgy Dick and Wendy filtered into Lark's mind. She hoped they wouldn't show up, though she knew none of the staff would have sold them tickets. And if they'd procured them by other means, they still wouldn't be given admission. All the same, Lark hoped the event would be trouble-free and that Florrie and Ed could enjoy it.

As they inched their way to their seats, Lark was pleasantly surprised to see Louisa. She was sitting four rows back at the opposite end. The curator was deep in conversation with a woman in the seat next to her. Talk about fortuitous! Lark took this as a good sign; it would be the perfect opportunity to introduce her father to Louisa. She tried to catch the curator's eye, but to no avail. Since the room was quickly filling up, and the reading was about to start, she decided to leave it for now and speak to her afterwards. There'd be plenty of time then, with drinks and nibbles being laid on in the tearoom. She'd be sure to catch Louisa before she headed off.

She settled herself in her seat beside Nate, who was talking calmly to Buddy and helping him get settled. She watched as he obediently followed Nate's command telling him to sit, and was rewarded with a scratch behind the ear. It was clear the Labrador had been well trained by whoever owned him. As much as she didn't want whoever that might be to be feeling sad at losing him, she couldn't help but think Nate and Buddy went well together, like they were somehow meant to be. Maybe he'd been sent to Nate? Lark strongly believed that everything happened for a reason.

It wasn't long before the lights dimmed and the music stopped.

The atmosphere suddenly became more intimate. Lark turned her attention to the matter in hand as a murmur of anticipation ran around the room. Buddy looked on, his velvety ears cocked in interest. Lark met Nate's eye and they shared a smile. Buddy certainly had plenty of character.

TWENTY-ONE

Jenna came into the room first. She was wearing a silk shirtdress in her trademark pink, black tights, and a pair of black suede Mary-Janes. Her softly highlighted hair was scraped back and fixed with a crocodile clip. Jack followed close behind, sporting a smart wool jacket, blue shirt and mustard-coloured chinos.

Applause bounced around the room. Lark joined in, clapping her still-cold hands together, thrilled her dad was there to share the experience, knowing how much he'd enjoy it. She stole a look his way to see him smiling, his expression relaxed.

A sense of happiness shimmered through her. She had a feeling it was going to be a great night.

'Now then, good people of Micklewick Bay, welcome to The Happy Hartes Bookshop, and on behalf of Jenna and myself, I'd like to thank you all for turning out on such a freezing cold winter's evening. I assume the expression you're all wearing at the minute is down to the fact you were absolutely nithered out there and are still thawing out, and it has nowt at all to do with the fear of having to listen to me blatherin' on in my usual tedious way for the next hour – at least, I hope that's the case.' His deep chuckle was met with laughter from the audience.

Jack's slightly craggy face and dour expression belied his self-deprecating sense of humour which was always well received by his legions of adoring fans. He'd acknowledged publicly many times that blowing your own trumpet didn't go down well with his fellow Yorkshire folk, and was a surefire way of getting yourself somewhat unceremoniously brought down a peg or two. And he didn't fancy risking that. Despite being a nationally revered author and poet, he was down to earth and unassuming and shared privately that he was prone to suffering from the dreaded imposter syndrome. It was the same with Jenna. She hailed from Newcastle and was a successful romcom author whose books had been commissioned for television. Both writers were hugely popular and their eagerness to take part in such events had boosted the bookshop's fortunes, along with Florrie and Ed's forward-thinking approach.

'So, tonight we thought we'd try something a bit different,' said Jenna in her sing-song Geordie accent. 'Instead of us each reading a passage from one of our own books, we thought it would be a bit of a giggle if we read from my last book, with me taking the role of the heroine and Jack the hero.'

'Always happy to be your hero, lass.' Jack pressed his hand to his heart and feigned a sincere expression, making the audience hoot with laughter.

'Honest to God.' Jenna shook her head fondly. 'Daft lad.'

Jack treated her to a cheesy grin.

Turning his attention to the paperback in his hand, he said, 'So, without further ado, let's get cracking.'

The couple made themselves comfortable in the leather seats, Jenna tilting the lamp next to her chair so it angled over the pages of her book.

For the next forty-five minutes, they had the audience in fits of laughter as they made their way through the book. The couple occasionally had to pause in order to get their own giggles under control, particularly when Jack mistakenly read lines that were Jenna's. It only added to the entertainment factor.

Cries of 'Encore!' filled the room when the couple closed their books, drawing the reading to a close. They both looked on in humble disbelief as they were treated to a standing ovation.

'That was fantastic!' said Silas, vigorously clapping his hands together. 'I had no idea what to expect, but that was *amazing*!'

'It's usually a really great night, but that was the best ever,' said Lark, clapping as hard as her dad, a huge grin on her face, happy that he'd enjoyed himself so much.

He was right, the reading had been fantastic, though Lark had found herself distracted at times thanks to the feel of Nate's leg pressed against hers, the touch of his skin as his hand had accidentally brushed against her fingers. She felt sure he must've experienced the electricity just as she had.

Jack, looking more than a little embarrassed by the enthusiastic response, gestured for the applause to cease. 'Haven't you lot got homes to go to?' he called out, a laugh in his voice.

'Encore! Encore!' came the reply from the audience.

Jack looked over to Jenna, his eyebrows raised in question. She replied with a nod.

'Okay, okay! If we read you another chapter, will you stop clapping and get yourselves home?' he said, still having to shout to be heard.

The response was a resounding yes.

'Eee, I'll tell you what, you lot aren't half easy pleased,' said Jenna.

She and Jack exchanged another glance, their eyes twinkling with hidden meaning.

'Right then, before we do that, we've got some rather exciting news – well, when you hear what it is, you'll agree that the prospect's a heck of a lot more exciting for me than it is for Jenna.' He chuckled as Jenna shook her head and jokingly rolled her eyes.

'Come on, Jack, lad, spit it out!' came a voice from the audience.

'Aye, righto.' He reached for Jenna's hand. 'So, earlier today, I got down on these creaking old knees of mine – no idea how I managed, it's still a mystery – and asked Jenna to be my wife.'

A collective 'Ahh' ran around the room.

'You can tell me later if that was an "ahh" for my knees, or an "ahh" for me proposing to Jen. Anyroad, I'm chuffed to bits to tell you she said yes. Mind, she took that long to make her decision, my knees had locked and she had to help me up. I was seriously worried we were going to have to call the fire brigade to winch me to my feet. Thought she was going to regret saying yes when she realised what an old codger she was getting herself tied to.'

'Eee! You don't half tell a good story, Jack Playforth, talk about gilding the bloomin' lily,' Jenna said, giving one of her throaty laughs, the room filling with yet more applause.

Lark's gaze slid to where Jack's mother, Jean, was standing by the door, her face wreathed in smiles. *So that explains the glow!* She was clearly thrilled by the anticipation of her son sharing his happy news. And Lark couldn't blame her.

The spark between Jenna and Jack had been obvious when Jenna had first visited the town and the pair had been inseparable ever since. She didn't seem in the least bit bothered by the nine-year age gap between her and her future husband. The observation made Lark pause. Though the age gap wasn't the main reason Lark had resisted the temptation of starting a relationship with Nate, it was a factor, albeit a small one. But, if nine years didn't bother Jenna and Jack, why should the seven between her and Nate be a problem to her?

'Someone excelled himself.' Alex nodded towards Buddy who was sitting patiently at Nate's feet.

'Aye, he was a good lad,' agreed Ed.

'He was,' said Nate. 'Mind, I was a bit worried when he started snoring, just in case it was going to get loud. We had a Labrador when I was a kid, used to snore like a pig! Just about made the windows rattle. Luckily this one's don't seem to be too bad.' He gave Buddy a pat, triggering a bout of tail swishing.

They'd reconvened to the tearoom where an array of tasty

nibbles had been laid out along with glasses of mulled wine and spiced cider, with non-alcoholic alternatives for those who preferred it or who were driving. Jack and Jenna were mingling, people heaping congratulations and good wishes onto them. Nate had been given the go ahead for Buddy to join them as a one-off which was an honour since Gerty wasn't allowed to venture up there.

Lark was in conversation with Florrie and Stella when she felt a nudge on her arm. She turned to see Nate smiling down at her.

'Have you seen this?'

Lark followed his gaze to see her father enjoying an animated conversation with Louisa. He looked relaxed and happy while Louisa was playing with her hair, smiling up at him.

She pressed her hand to her chest, her heart filling with love for her dad. This was huge!

She hadn't had a chance to speak to Louisa immediately after the reading, but she'd spotted her heading up the stairs and decided to catch the curator at some point before she left, introduce her to her dad then.

But it would seem they didn't need her involvement. And from what she could see, they were getting on like a house on fire.

Lark glanced back at Nate, a smile on her face. 'I had a feeling they'd get along.'

'Aye, watch this space.' He waggled his eyebrows, making her giggle.

TWENTY-TWO

'Anyone fancy heading to The Cellar for a quick drink after this?' asked Max. His son, Connor, and Jasmine's two children had gone back to his house, Njord's View, where they were staying overnight while Jasmine's parents babysat. Jasmine was staying over at his place that night, which she and her kids did occasionally, and her parents had encouraged her to make the most of the evening.

Stella checked her watch. 'Don't know about you, Al, but I've got time for a quick drink before I need to head back. I'll stick to fizzy water with me driving. Plus, I still have a bit of prep to do for the trial tomorrow.'

'Yeah, I'm good with that,' Alex replied.

Lark checked Maggie and Bear for their reaction. She'd take their lead. If they felt the need to go home to relieve his mum, Chrissie, from her babysitting duties, then she thought it would be best if she and her dad headed back with them rather than them having to walk back.

She was pleased when they were keen to call at The Cellar and made her way over to where her dad was talking to Louisa.

'Sorry to interrupt,' she said, smiling as she rested her hand on her father's arm. 'Dad, there's been a suggestion for our group to head to The Cellar for a quick drink, not sure if you're interested?'

'Oh... um.' Silas's face fell, his eyes darting back to Louisa. 'I—'

Reading his mind, Lark acted quickly. 'Maggie and Bear are going, so we can still get a lift back with them. And you're very welcome to join us, if you'd like, Louisa.'

She pretended not to notice the hopeful look in her dad's eyes, the tentative smile that danced over his mouth.

'Are you sure your friends won't mind?' Louisa glanced between Silas and Lark, her cheeks flushed pink.

'They wouldn't mind at all, the more the merrier. It'd be great if you could join us.' Lark bit back on her smile, not wanting to betray how happy she felt seeing her dad enjoying himself. He'd actually got some colour back in his cheeks and she was sure it was all down to Louisa. *Woohoo!*

'Sounds like a good plan to me. That way we'd be able to continue our conversation over a nice glass of wine,' Silas said.

'In that case, how could I refuse?' Louisa beamed at him.

'Great. We're heading off in about five minutes.' Lark could barely contain her happiness, as she made her way back to her friends.

'Oh, this place is amazing!' exclaimed Louisa as she walked over the threshold of The Cellar, Silas holding the door open for her. The place was busy but not crazily so, and the gentle burble of conversation blended with the hostelry's playlist of indie folk-rock fusion. 'I can't believe I haven't been here before now.'

The Cellar was the town's fashionable microbrewery that was situated on Endeavour Road. Its reputation for brewing outstanding beers, including Micklewick Magic and Micklewick Mischief was rapidly gaining pace. The décor was a contemporary take on rustic chic, with waxed floorboards alongside a solid oak bar where a row of gleaming beer pumps sat in a line. A mix of statement lighting illuminated the space. This evening, it was decorated for the festive season with a Christmas tree on the far wall by the door to the private quarters and baubles dangling from the antlers of silver stag heads.

'Ooh, look, there's a cheeky booth free over there. We should all just about be able to squeeze in,' said Maggie.

'Right, missus, you go and grab it for us while I head to the bar. Glass of Pinot?' said Bear.

'Fizzy water for tonight, thanks. I've got some serious bear-making to contend with in the morning and I want to keep a clear head.'

'Aye, righto,' said Bear as Maggie headed over to the booth with Jasmine and Florrie.

'Hi, folks.' The Cellar's co-owner, Netherlands-born Pim greeted them with a warm smile. 'How's things, big sis?' he asked, fixing his gaze on Stella. The pair had discovered they were half-siblings a year ago, the revelation coming as a massive shock. It was only then that their resemblance to one another had become so obvious. Both were above average height with strong shoulders, blond hair, and straight eyebrows above bright-blue eyes.

'Hi, little brother, things are fine and dandy, how about you?'

'Good, thanks. Have you come from the reading at the bookshop?'

'We have, it was amazing,' said Alex, his hand resting on Stella's hip.

'Cool. So, what can I get you all?' Pim asked in his lilting Dutch accent as he scraped his hair back, revealing a tattoo on his wrist.

Pim's partner and co-owner, Bill, landed back at the bar as the friends were placing their drinks order. Both men were wearing The Cellar's uniform of jeans and a white shirt with The Cellar's signature black apron tied at the waist and emblazoned with the microbrewery's logo. Over their shirts they wore fitted tweed waistcoats. The staff uniform was the same, though their waistcoats were a slightly different fabric. Appearance-wise, small-framed Bill was the polar opposite to his husband. Whereas Pim's thick locks were chin-length, Bill's hair was cut close and revealed it was starting to thin. And he wore a neatly clipped beard while Pim was clean-shaven.

'Right then, who's next?' Bill asked in his usual friendly manner, his eyes growing wide when he spotted Lark's father. 'Silas! How lovely to see you.' His eyes slid to Louisa standing beside him. 'I see you've brought a friend.'

Lark left her father and Louisa chatting about the heritage museum with Bill while she headed over to her friends.

Silas and Louisa were the last to arrive at the booth and despite everyone inching up and making room for them, they agreed that the arrangement was going to be a little snug. Instead, they opted for a cosy table for two tucked away in a corner and set with a flickering candle. It pleased Lark no end that her dad felt he was okay to do something like this. He would've recoiled from the idea a couple of months ago.

As the evening progressed, Lark and Nate shared with their friends what had happened at Crayke's Cottage, the suitcases and the meeting with Louisa, the group listening attentively, occasionally asking questions. All the while, Buddy sat quietly at Nate's feet as if it was nothing out of the ordinary.

Lark found herself sneaking surreptitious glances in her father and Louisa's direction. It gladdened her heart to see them both looking so happy and comfortable in one another's company, reminding herself that it wasn't only her dad who'd experienced great sadness, that she'd sensed Louisa had, too.

Florrie caught her eye from the opposite side of the booth, giving a quick hitch of her eyebrows. The mutual attraction going on at the cosy table for two evidently hadn't escaped her attention either. The two friends exchanged a knowing smile.

Though it was very, *very*, early days, and she hardly dared to think about it too much, Lark hoped it signalled a fresh start for her dad.

TWENTY-THREE
FRIDAY 5TH DECEMBER

Lark gave in to a wide yawn as she followed the sound of whistling to the kitchen. There, she found her dad still in his pyjamas, rummaging through the cutlery drawer. He, too, was an early riser.

The pot of tea on the table, with its woolly cosy pulled tightly over it, drew her eyes. It was a welcome sight. Lark couldn't function until she'd started the day with at least one cup of proper builder's tea inside her. She drank herbal teas and green tea at other times during the day, but proper, strong tea you could stand a spoon in was her favourite.

'Morning, Dad,' she said sleepily, wisps of golden hair framing her face, her cheeks pink and crumpled from slumber.

'Morning, sweetheart.' He turned to her, his eyes shining. 'Sleep well?'

'Mm. I did, thanks. You?' She headed over to him, pressing a kiss to his unshaven face, his stubble tickling her cheek, reminding her of when she was a little girl. It wasn't hard to work out why he was so chirpy this morning.

'Like the proverbial baby. As soon as my head hit the pillow, that was it' – he clicked his fingers – 'I was out like a light. I can't remember the last time I slept so well. Must be the sea air, or the aromatherapy oils you have dotted about the place in various guises. Whatever it is, it knocked me out.'

More like a certain curator who lives not too far from here. Lark kept her thoughts to herself as she observed him quietly from the corner of her eye, stifling another yawn. Even his body language seemed different, more positive.

'You look busy,' she said, as she reached for the teapot, splashing tea into her mug.

'Thought I'd make us some breakfast. Smashed avocado on toast topped with a poached egg and a pinch of smoked paprika. Oh, and a handful of crushed pecan nuts. Sound okay?'

'Mmm. Sounds wonderful, thanks.' She held the teapot above his mug. 'Need a top up?'

'Please.' He shot her a smile as he closed the drawer and set the cutlery down on the table. 'Seems the sea air has worked its magic on my appetite, too. I woke up absolutely famished despite that hearty meal we had last night.'

Lark could've danced with happiness. She hadn't expected to see such a change in her dad so quickly, but she was overjoyed. He had a real spring in his step today.

Over breakfast, they chatted about the events of the previous evening, how much they'd both enjoyed the reading and nibbles afterwards.

'You seemed to be having a good chat with Louisa,' she ventured, slicing through the perfectly poached egg, its golden yolk oozing over the toast. 'Did she mention the suitcase?'

'Mm.' Silas nodded, swallowing his mouthful. 'She did. She enthused about it actually. She's over the moon you and Nate have donated it to the heritage centre.'

'To be honest, Dad, the heritage centre's the best place for it.'

'I totally agree.' He took a slurp of tea. 'She's all fired up about a new exhibition for it, says the items will be a real draw. Judging by her plans for the place, she's going to turn it around.' He paused a moment, knife and fork in hand, as if he was contemplating something.

'That's what we thought, too.' She waited to see if her dad would share what was on his mind. When he remained quiet, she said, 'So are you still wanting to do a spot of house-hunting this weekend?' Lark had asked Zara to cover for her over the next couple of days so she could spend time with her dad.

'Very much so,' he said. 'Once I've got the training session out of the way this morning – shouldn't take long – we can check the internet, see what's available in Micklewick Bay.'

'And you know how on Friday nights I join the lasses at the Jolly? It's usually a man-free zone, but I know they'll make an exception for you.' Lark didn't want him to think he had to spend the evening in on his own; he'd done enough of that over the last three years, and her friends wouldn't want him to either. All but Maggie had known him since they were children.

He cleared his throat. 'Well... um... I'm very happy to *head* to the Jolly with you...'

'Oh?' She'd picked up on his emphasis on the word "head", wondering where this was going, noting he looked suddenly bashful.

'Yes, but I won't be imposing myself on you and your friends since I've actually arranged to meet Louisa there. We're going to continue our chat about local history over a dinner of fish and chips and a bottle of wine.' He looked at her, almost shyly. 'I hope you don't mind.'

Lark reached for his hand, a smile spreading across her face. 'Of course I don't mind, Dad. Louisa's lovely, I'm glad you've found a new friend.'

He beamed. 'Well, unexpected as it is, so am I.'

TWENTY-FOUR

Lark linked her father's arm as they left Seashell Cottage and made their way along the cobbles, her teeth chattering noisily. According to the weather app on her mobile the current temperature in Micklewick Bay was minus two degrees, but that didn't account for the northerly wind that Lark was sure made it feel more like minus ten. It was so cold it actually hurt! And though there'd been no more snow, underfoot was treacherous, icy patches glittering in the moonlight. Despite being layered up with a long-sleeved T-shirt under her thick hand-knitted jumper in ombre shades of pink, and knitted purple tights under her heavy purple skirt, Lark was still glad they didn't have far to walk to the Jolly.

'So, are you tempted to book a viewing at any of the houses you found online today?' she asked, her breath floating in the air in front of her. They'd spent a couple of hours trawling the internet, and having a drive around the town in search of somewhere suitable.

'The one near to where Stella's mum lives is an option, but I think I prefer the one on Saffron Street with it having a view out to sea. Both need a bit of TLC, but they've both got good-sized gardens, so they tick those boxes.'

'True. Having a look around them will help give you a better idea, give you a feel for a place.'

'You're right. You can accompany me, tell me what kind of vibes you pick up. Hopefully neither place will make you feel like Crayke's Cottage did.' He gave a laugh.

'Ugh! No, you really don't want anywhere like that! I'd struggle to come and see you. Though, in fairness, the building itself is stunning; right up your street actually, with all its original features. It's full of character.'

'That much is obvious from the information in the books I brought. It's just the unseen things that go with it don't seem so appealing.' He gave a mock shiver, making her laugh.

They turned the corner onto the seafront, the wind hitting them full on. They strode along, passing the stack of lobster pots lined up against the sandstone wall, which were still covered in a dusting of snow though it looked frozen solid now. The whoosh of the waves was never far away down here, nor the cry of a gull, even at night. Soon the pub came into view, its lights casting a glow onto the outside seating area which was unsurprisingly empty but for a couple having a heated argument.

The Jolly Sailors was a whitewashed sixteenth century inn, with thick, uneven walls and stout windows. It sat in the embrace of the cliffs where it faced out to sea, stoically taking whatever the unforgiving elements threw at it. Which had been plenty over the centuries, not least the high spring tides that had been known to rush in, flooding the ground floor and the cellar – and tunnels, if local rumours were to be believed.

'It feels like an age since I was last in here,' said Silas, pushing on the solid oak door. In an instant they were hit by a wave of warmth, closely followed by the sound of jaunty fiddle music that floated over the top of lively conversation. It was rounded off by the delicious aroma of the award-winning fish and chips the Jolly was famous for. They couldn't have asked for a better welcome.

Stepping into the bar, with its soft lighting courtesy of recommissioned storm lanterns, the smell of woodsmoke from the fire curled around them. Thick, tweed curtains were drawn against the night, while a bushy Christmas tree, groaning with baubles and tinsel, glowed against the wall near the bar. Yet more tinsel and garlands were strewn across the age-darkened beams of the low ceiling and, in an amusing twist, an original figurehead of a barebreasted woman, which had been washed up on the beach directly in front of the pub, had been given a festive makeover. She was sporting a sparkling tinsel halo and large, red baubles dangling from her ears. It was the same for the highly polished old ship's bell, with tinsel wrapped around it.

Lark watched as her father's face broke out into a smile.

'Oh, wow!' he exclaimed. 'It's heaving.'

He wasn't wrong. There wasn't much that could deter the Jolly's loyal clientele from venturing out.

'Oh, and there's Jacob Crayke's decommissioned pistol – I'd forgotten about that,' Silas said, intrigued. 'I wouldn't mind taking a closer look at it sometime.'

The pistol, which was alleged to have belonged to the town's infamous smuggler, was kept in a glass case behind the bar. It was much plainer than the one in the suitcase from Crayke's Cottage, which would make sense if it had belonged to the wealthy Benjamin Fitzgilbert.

'Is Louisa here yet?' Lark asked, scanning the room. She spotted Jasmine and Stella at the friends' usual table by the fire, and gave them a wave.

'I can't see her.'

'You're welcome to sit with us until she arrives.'

'If it's okay with you, I think I'll loiter at the bar. That way, I'll see her coming in. She might not spot me if I'm tucked away in the corner. I'd hate for her to think I haven't turned up.'

'Good point.' She noted her father looked more than a little apprehensive. Him having a date – if indeed that's what this was – felt unusual to her, so she couldn't imagine how it felt to him. She squeezed his arm. 'I'll leave you to it. Have a lovely time, Dad.'

'Thank you, sweetheart, you too.'

Lark was just about to head over to her friends when Louisa appeared beside them wearing a thick, padded coat and chunky scarf, her hair fanning out from beneath a woolly hat. Her eyes were shining and she smelt of fresh, frosty air.

Silas's face lit up. 'Louisa!'

'Hi, Louisa.' Pleased to see her, Lark gave the curator a warm smile.

'Hi.' The smile Louisa returned was a mix of excitement and uncertainty. 'I hope you haven't been waiting long.'

'We've just got here,' said Lark. 'And I'm about to join my friends at that table over there as I do every Friday evening.'

'Oh, okay.' Louisa's gaze followed to where Lark was pointing, Jasmine and Stella looking over with interest.

'I'll leave you to it. Enjoy your evening.' Lark smiled, giving her dad a wink as she walked away. She secretly crossed her fingers that his evening went well.

Lark was yet to warm through and was pleased to see a lively fire blazing in the inglenook of the old sandstone fireplace that sat beside the friends' table.

'Now then, missus.' Jasmine, who was in her usual seat at the head of the table, treated her to a wide smile as Lark shrugged off her coat and slid along the settle opposite Stella. It still felt odd to Lark to see Jazz here on time. Not so long ago, she was always late, arriving out of breath and stressed, edible glitter or icing sugar in her hair, smears of it on her face; the evidence of her cake-baking side hustle. But all that had changed since she'd given up her job at the bakery and all-but-one of her cleaning shifts for Stella's mum who owned and ran a cleaning business. Having just her celebration cake business kept her busy but it made her time more manageable and meant she wasn't living life racing around trying to get things done while still feeling she was being a good mum to Zak and Chloe – something she constantly beat herself up about. But dating Max Grainger had put an end to her races down Skitey Bank on a Friday night. All of the friends agreed it was good to see this new, relaxed version of their friend. Well, it wasn't new exactly; it was the Jasmine they'd all known before her relationship with Bart Forster had taken its toll. But tonight she was looking happy and relaxed in an olive-green hoodie that emphasised her sharp green eyes and brightly dyed red hair to perfection.

'Hi, flower.' Stella passed Lark a freshly poured glass of Pinot Grigio. Whereas Jasmine favoured a casual style, Stella was always groomed – her friends regularly teased her that she even looked immaculate when she went for a run on the beach, with her hair neatly tied back and her pristine running gear. Tonight she was wearing a caramel-coloured turtleneck jumper and black bootleg jeans. Her sleek blonde hair was hanging in a glossy curtain down her back, while a designer handbag was tucked on the settle beside her. 'Looks like your dad's getting on well with the heritage centre's new curator.'

Lark stole a look over to where her dad and Louisa were standing at the bar waiting to order their drinks. Louisa said something that made them both laugh, the sight gladdening Lark's heart. She couldn't help but smile.

'Yeah, Dad said they have a lot of things in common, one of which is the history of Micklewick Bay. It would seem they agreed to continue last night's conversation at The Cellar and meet up here tonight.'

'They actually look really cute together,' said Jasmine.

'I agree,' said Stella, just as Florrie arrived, bundled up in her duffle coat and red bobble hat.

'Sorry I'm late, lasses. I'll tell you why when Mags gets here. Blimey, it's raw out there. That wind's picked up and it's trying to snow again.'

Stella reached for the bottle of wine in the cooler and poured another glass as Florrie undid the toggles of her coat.

She'd just got sat down when Maggie landed. 'Hi, lasses,' she said, before directing her gaze at Lark. 'Have I just seen your dad and Louisa at a cosy table for two over by the window?'

'You have.' Lark nodded before taking a sip of wine.

'Apparently they're continuing their local history anorak

conversation from last night.' Jasmine gave an exaggerated wink, making the friends laugh.

'I thought I saw someone who looked like Silas when I first came in,' said Florrie. 'Must be a relief he's getting himself out at last.' She was wearing a dark denim pinafore over a blue and white striped Breton top with a navy-blue cardigan as an extra layer of warmth.

Lark nodded. She'd shared her concerns about her dad with her friends and they'd all listened, offering words of support.

'Are you having a glass of wine with us tonight, Mags?' Stella asked, the bottle poised over the remaining empty glass.

'I am, indeed, thanks, Stells. I'm completely done breastfeeding, so I can guzzle whatever I fancy.' Maggie chuckled. She was wearing a cheerful looking cherry-red jumper with sky-blue dots over a pair of boyfriend jeans; her rich chestnut curls were piled up on top of her head and kept in place with a scarf in a matching shade of blue. She always favoured bright colours which suited her personality well.

With everyone settled, and Jasmine having placed an order for their fish and chips at the bar, Stella said, 'So, how's everyone's week been? I know we had a bit of a catch-up last night, but we always hold back a bit when the menfolk are there.'

All eyes turned to Florrie who'd puffed out a sigh.

'What's up?' asked Jasmine.

'Please don't tell me it's Dodgy Dick and Wendy,' said Lark. She briefly told the others how the obnoxious pair had turned up in the bookshop's tearoom.

'You're kidding?' Maggie's eyes were filled with concern.

'I don't think I like where this is going,' said Stella.

'It's not Dodgy Dick... well, that's not strictly true... I mean... Ugh!' Florrie rubbed her forehead in frustration. 'It looks like we've had some out-of-print books stolen.'

'No way.' Lark's heart went out to her friend.

'Were they worth much?' asked Stella. 'And did you capture

any of it on the shop's CCTV?' Her lawyer's brain was always switched on.

'They were of mixed value, totalling just under five hundred pounds.'

Maggie tutted and shook her head in disgust.

'They're all books on the history of Micklewick Bay.' Florrie swept her gaze around her friends. 'And they weren't all together. Some were in a separate display while the others were on one of the shelves.'

'Hmm.' Stella looked thoughtful. 'It sounds to me like it wasn't just a case of opportunist theft. I get the impression whoever it was, has specifically chosen those books.'

'That's what Ed and I thought,' said Florrie. 'But there is a definite market for them. And there's been a considerable increase in interest recently. If they've been stolen to sell on, whoever it is stands to make a tidy sum.'

'It's disgusting! I don't know why some people think it's okay to take something that belongs to someone else rather than paying for it. And if they can't afford it, save for whatever it is or bloomin' well do without.' Jasmine's face had flushed red as it always did when something had annoyed her. When she'd been with Bart and after he'd passed away, she'd had years when she'd had to do without so her kids could have whatever it was they needed. She'd worked herself ragged to make sure they didn't go without. Which was why she got so annoyed by people who thought it was okay to steal from others.

'It's cos they have no self-respect, no morals, and are deeply lacking in remorse. That's why,' added Maggie.

'Couldn't have put it better myself,' said Stella.

'Anyway, Ed's going to check the camera footage while I'm out. We placed one to cover that area, with some of the books being quite valuable. Hopefully, it's captured whoever's responsible.' Florrie huffed out a sigh before reaching for her glass. 'Anyroad, that's enough of me bringing the mood down, how's everyone else's week been?'

'Ooh, I know what I meant to ask,' said Maggie. 'Has Nate made any progress with finding out who Buddy belongs to?'

Lark shook her head. 'Not as far as I'm aware, but in fairness, I haven't heard much from him, with me being busy with my dad for most of the day.'

It had been good to spend time with her father, talking and catching up, hearing about how he'd spoken to the head at school with a view to putting his retirement plans into action. He'd told Lark how the headteacher had been supportive and could fully understand why he'd want to move back to Micklewick Bay. And, even better, when they'd been chatting there'd been several times when he'd been able to speak about Greer without his eyes filling with tears, or a shadow crossing his face. Lark saw this as a massive step forward. He was now able to speak of the happy times they'd shared with a smile on his face, these memories gently pushing their way through and nudging his grief out of the way. And she had a feeling Louisa was going to help him with this process. Hopefully, he'd help her, too.

Before long, plates piled high with the legendary Jolly Sailors fish and chips arrived, with sides of mushy peas and curry sauce. The friends tucked in with gusto, chatting and chuckling as they ate. Stella had them laughing so hard there were tears running down Lark's cheeks as she recounted a trial she'd prosecuted recently. The defendant had complained about her "verbally aggressive" cross-examination, and when the judge told him he could see no problem with it, the defendant proceeded to strip off down to his underpants in protest.

'How did he think that was going to help?' asked Florrie as she nudged her glasses back up her nose.

'His underpants were pretty grim-looking. I s'pose a barrister with a softer heart than me might've weakened,' she said, straight-faced.

Jasmine gave a snort of laughter, setting the others off.

'It did get a few sniggers from the jury,' Stella said. 'I even noticed Judge Hartley's mouth twitching.'

'Knowing you as I do, Stells, I'm guessing the defendant's display didn't make you feel you had to take the softly-softly approach,' said Maggie, popping a chip into her mouth and chewing.

'Too right. I pointed out to his barrister that his client didn't have any qualms about being "verbally aggressive" when he carried out the robbery at the off-licence and absolutely terrifying the shopkeeper and his wife in the process. I advised that he tell his pathetic little wimp of a client that he could get himself dressed and man-up. And that his ridiculous performance ensured that he didn't have a hope in hell of me taking his delicate little feelings into account.'

'Mess with our Stells at your peril,' said Jasmine.

'I'm pleased to report, the jury potted him of every count; a guilty verdict all the way.' Stella gave a satisfied smile as she dusted her hands off. She had a reputation for being a fearless and no-nonsense prosecutor and had a busier practice than many barristers with years' more call than she had, which didn't go down well in some quarters.

'There's a moral to that story,' said Florrie.

'Oh, aye?' said Maggie.

'Don't strip down to your undies in public,' Florrie said matter-of-factly.

'Wise words,' agreed Jasmine, feigning a serious expression, making them all laugh.

With the food devoured and the plates cleared from the table, the friends sat back, replete and relaxed. On a trip to the loo, Lark had stolen a quick look at her dad and Louisa as she'd made her way across the bar. She was beyond thrilled to see they still seemed to be enjoying one another's company. They were tucking into their food, and chatting away as if they'd known each other for years, not a hint of awkwardness in sight. Lark could've done a happy jig on the spot but thought better of it, not wanting to draw their attention to her.

'Did I hear you say Nate was going to head back to Crayke's

Cottage again, Lark?' asked Maggie when Lark had returned to the table.

'Mm. He wants to have a final check round – Mr Thurston's very keen for him to make sure it's been completely cleared, then he and his brother can put it on the market. Ed seems to think there's a panel or door that might have something left behind it but I'm not so sure. I think it's a bit of wishful thinking.'

'Don't suppose there's a chance of him sneaking out of the friend zone, is there? I mean, it is nearly Christmas.' Jasmine gave an exaggerated wink.

'Jazz's got a point, flower. Have you seen the way he looks at you? He adores you,' added Maggie.

'Hmm. And if I'm not mistaken, I think your feelings have grown for him too.' Not much got past Stella. Her ferocious lawyer's instincts were finely honed and she'd developed an unnerving gift for rooting things out.

With her thoughts being drawn back to Nate, Lark made a mental note to send him a message, see how he was getting on with Buddy, whether he'd made any progress finding his owner.

But that wasn't all that was circling her mind.

She took a fortifying breath...

TWENTY-FIVE

'Joking aside, I wouldn't mind running something past you, if that's okay?' Lark said, her usual gentle tones taking on a serious note.

That, and the grave look on her face got her friends' full attention. All traces of laughter drained away.

''Course, flower. What's up?' asked Stella, her smile falling.

Lark glanced around them to see four pairs of eyes looking back at her intently.

She paused a moment, making sure she felt comfortable to vocalise her concerns. Her hand went to the rose quartz crystal pendant hanging around her neck on the end of a silver chain, sending her bracelets jangling as they slid along her arm. She trusted these four women with her life. They'd been through thick and thin together, supporting one another along the way. They were, without a doubt, the best friends anyone could wish to have. She'd known all of them but Maggie since primary school and they'd been best friends since that time. Maggie had become part of their group after meeting Florrie at university in York. On her first visit to Micklewick Bay she'd met and fallen in love with Bear, moving to the town once she'd finished at uni. The differing personalities of the five friends had helped unite them, rather than pushing them apart. Each one had a strong moral compass that kept them on the same track and pulled them together. And heaven help anyone who decided to give one of them a rough time; they'd face the wrath of the other four, which was a fearsome prospect.

'I want you all to swear you'll keep it to yourselves and not repeat it to anyone else.' Lark glanced around her friends, an earnest expression on her face, knowing she could trust them to do exactly that.

''Course, goes without saying,' said Maggie.

'Absolutely,' added Jasmine.

'Are you okay, Lark?' Florrie, who was sitting beside her, reached for her hand, giving it a squeeze.

'I'm fine, it's not me. It's…' She closed her eyes. Why was it so difficult to put it into words?

'You're scaring me now, Lark,' said Jasmine.

Lark opened her eyes. 'Sorry, don't be scared, Jazz.'

'Is it Nate?' asked Stella.

The question made Lark's insides squeeze with tension, and her breath caught in her throat. Had Stella noticed, too?

Lark nodded. 'Yes. Why do you ask?' Her heart was thumping as she anticipated her friend's response.

Stella pressed her lips together, thoughts running behind her eyes. 'I've just noticed he hasn't been looking himself recently. Seems to look tired, has bags under his eyes.'

Lark felt her throat constrict and her eyes prickle with tears. *No!* She was hoping her friends would say they hadn't noticed anything, that she was imagining things. Worrying unnecessarily.

'Why d'you ask, flower? Have you sensed something?' said Florrie.

Lark nodded. 'I've just been getting the strangest vibes, been telling myself it's because of him wearing vintage clothing and working with reclaimed furniture so he's been absorbing the energy from those.'

'But…' said Maggie.

'I'd almost convinced myself of that but then I noticed the dark circles under his eyes and this feeling I can't shake off that something isn't right.' Despite her best efforts, her voice wavered. 'He's my friend, it's horrible having these feelings.'

'Listen to me, lovey.' Maggie reached across the table and took Lark's hands in hers. 'You yourself said the other day how he's been rushed off his feet recently. He has loads of orders to get ready for Christmas, he's been dealing with that grouchy Mr Thurston about Crayke's Cottage and now he's looking after a stray Labrador. There's no wonder he's got bags under his eyes. Anyone would.'

'Mags is right,' said Florrie. 'Ed called round to his workshop the other day to pick up another bookcase for our cottage and—'

'How the heck can you fit another bookcase in your tiny little home, Florrie Appleton? You must have half a dozen already.' Jasmine looked at their friend in disbelief, making the rest of the group laugh.

'We measured up and worked out we can squeeze another one in the attic room.'

'Where there's a will there's a way with our Florrie and her books,' said Stella fondly.

'I hold my hands up, guilty as charged.' Florrie grinned before turning back to the conversation in hand. 'Anyroad, it was clear to Ed that Nate was backed up with work. Said Nate had told him he had a big order from a couple who'd reserved a load of free-standing units for their kitchen which Nate needed to get ready for them, but that it was quite a big job.'

Florrie had a point. Nate had told her he'd taken a big order of reclaimed units he'd yet to have a chance to fix and wax. The couple, who were from Lingthorpe, had been hounding him to get them done before Christmas even though Nate had told them from the start there was no way he could get them ready until the New Year. He had too many other orders to honour before then. But rather than listening, they seemed to think being pushy and hassling him would get them to the front of the queue. They didn't seem to understand it didn't work that way for Nate.

Customers would regularly amble into his workshop where

items awaiting repairs would catch their eye and they'd reserve them before they'd even got through to the shop. Most people were happy to wait their turn, but Lark was aware this couple were a little different. Though, with Nate taking everything in his stride as he usually did, she hadn't realised it was starting to become a bit of a problem.

'I'm getting a feeling of déjà vu here,' said Jasmine. 'It wasn't that long ago you lot were saying the self-same thing about me having bags under my eyes and looking knackered. And, much as I know I denied it till I was blue in the face, you were all absolutely right. I was heading for burn out – not that I'm saying it's like that for Nate; he'll just be tired trying to keep on top of things.'

'True.' Stella nodded. 'We were worried about you, the way you were running around and trying to keep so many plates spinning.'

Lark nodded her agreement.

'And even I can see the dark circles have gone now I've got my life back under control,' Jasmine said cheerfully.

'You're only worried cos you care.' Stella fixed Lark with a pointed look, and Lark tried to ignore what she saw in her friend's ice-blue eyes.

TWENTY-SIX
SATURDAY 6TH DECEMBER

Lark woke to the sound of her dad whistling along to the radio and the aroma of frying bacon. She blinked sleep from her eyes and let her thoughts slowly filter into her mind. It was still dark outside and her bed was nice and toasty, perfect for snuggling under for another half hour or so. But she was eager to find out how her dad's date with Louisa had gone – though she reminded herself not to refer to it as a "date" when she was speaking to him. For the moment, "meal" or "get-together" was a much better way of putting it.

She threw the duvet back and slid her feet into her slippers, then pushed herself off the bed, grabbing her dressing gown as she passed the door. It registered with her that there was no sign of Luna, nor the usual dent in the duvet at the bottom of her bed.

Downstairs, Lark was surprised to see the wood burner had been cleaned out and re-laid, and now a lively fire danced behind the glass, the hearth swept clean. Luna was curled up in her favourite armchair, savouring the warmth being thrown out into the room. Lark smiled fondly. *Ah, so that's where you are, miss.*

Lark headed into the kitchen, her smile growing wider as she saw her dad bopping along to an upbeat song that was playing on the radio, his back to her as he flipped bacon rashers in a pan. Like yesterday morning, he was still in his pyjamas, his blond hair uncombed. She leant against the door frame, observing this light-hearted version of him she hadn't seen for years. She bit down on a giggle as he gave an exaggerated hip-wiggle.

As if sensing he was being watched, Silas turned, his eyes widening before his face broke out into a smile. 'Morning, sweetheart. What d'you think of my funky dance moves?' He proceeded to strut around the kitchen, fish slice in hand, just as he used to do when she was a child and he was trying to make her laugh. It worked every time. And today was no exception.

She giggled – he'd always been uncoordinated which he'd blamed on being tall, but him losing so much weight only seemed to emphasise the fact. 'Morning, Dad. If you want my honest opinion, I reckon you shouldn't give up your day job.'

'Shame you say that. Especially with me about to give up teaching. I was planning on offering my services as a freelance dancer or even choreographer. Show the young whippersnappers a thing or two about body-popping, break dancing and the like. What's that expression? *Dance like nobody's watching*. I live by that mantra.' He attempted a dubious looking body-popping move, which had Lark doubled over with laughter.

'No, Dad! Please stop! Much as I love you to bits, I reckon you should save your dancing for when nobody is actually watching. And, anyroad, isn't body-popping and break dancing a bit outdated?'

'Ah, well, I'm thinking of bringing it back.' He tried his hand at a couple of robotic moves, his arm catching the bottle of ketchup and sending it whizzing across the kitchen floor, which only fuelled Lark's guffaws.

But Silas was undeterred and continued with his hip wiggling as he briefly turned his attention back to the frying pan. 'You of all people, as the owner of a vintage clothing company, should know that you can't beat a bit of retro.' He turned to face her again, treating her to a quick display of more crazy dance moves.

Luna sauntered into the kitchen to see what was going on,

pausing to watch Silas. The disapproving look she gave before turning and walking out had both father and daughter creased with laughter.

Lark wiped tears of mirth from her cheeks. It felt so good to laugh with her dad like this. He'd always had a well-developed sense of fun, and watching him fool around, his smile reaching all the way up to his eyes, felt just like the old days.

'Well, if you're not impressed with my dance moves, how about I get you a cup of tea? Allow me to at least redeem myself with that.' Silas grinned at her, his cheeks flushed as much from the warmth of the kitchen as his exertions.

'That sounds more like it, and I can say, hand on heart, your tea making skills are excellent.'

'Phew! That's a relief.'

Over yet another hearty breakfast – this one was comprised of bacon, scrambled eggs, fried tomatoes, sautéed mushrooms and chunky doorsteps of granary toast, so different from her usual granola and Greek yoghurt or porridge with honey, not that she was complaining! – father and daughter chatted about the previous night at the Jolly. As fond as she knew her dad was of Nate, Lark decided to keep her concerns about him to herself. She didn't want to put a cloud over her father's newly restored happiness, especially when she knew it was at such a potentially delicate stage. In fact, she was determined to do all she could to encourage it. And besides, she reminded herself, her friends had helped assuage her worries about Nate. She really needed to convince herself they and her theory of him absorbing the energy of his second-hand clothes and furniture were right.

Her dad told her how he and Louisa had not only talked about their shared interest in local history, but that their conversation had continued on a more personal level, with them sharing that they'd both lost someone close. Though Lark didn't say anything, she knew talking about Greer to someone else was a huge step for her father, and she resisted the urge to rush over and wrap her arms around him, not wanting to interrupt his flow or trigger tears.

Instead, she listened intently as he told her that Louisa's husband had died of Motor Neurone Disease three and a half years ago. It had cruelly taken him less than a year after his diagnosis, though she'd said watching him deteriorate had been the hardest part. Like Silas, she'd hidden away and thrown herself into work, but unlike him she had no children, or family close by. It was moving to Micklewick Bay that had been a turning point for her. She was ready to make a fresh start and her role at the heritage centre fitted in with her new plans perfectly.

'She said she's looking at it like it's a new chapter in her life, one she can look forward to, which is exactly how I feel about moving back home.'

Her dad's use of the word "home" hadn't gone unnoticed by Lark. It gladdened her heart that he thought of Micklewick Bay that way.

With her being right about Louisa, and that she'd sensed the curator had experienced a painful loss, it made Lark wonder about Nate once more. Could she be right about that, too? *Ugh!* She really needed to stop to-ing and fro-ing with this. She pushed it to the back of her mind for now while she concentrated on her dad.

'So, what are your plans for today? More house-hunting?' She picked up her mug, peering over the rim at him as she took a sip.

'Well...' He set his knife and fork down on the edge of the plate. 'Louisa's invited me to take a look around the heritage centre. She's going to show me her plans for the new exhibition, as well as the suitcase you and Nate donated.' He looked at her. 'But if you have anything planned for us, I can always postpone until next time I'm here.'

'Honestly, Dad, I think the heritage centre visit sounds like a fab idea. You should definitely do that, it's amazing.'

A look of relief flittered across his face. 'Are you sure you don't mind? After all, the reason I'm here is to see you, not go gadding about.'

''Course I don't mind. I think Louisa's lovely.' There was no way she was going to make her dad change his plans, especially when spending time with his new friend was clearly doing him good. That it might also be helping Louisa move on from her loss confirmed her thoughts. They were a breath of fresh air for one another. 'And you never know, you might unearth something interesting about Crayke's Cottage or the stuff in the suitcase.'

'I'll do my best,' Silas said, smiling. He picked up his knife and fork and started slicing into some bacon. 'So how was your night?'

Lark went on to tell him about the theft of the out-of-print books from The Happy Hartes Bookshop, and how Ed was hoping to find the thief on the store's CCTV. Silas had shaken his head, tutting disapprovingly. Talking about it reminded her that she should text Florrie. A thought had struck her last night when she'd first gone to bed, her mind winding down in preparation for sleep. Lark had been thinking about what her friend had told them regarding the theft of the books, when Dodgy Dick and Wendy popped into her thoughts along with the couple they'd joined at the tearoom. Something told her they were involved one way or another. Lark recalled she'd had a conversation with Florrie in which they'd discussed old books on local history, and how collectible some of them were, but she wasn't certain if it was before or after Dodgy Dick and Wendy had arrived at the tearoom. If it was after, then there was a risk the unscrupulous duo had overheard them. They'd know being out of print would make the books difficult, if not impossible, to get hold of. And she wouldn't put it past Dodgy Dick and Wendy to do something simply out of spite. She knew they were still smarting over Florrie and Ed's refusal to sell the bookshop. And the more she'd thought about it, the more she could see it had all the hallmarks of their previous behaviour. Stealing the books, or having someone else do it on their behalf, was exactly the sort of thing they'd do. They'd get enormous pleasure out of the distress the theft would cause. Lark had given up trying to get her head around their nastiness. Their behaviour and values were so far removed from her own, she couldn't apply any logic to it.

When she ran her theory about the books by her dad, who was

all too well aware of the slippery businessman's reputation, it was his strenuous agreement of it that made her resolve to text Florrie straight after breakfast and mention her suspicions. She hoped there'd be a chance they could get the books returned undamaged, though an uneasy feeling told her otherwise.

TWENTY-SEVEN

With her dad out at the heritage centre, Lark was pottering around Seashell Cottage, tidying up, having just woven a number of tiny plaits into her hair and fixed them with beads. She'd already booked Zara to work in the shop for the day and didn't want to mess her about by cancelling, so she decided to make the most of having some time to herself. She'd do a spot of meditating, hope it would help clear the clutter from her mind, restore its usual sense of calm. But what was calling out to her the loudest was the suitcase of Betty's clothes. She felt the need to take another look at them, which was something she hadn't had a chance to do all week. It crossed her mind that maybe she should pass the suitcase and its contents on to the heritage centre too, rather than putting them up for sale in Lark's Vintage Bazaar. After all, it wasn't just a museum about smuggling, it was about the heritage and history of Micklewick Bay. And Betty's story was a part of that, especially with the newspaper articles Louisa had unearthed.

She was about to retrieve the suitcase from the cupboard under the stairs where she'd tucked it out of the way, when there was a knock at the door.

She opened it to find Nate standing there, his easy smile

making her stomach flip. It took her a moment to register he had Buddy by his side.

'Nate!'

'Hi, Lark.'

'Come in out of the cold.'

He hesitated a moment. 'Am I okay to bring Buddy inside?'

'Of course! We can't leave the poor fella on the doorstep. I should imagine he's done enough of that recently.'

'Thought I'd better check since I wasn't sure how Luna was with dogs, not that I would leave him on the doorstep, of course. I'd take him for a walk instead.'

Buddy's gaze darted between the two of them as they spoke.

'I'm sure he'll be fine in here. Buddy's a good lad. Come on in, the pair of you.' She held the door open wide.

Buddy wagged his tail on hearing his temporary name. Taking Nate's cue he stepped into the vestibule. Lark bent to fuss him, her bracelets jangling, while Nate heeled off his boots and hung up his coat.

'Ahh, you're a gorgeous lad, aren't you?' She ruffled Buddy's ears.

'That's what all the lasses say,' said Nate, shooting her a jokey grin.

Lark rolled her eyes. 'I was talking about this boy here, wasn't I, Buddy?'

Buddy closed his eyes, basking in the attention, his tail thudding against the door frame. He was oblivious to Luna eyeing him from her chair by the stove.

Lark unhooked the Labrador's lead and hung it over Nate's coat. Buddy didn't waste a moment and trotted off into the living room, giving everywhere a thorough sniffing. He stopped abruptly when he got to Luna's chair, Lark and Nate observing them.

'I'd love to know what he's thinking.' Lark chuckled.

They watched as Buddy stretched his neck, coming nose-to-nose with the cat, his tail wagging. Lark was just about to say he'd made yet another new friend when Luna's paw shot out and swiped Buddy on the nose. His head darted back, his eyes wide with shock. After a couple of seconds, he turned to Nate wearing an expression that said, 'Did you see that?'

Nate and Lark burst out laughing.

'I think we know what's going through Luna's mind,' said Nate, his shoulders shaking with mirth.

'Oh, poor Buddy,' Lark said through her giggles.

''Fraid that's women for you, fella. It's called keeping you on your toes.' Nate's comment earned him a nudge from Lark. Buddy backed away from Luna and plodded into the kitchen, his nose stuck to the ground.

'Have you got time for a cuppa?' She tilted her head to look up at Nate.

'Aye, why not?' He playfully tugged on one of her plaits as he followed her toward the kitchen.

'How're things going?' She got the feeling he had something on his mind.

Nate pulled out a chair at the table and flopped into it, dragging his hand down his face. 'I've got a massive backlog, but I thought Buddy needed a break. He's been very patient just sitting in the workshop, watching me as I work. And to be honest, I needed a change of scenery myself. I'm feeling a bit knackered. What with sorting out the stuff from Crayke's Cottage and making space for it, I've been starting early and finishing late. And on top of that, I'm being hassled by a couple from Lingthorpe expecting their stuff to take priority. The bloke rang this morning telling me his wife was going to be disappointed if the units weren't in situ at their house by Christmas. It was all said in a bit of a weird manner, kind of friendly but with a slightly menacing undertone. He finished off by saying that he does what it takes to make sure his wife's never disappointed.'

'Ugh!' Lark shuddered as she went to fill the kettle at the sink. 'He sounds *awful*.'

'Aye, he's not my favourite customer, I have to say. He even said he was going to pay the workshop a visit to check on progress.'

He raked his fingers through his hair. 'I'm beginning to regret selling the flaming things to him. Seemed like a good thing at the time, but dealing with the pair of them, with their never-ending phone calls and texts, has started to take the pleasure out of my work. Would you believe he rang three times yesterday? And that doesn't factor in the texts, reminding me what wax finish they want and stuff like that. It's not as if I'm likely to forget with the amount of times they remind me.'

'I'm really sorry to hear that.' Nate usually loved his job, and you rarely heard him complain, so things must be getting him down. Her mind went to what Florrie had told her when they were at the Jolly. It matched what Nate had just shared and made her think her friend's theory could be right, which was slightly bittersweet. Much as she didn't want him to be ill, she didn't like the thought of an obnoxious customer piling stress onto him. 'But a break will do you good, help recharge your batteries. Let me know if there's anything I can do to help, won't you?'

'Thanks, Lark. So, how's things with your dad? He seemed to be enjoying himself with Louisa on Thursday night.' It was clear Nate was ready to change the subject.

'He's doing really well, actually,' she said over her shoulder as she gathered a brace of mugs from the cupboard.

'That's good to hear. I thought he looked chirpier the other night at The Cellar. He's lost a fair bit of weight, mind – not that I'm saying it to worry you. It's probably more noticeable with him being so tall.'

'You're not saying anything I hadn't spotted myself. Though from the way his appetite's returned since he got here, I think he won't be too skinny for much longer. You wouldn't believe the breakfasts he's been making for us both.'

They shared a pot of tea as she filled him in on everything that had happened with her dad since Thursday night, including catching him dancing in the kitchen that morning which had tickled Nate no end.

'Now that would've been worth seeing – your dad body-popping!'

'It was hilarious, Luna looked at him like he'd lost the plot.' She smiled at the image in her mind of the cat's look of disapproval. 'He's at the heritage centre right now, actually. From what I can gather, Louisa seems to be as taken with my dad as he is with her. I only hope she doesn't have a change of heart. They're both in quite a delicate place right now. I wouldn't want anything to set him back when he's come this far.'

'I reckon he'll be all right. She seems a decent person and I certainly didn't get the impression she's the sort who'd mess with anyone's head,' Nate said casually.

Lark's brow crumpled, his words striking an unexpected chord. Did Nate think that's what she did with him? Mess with his head? She knew some people struggled to understand how they were able to be such close friends when it was obvious Nate would rather it was so much more. But then again, she told herself, she'd made her feelings clear right from the start. He could've walked away, kept her at arm's length if being nothing more than friends was something that wouldn't work for him. And they were good friends. Close. Comfortable together. She flicked a quick glance his way. He seemed okay with her, seemed content with things. Surely he wouldn't be there if he wasn't? And then there was what appeared to be a throwaway comment to Buddy after Luna had swiped at him, about women "keeping you on your toes". Is that how he thought of her? That she was deliberately... what? Did he think she was keeping him dangling?

Guilt started to swirl in her stomach. Was she being selfish, putting her own feelings first? That was never what she'd intended. She cared deeply for Nate.

And what exactly are your feelings?

She rubbed her brow with her fingertips as something started inching forward from the dark corners of her mind. The place she tucked the issues and thoughts that were never easy to resolve, the ones that gave her emotions an exhausting workout. Was *she* content with being just friends? Or was she ready to take things further? She groaned inwardly. Now really wasn't the time to be thinking about it. There were so many other things going on, what with her dad dipping his toe in the dating pool. The potential risk that it might not work out, the fallout from that – not that she wanted to be negative, but Lark wanted to be there, just in case. She wanted to be able to give him her full attention, especially since he was ready to face the world again which had been a massive step for him. It was important that her father knew she was there to support him, and the last thing she wanted was for him to think she was too wrapped up in her own life or too busy for him to talk to her, or share his worries.

And if that wasn't enough, she still felt unsettled after the events at Crayke's Cottage and the suitcase incident. Even after doing all she could to clear any residual negative energy using her knowledge of crystals and cleansing rituals, she was still conscious of a sense of unease thrumming away in the background. It had never taken so long to shake anything off.

Taking everything into account, Lark decided it was probably for the best if her relationship with Nate remained as it was. Being able to call him her friend was a good thing. Maybe when she had more headspace, she could give it the consideration it deserved, but jumping in right now wasn't a good idea, and it wasn't her style.

Before she had a chance to close the subject down in her mind, another thought sneaked in. Maybe she should talk it over with her friends? She hung on to the notion for a couple of seconds before dismissing it. *What are you thinking?!* She could only imagine the excitement that admission would generate, not to mention full-on encouragement and the ensuing grilling session, with them wanting to know every teeny-tiny detail of when her feelings had changed. She'd witnessed it enough times when one of them had been in the hot seat. *Nope, sharing with her friends was a seriously bad idea.*

'What's up?'

Lark blinked to see Nate looking over at her.

'You were miles away.'

She pushed up a smile. 'I was just thinking about what you said about Louisa being a decent person. I'm glad you think so too. I warmed to her straight away and, so it seems, did my dad.'

'Aye, he did, and from where I was standing, it was mutual. I hope it all works out for both of them.' Nate drained his tea and set his mug down.

'Me too.' His words were the perfect cue to move away from the subject of romance. Lark seized on it. 'So, have you made any progress with finding out who Buddy belongs to?'

'Well, that's actually what I've come to tell you.' There was a note of intrigue in his voice.

'Ooh, sounds interesting. Would I be right in thinking this calls for another pot of tea and a slice of Christmas tiffin?'

'You'd very definitely be right, especially the part about the tiffin.'

'Two ticks.'

With fresh tea poured and them each having a chunky slice of tiffin in front of them, Nate set about filling Lark in on what he'd discovered.

'As you know, I put a post on the town's social media pages and included a photo of Buddy.'

'Mm-hm.' Lark nodded, chewing on a mouthful, the gingery heat making her tastebuds tingle. She'd seen the photo Nate had taken, and thought Buddy looked adorable, all big woeful eyes and velvety ears.

'And I was surprised to find I received a few responses identifying him.'

'You did?' It was clear to Lark that Nate had grown fond of Buddy over the last couple of days, and she wasn't so sure this was good news for her friend. 'Did you find out his name?'

'I did.' He popped a piece of tiffin into his mouth.

'And?'

'He's called Bobby,' he said through his mouthful. 'I guess it's because they sound so similar that he responded to Buddy straight away.'

'Good point. Bobby's a cute name for him too.'

A fond smile flickered over Nate's face. 'I agree.'

'And what else did you find out?'

He drew in a deep breath. 'It's quite sad actually...'

Lark listened as Nate told her that a few people had responded to his Facebook post, identifying Bobby and providing him with details of what had happened. It turned out Bobby's owner was an elderly widower called Cyril Millington who'd suffered a nasty fall three weeks earlier, breaking his hip and a couple of ribs in the process. Since Cyril lived alone, his son and daughter-in-law were looking after Bobby while Cyril was recovering in hospital, but the set-up had proved less than ideal since both Eric and Sue Millington worked full time. Because of this, they'd refused to leave him in the house on his own all day, not wanting to risk coming back to accidents and mess. So Bobby had been left out in the garden with a bowl of water, and only a kennel for shelter. It would seem Bobby was as unhappy with the arrangements as his owner's son and daughter-in-law and had made a bid for freedom, escaping through a broken panel in the fence. He'd been wandering the roads, cold and hungry until he'd turned up at Nate's workshop.

'Oh, poor Bobby!' Lark's heart ached for him – it was horrible to think that's what his life had become. 'So what happens now? Does he have to go back to the Millingtons?' Lark sincerely hoped that wouldn't be the case.

'A couple of the people who contacted me gave me Cyril's son's phone number and when I called them and told them I had Bobby, let's just say they were less than thrilled to hear from me. They even tried to deny the dog was Bobby.'

Sadness washed over Lark. 'How could they be like that? Bobby's a gorgeous boy.'

'I know, I couldn't believe it either. They pretty much bit my hand off when I offered to look after him while Cyril's incapacitated. I asked Eric to double check with his dad that he was okay with the arrangements, and he called back less than an hour later to say he'd spoken to him and that his dad was happy with it, but I'm not so sure I believe him.'

Lark puffed out a sigh. 'At least we know Bobby's in good hands now. I think I'd be worried about him if he had to go back to the Millingtons.' She paused for a moment. 'Did they give you any idea of how long Cyril's likely to be in hospital?' The longer Bobby was with Nate, the stronger the attachment between them would grow. She knew Nate would be gutted when the time came for him to hand Bobby back, but equally, she appreciated that he would no doubt be a much-loved companion for Cyril.

Nate sucked in a deep breath. 'That's the thing, from the way they were talking, I got the impression Cyril had been struggling with his mobility for quite a while. Eric and Sue seemed to think he wouldn't be in a position to look after himself, never mind a pet, when he was discharged from hospital. And in fairness, the state Buddy – I mean, *Bobby* – was in when he turned up at the workshop... I'm reluctant to say he wasn't cared for; I'm sure Cyril cared for him a lot, but Bobby's coat was matted and it'll have taken a while for it to get that grubby.' He gave a shrug. 'I feel sorry for him and Cyril, they've both had their lives turned upside down.'

'Yeah, it's a sad situation,' Lark said softly.

'So, the upshot is, I told them I'd be happy to keep the little fella if Cyril feels he won't be able to manage him anymore. I told him I'd take Bobby to visit him. Makes sense, he's settled quickly with me, and we've been rubbing along nicely. Mind, his snoring's a bit of an issue and don't get me onto his breath...' The face Nate pulled made Lark laugh out loud. But there was no mistaking the affection in his eyes.

Nate glanced around the kitchen. 'Come to think of it, where is he? Whenever there's food on the go, he's usually glued to my side in typical Labrador fashion.'

Lark peered under the table, but there was no sign of him

there. 'I'm sure he came in here with us after his less-than-warm welcome from Luna.'

Wearing a puzzled expression, Nate got to his feet and headed towards the living room. Moments later, he peered around the door. He pressed his finger to his lips then gestured for Lark to join him.

Tiptoeing across the room, she leant around Nate to see Bobby stretched out on the rug in front of the stove with Luna snuggled up close to him. Both were sleeping contentedly.

Lark pressed her hands to her heart, the soft jingling of her silver bangles making Luna stir. It was quickly followed by Bobby emitting a loud snore which had the cat leaping up and stalking off in disgust. The Labrador raised his head and glanced around as if searching for whatever it was that had disturbed him. Failing to find anything, he rested his head back down on the floor and gave a contented sigh. Lark couldn't help but laugh.

'You'd never guess he was homeless a couple of days ago,' she said, watching the steady rise and fall of his body.

'You wouldn't, he just seems to fit in anywhere, which makes how the Millingtons treated him seem even worse.' Nate shook his head in disgust, his smile falling. 'If it was up to them, he'd still be running the roads. Makes my bloomin' blood boil.'

Lark rested her hand on his arm. It took a lot to generate such a reaction from the usually mild-mannered Nate. 'Don't think about it anymore. Bobby's fine now – looking at him, he seems to have forgotten all about it – everything's worked out well for him. And you.' She gave him a nudge with her hip and caught his eye, smiling. The shadow lifted from his face and he smiled back.

'Aye, I suppose you're right.'

Lark turned and headed back to the kitchen, Nate following. 'So, what are you doing with the rest of your day? Heading back to the workshop?'

'Thought I'd save the workshop for later this afternoon. I'd originally called to see if you or your dad fancied joining Bobby and me for a walk on the beach. And after what we've just witnessed, I reckon Luna might think it's a good idea.'

'A walk on the beach? A good idea?' Lark looked horrified at the suggestion. 'Won't it be absolutely freezing?'

'I can't deny, it is pretty chilly out there, but there's no wind and the sun's shining. And I discovered yesterday that Bobby loves a tear about on the sand and a game of fetch. If you wrap up warm, you should be okay.'

'Go on, then, you've talked me into it. My dad's got a key, so he'll be able to let himself in if I'm still out when he gets back.' Lark found herself suddenly quite taken with the idea of a cobweb-clearing walk along the beach, watching Bobby race around. And just maybe, spending a bit more time with Nate had something to do with it, too...

TWENTY-EIGHT

Nate was absolutely right, it was cold, but there was a freshness to the air that felt inexorably good for the soul. The winter sunshine and clear blue sky overhead only added to the feeling.

The beach was empty but for a couple of other dog walkers up ahead, the sound of barking in the distance, and the cawing of a seagull up above. Lark's gaze drifted towards the sea. It looked dark and brooding, salty spray filling the air as the waves crashed onto the shore.

Nate let Bobby off the lead, then threw a ball. The Labrador shot off like a rocket, kicking up sand as he chased after it, bounding back with it clenched between his teeth. He dropped it at Nate's feet, looking up at him expectantly, his tail wagging excitedly. Nate threw the ball again and Bobby raced after it.

'Bobby never tires of this game.' Nate chuckled. 'I suspect he'd do it all day, or at least until the tide came in and there was no sand left for him to run on.'

Lark smiled as she watched Bobby scoop up the ball with his mouth, the eagerness on his face as he raced towards them, ears flapping. He was sociable and had a huge zest for life. It saddened her to think that not long ago he'd been left on his own in the cold for hours at a time. She took reassurance from the knowledge that those days were behind him now, especially after Nate had told her he'd been shopping and bought Bobby a new "luxury" bed, lined with sheepskin, as well as a red leather lead and matching collar with name disc attached. He'd also picked up a new food and water bowl and couple of squeaky toys, adding a large bag of dog food and a box of dog treats to the list.

'Cost me a bloomin' fortune,' Nate said, feigning outrage, but the look in his eyes was pure affection.

He'd also made an appointment at the vets for the Labrador to get vaccinated – enquiries made with the Millingtons had confirmed Bobby's vaccinations hadn't been kept up to date. While the Labrador was there, he was also getting chipped and having his claws trimmed.

It looked like Bobby was here to stay.

They walked along the wide stretch of beach, taking it in turns to throw the ball and laughing at Bobby's boundless energy and enthusiasm. Despite the sun, it was bitterly cold but, unlike Lark, the Labrador didn't seem to notice. She looked on, snuggling her chin into her scarf and stuffing her gloved hands deeper into her pockets.

'Don't suppose you've had a chance to take another look at the clothes in the suitcase with everything else that's been going on.' Nate hurled the ball with all his might before glancing over at her.

'It's funny you should say that, but I was going to fetch it from the cupboard under the stairs just before you arrived. I haven't had time since I first opened it. But a thought struck me and I...' Bobby came back and dropped the ball in front of her, his eyes hopeful, tongue lolling. 'Go fetch, Bobby!' she said as she reached down and picked up the sand-covered ball before hurling it down the beach. 'He'll sleep like a log tonight.'

'He will, and then the torture by snoring will commence. I've never heard anything like it,' Nate said dryly, shaking his head. 'Anyroad, you said something struck you about the suitcase.'

'Yeah, it did.' She switched her gaze to him, keen to see his reaction. 'What do you think about us donating Betty's suitcase and the contents to the heritage centre?'

His dark eyebrows flicked up in surprise. 'Oh, right... I wasn't expecting you to say that.' He turned his face to her, listening as she explained the reasons behind her suggestion.

When she'd finished, he said, 'I think it sounds like a brilliant idea, as long as you're sure you won't regret not putting them in your shop.'

'I won't, I'm totally fine with it. In fact, I think it would be a wonderful way to remember such a lively member of the town's wartime community, especially with Betty's wedding dress possibly being made from parachute silk.'

'I agree.'

'I wonder if any of Betty's relatives still live here in Micklewick Bay? And if so, do they know about her singing at the dance hall? And what a huge deal it was at the time, when morale needed a boost. How lovely would it be for them to see some of the things that actually belonged to her? That she actually wore.' Her eyes shone as she felt her enthusiasm for the idea growing. She hoped Louisa would be as taken with it as she was.

'I daresay it wouldn't be too difficult to track down living relatives.'

'I think you're right.' Lark tapped her finger against her lip in thought. Did she have time to pay the records office in Middleton-le-Moors a visit? Though you could probably access them online these days. 'I wonder where I could start looking?'

Nate let out a laugh. 'You've turned into a right little history geek since you opened those suitcases from Crayke's Cottage.'

'I'm evidently my father's daughter.' She grinned back at him, his smile melting her heart a little. 'I'll speak to Louisa about Betty's clothes, see if she's interested.'

'I can't see why she wouldn't be. From what you described, they sound amazing.'

Mention of her father meant she found her thoughts veering

away from Betty's potential exhibition. 'I wonder how Louisa and my dad are getting along?'

'Like a house on fire, I reckon.'

'I've got a feeling you're right.' The thought sent a wave of warmth spreading through her as she pictured them both smiling and laughing together, the way she'd seen them at the Jolly the night before.

Lark and Nate ambled along, the cold biting at their heels. Arriving at the pier, the halfway point along the beach, they stopped. The iconic landmark was a feat of Victorian engineering, as was the nearby funicular which was built to give Victorian holidaymakers easy access to and from the bottom prom without them having to trouble the one hundred and ninety-nine steps or Skitey Bank. The lift used a system of pulleys and water-filled weights to power each journey and was still in use today.

Seagulls screeched noisily overhead as Nate turned to face her, his cheeks and nose glowing red, his fringe fluttering beneath his woolly hat.

'What are your plans for the rest of the day?' she asked, the cold nipping at her cheeks, the breeze that had suddenly appeared lifting her hair. She took the opportunity to scrutinise his face in the daylight, taking in the shadows under his eyes. There was no escaping the fact he looked tired. If it was down to that couple hounding him, then that was just awful. But, she told herself, rather that than something serious to do with his health, which was what she'd originally feared the weird feelings she'd been picking up were trying to tell her.

'I'm going to head home, grab a bite to eat, then head back to the workshop, tackle those units, see if I can get them finished.'

'You shouldn't let that couple bully you, Nate.'

'I know, but this break away from the workshop has been good, it's helped clear my thoughts. I feel ready to get back to work now.'

'Well, don't overdo it, will you?' She knew he worked every day, and often late into the evening, and he rarely had a full day off unless they were on a sourcing trip.

'I'll be fine, there's no need to fret about me.' He smiled down at her, making her heart melt just a little.

It seemed to be happening with increasing frequency.

'You're welcome to join me for some soup before you head off. It's sweet potato and thyme, I made a batch for my dad's visit so there's plenty to go round.'

'Mmm. That does sound tempting.' He rubbed his gloved hands briskly together. 'If you're sure?'

''Course I'm sure. Come on, let's head back, it's *freezing*. I can't feel my toes anymore.'

'Yeah, I suppose it is a bit parky.'

'A *bit* parky?' Lark echoed, incredulous. 'Talk about master of the understatement.'

Nate laughed then whistled for Bobby who came tearing over, thrilled to be rewarded with a dog treat.

That done, Lark linked her arm through Nate's, who jokingly complained as she tried to hurry him along, Bobby racing around them, eager to join in the fun.

'Okay, okay! I get the message!' Nate said. In the next moment, he grabbed Lark's hand and started running as fast as he could. She let out a squeal as her legs raced to keep up with his long strides, Bobby barking in delight as he ran alongside them. 'Come on, Lark! *Keep* up!' Nate cried.

The breeze scooped up their peals of laughter, carrying them along the sand.

TWENTY-NINE

Lark was folding Betty's clothes and replacing them neatly in the suitcase when she heard the key in the front door – she'd treated herself to one last look at them before she handed them over to the heritage centre – followed by the sound of it opening and closing. A draught sneaked in, curling around where she sat on the rug in front of the fire. A shuffling indicating the removal of shoes and coats ensued before the living room door opened. She looked up to see her dad looking bright-eyed and windswept.

'Hi, Dad.' She beamed at him, thinking what a difference a couple of days had made. He looked a far cry from the weary-looking man who'd arrived on Thursday evening. In fact, she'd go as far as to say he looked years younger.

'Hello, sweetheart. Had a good day?' He rubbed his hands together, blowing into them. 'Brr. It's cold out there.'

'Yes, thanks. You?' From the way he was smiling, she already knew the answer to that. She closed the lid of the suitcase and pushed herself up, straightening her jumper.

'I have actually. The heritage centre's fascinating and Louisa's great company; she's so knowledgeable.'

Luna jumped down from the armchair, slinking over to meet him, mewing as she went.

'Hello, there, Luna.' He reached down and smoothed his hand along the cat's back as she pressed herself against his legs.

'Fancy a cup of tea while you tell me all about it?' Lark glanced at the clock, which told her it was twenty past two. The light outside was already fading as dusk sidled its way in. 'I take it you had some lunch while you were out?'

'I have, thanks. Louisa and I treated ourselves to takeaway sandwiches from the deli – delicious they were, too. We might've had a slice of chocolate fudge cake each as well.'

'Good for you, the deli's chocolate fudge cake's really good – not as yummy as Jazz's though.'

Silas patted his stomach. 'I feel like all I've done while I've been here is eat. I'll be heading back to High Nedderton a good half a stone heavier. Not that I'm grumbling, I've enjoyed every mouthful.'

'It's done you good to get some hearty meals inside you. I mean it kindly when I say you're looking loads better than when you arrived; got more colour in your cheeks, too.'

'That's probably down to the savage winds that batter this place. I'd forgotten just how abrasive they can be. They've certainly woken me up. Feel like I've had a thorough shaking.' He gave a deep chuckle.

In the kitchen, Silas poured the tea while Lark retrieved the biscuit tin from the tiny pantry. Popping the lid, she set it down between them.

Lark observed her dad as he helped himself to a chocolate digestive, noting how his whole demeanour had changed. On his last visit, he'd sat in this kitchen, his posture slumped in defeat, his eyes pitiful pools of sadness. It had just about torn her in two to see it. But now, he sat upright and confident, his eyes dancing, just as they used to. And she couldn't help but pick up on the happiness and glow that radiated from him. It filled her with joy to see him like this. He'd not so much turned a corner, but taken a great, broad swoop into new, happier territory, keen to embrace new challenges.

'So, did Louisa share her plans for the heritage centre?' She reached into the tin for a chocolate-dipped shortbread and took a bite, the chocolate melting over her tongue.

'She did. She's got so many wonderful plans, so much energy. She's a total breath of fresh air for the place. Her ideas are going to make it a real draw for the town,' he said, animatedly. 'I think you already know about the grant the centre's been awarded, and how the money's going to be put to linking the cottage next to it, and making that part of the exhibition.'

Lark nodded, chomping on her biscuit. 'Yes, Louisa's got real vision, which is why Nate and I have decided to donate the suitcase containing Betty's clothes to the heritage centre.'

'I think she'd be absolutely thrilled if you did that. She was saying just this morning how she wanted to make the exhibitions more than just about smuggling. Betty's things would be perfect for that.'

'That's what we thought.' She picked up her mug, taking a sip of tea.

Silas wiped a crumb from the corner of his mouth. 'While I was there, I took the opportunity to ask Louisa if there were any volunteer roles available – you'll recall I mentioned volunteering was something I was interested in doing once I'd retired.'

'I do, yes.' *This is getting better and better!*

'Turns out, the centre's always glad of local volunteers, especially after the last curator scared most of them away,' he chortled. 'Though Louisa did say she was going to contact the ones who used to help out, see if they'd consider coming back.'

'That's good, I'm sure they will when they hear how friendly she is.'

'I hope so.' He took a glug of his tea. 'And not just that, Louisa says there's a new role being created for a part-time assistant with a start date of July. I'm thinking of applying.'

'Oh, Dad, that's fantastic news!' Talk about serendipity! Her dad was meant to come to Micklewick Bay for this weekend. Everything was falling into place, and she couldn't be happier for him.

'If I didn't know better, I'd think you'd been doing some sort of manifesting for me – is it possible to do it on behalf of someone else?' he said, sounding like he was only half joking. 'I did notice you'd placed some crystal in my room.'

'I hold my hands up when I say I have been carrying out some positivity rituals for you and trying to send happiness vibes your way, but I had nothing whatsoever to do with Louisa arriving in town or the events with the suitcase or you coming to visit when you did. Having said that, as you know, I strongly believe in fate and that everything happens for a reason.'

'I, for one, can't argue with you about that, sweetheart.' He sat back looking thoughtful. 'It does feel as if someone somewhere has taken me in hand and is guiding me down a new path. Whoever it is, I hope they know I'm truly grateful.'

'I think you don't realise just how much you've been helping yourself, too, Dad. Taking the steps to come here and go to the book reading, your friendship with Louisa...'

'Talking of my friendship with Louisa,' he said, looking suddenly bashful. 'She's asked if I'll join her for a meal at Oscar's Bistro this evening. Told me it's her way of saying thank you for helping at the heritage centre today – not that I'm going to let her pay; I'm too old-fashioned for that. Would you mind very much if I went?'

'Not at all, and you don't need my permission.' It was impossible to control the huge grin that was currently spreading across her face. She wouldn't mention the chicken shawarma she'd taken out of the freezer for their evening meal – one of the dishes she'd prepped earlier in the week in readiness for his visit. 'I think it's right that you go out, though I should probably warn you, you might have to put your old-fashioned values to one side if Louisa insists on paying.' It had been a long time since he'd dated and she knew he'd be unaware that the climate had changed as far as things like that were concerned.

'Will I?' Lark could see him wrestling with her advice. 'I'm not sure I'll be able to do that.'

'Give it a try, or at least make do with paying half if you can talk her into that.'

'Okay.' He still didn't look happy about the suggestion.

'Just one more thing.'

'Oh dear.' His expression made her giggle.

'Don't look so worried. I was only going to ask you to promise me one little thing.'

'Go on.'

'Please swear you won't revisit any of those wild dance moves you were doing in here this morning. I don't think Micklewick Bay's ready to see them, never mind poor Louisa.'

Relief spread across Silas's face. He threw his head back and roared with laughter. 'Now that I think I can manage.'

'Pinkie promise?'

'Pinkie promise,' he said, still laughing as he held out his little finger.

THIRTY

Lark and Silas had sat chatting for another half hour. She'd updated him on the situation with Buddy, telling him they were now to call him Bobby. Her father's thoughts had echoed her own when he said Nate would've been gutted to hand Bobby back.

When Silas mentioned he'd thought Nate was looking tired, Lark filled him in on the backlog of work he had, and the couple from Lingthorpe who were hassling him. Her father had rubbed his chin, looking thoughtful.

'You know, I might offer to give him a hand tomorrow before I head back to High Nedderton. I can sand pieces down, give things a lick of varnish or paint, which would free him up to focus on the other, more complicated stuff. I quite enjoy pottering about with things like that.' He looked across the table at her. 'Do you think he'd mind me helping out?'

'I think he'd be chuffed to bits if you did. He told me he liked having you around when you helped him with that huge dresser a few years back.'

'In that case, I'll send him a text,' Silas said decisively.

They spent the rest of the afternoon poring over their laptops at the kitchen table, searching for properties for sale in the town. Lark took the opportunity to place an order for more aromatherapy oils as well as bottles and sprays to use for her own blends. She ordered more crystals too. Silas had been disappointed to find there were no houses that fitted his criteria, so ventured onto researching local history and, in particular, seeing what it would throw up regarding Betty Roberts, née Pearson.

Seashell Cottage seemed suddenly empty without her dad's cheerful presence. He'd spent the afternoon whistling or humming to himself as he'd scrolled through the searches on his laptop, sharing bits of information he found, scribbling away in his notebook. His endeavours had thrown up a few interesting facts, the most exciting being that he appeared to have traced a relative of Betty's who still lived in Micklewick Bay. He'd been so fired up by it, Lark had struggled to rein in his enthusiasm and stop him from calling the person in question. But it felt good to have him there in her home. Luna seemed to think so, too, since she'd abandoned the armchair in favour of curling up beside his feet.

Since Oscar's Bistro was located in the centre of town and quite a walk away from Old Micklewick on a cold, winter's night, it was agreed – after some persuasion, Silas not wanting to put his daughter out on a Saturday evening – that Lark would play taxi driver and ferry her dad to and from the eatery. In town, they'd take a quick detour, stopping off at Louisa's house and scooping her up before dropping them off at Oscar's door. The arrangement made perfect sense to Lark.

It had touched her to see that her dad had made an effort to look smart for his meal out, opting for a pair of mustard-coloured chinos, and a blue and white shirt with a dark moleskin jacket worn over the top. On his feet were his favourite chunky brogue shoes he'd polished specially for the occasion.

She was still mindful not to refer to it as a date, though she'd almost slipped up on one occasion, correcting herself just in time, grateful that he appeared not to have noticed.

Louisa had been watching for them from her living room

window and hurried down the path wrapped up in a smart woollen jacket, her hair fixed in a messy "updo", dangly earrings swinging from her ears. Frost sparkled on the hedges, creating a magical effect. Silas had jumped out of the front passenger seat, greeting her with a peck on the cheek and holding the car door open for her while she climbed in, filling the vehicle with her delicate floral perfume.

The bistro looked achingly inviting, the large, steamy windows trimmed with warm white fairy lights, with further lights wound around the sturdy olive trees that flanked the half-glazed door. As Louisa and Silas climbed out of the car, the delicious aroma of garlic and herbs flooded in. 'Have a wonderful time and text when you're ready for me to pick you up,' Lark had called after them, watching as her dad guided Louisa to the door, his hand at the small of her back. Lark's heart performed a little leap on her father's behalf.

But now she was back at the cottage, she felt at a loss for something to do, which was unlike her. She usually enjoyed her own company and could always busy herself whether it be altering garments for her shop, mixing up aromatherapy blends, or even doing a spot of meditation. Yet this evening, she was struggling to get her mind to settle on anything and before long she found herself pacing, her thoughts flitting from her dad and Louisa to the contents of the small suitcase to Crayke's Cottage. And to Nate.

Pushing her hair off her face, she spied her mobile on the sideboard and scooped it up. Finding the contact she was looking for, she pressed call.

It was answered after three rings.

'Ey up, Lark, how's things?'

'Hi, Nate, I was wondering if you'd eaten yet?'

'Not had time; I'm still in the workshop. Why?'

'I don't suppose you fancy a plate of homemade chicken shawarma, some herby smashed potatoes and fluffy flatbread, with lots of salady bits thrown in? My dad's out gallivanting with Louisa, so there's a portion going spare.'

She had the feeling Nate would be working well into the night and would make do with something quick to eat that wouldn't be particularly nourishing. He might as well enjoy a hot meal.

'Ah, man, lead me to it!' She could hear the smile in his voice.

'Great! Though if you're busy, I could always drop a plate off, it's entirely up to you.'

'If it's okay, I'd rather have some company than eat on my own.'

''Course, that's fine.' Though she lived alone, and regularly ate by herself, for some reason, tonight Lark felt the same.

'I'll just finish up what I'm doing here. Shouldn't take long, I'm almost done on this cupboard, then I'll get cleaned up and head straight over.'

'Fab! I'll pop the chicken and the potatoes in the oven, they just need a warm through so should be just about ready by the time you get here.'

'Cool! Can't wait.'

'Oh, and don't forget to bring Bobby.'

'Don't worry, there's no chance of that happening, he's glued to me and watches my every move. If I'm out of sight for more than a few seconds he starts whimpering.'

'Ahh, bless him. He's probably worried you're going to disappear like Cyril.'

'Yeah, that had crossed my mind. Hopefully, he'll realise I'm not going anywhere, and I'll be able to build his trust.'

'I'm sure it won't take long. I'll give you some crystals to place in your workshop to help soothe him.'

'Thanks, Lark, that'd be good.'

By the time Nate arrived, the table was set and a playlist of festive music was playing softly in the background. Bobby trotted in and headed straight for the armchair where Luna lay curled up. He stopped in front of her, wagging his tail, staying well out of swiping distance.

Nate chuckled. 'He's obviously not going to risk another whack across his snout.'

'Can't say I blame him.' Lark smiled. 'Come through, food's nearly ready.'

'Smells amazing. I'm that famished I could eat a scabby horse between two mattresses.'

Lark chuckled. 'I'm so glad you said that, the portion's much bigger than I remembered.' She reached for the cloth she used in place of an oven glove.

'Is there owt I can do to help?'

'It's all in hand, you just park yourself at the table.'

Instead, Nate loitered awkwardly while Lark hefted the tray with the sizzling chicken shawarma out of the oven, the aroma of spices intensifying as she slid it onto the heatproof mats waiting on the worktop.

'Is everything all right?' Lark shot him a puzzled look, her eyes flicking to his right hand. It was the first time she'd noticed he was holding something.

He scratched his head, looking a little uncomfortable. 'Thought you'd like this.' He handed her a small, square item wrapped in a paper bag. 'Don't worry, it's not from Crayke's Cottage. It was meant to be for Christmas, but with you feeding me so much recently and helping with Crayke's Cottage, I thought it'd be nice for you to have it now.'

'Thank you.' She reached inside the packet and eased out a small wooden box, its lid inlaid with mother-of-pearl. 'Oh, Nate, it's beautiful, but there was really no need to give me anything. You've helped me out loads in the past.'

Lark was instantly struck by the box's energy. She sensed happiness and warmth and an overwhelming feeling of affection. Her eyes roved over the intricate detail, the fine, iridescent slivers of shell arranged in a flowerhead design, the petals growing wider and fanning out. Lifting the lid revealed the box was lined with blue satin where a silver chain was coiled around an oval-shaped amethyst.

She couldn't stop the gasp that escaped her mouth.

'D'you like it?' he asked, looking uncertain.

'It's absolutely beautiful!'

His face broke out into a smile. 'I'm glad you think so, I thought of you as soon as I saw it.'

'But it's too generous, Nate. I really think you should save it for Christmas.'

'But I'd rather give it to you now.'

'But Christmas isn't far away. I can wait till then.' She smiled, hoping he didn't think she was being ungrateful.

'Early Christmas present, then.' He released a sigh. 'To be honest, I've been feeling guilty about the stuff with Crayke's Cottage. I know how you're sensitive to things like that, how they can affect you. I should've thought about it before dragging you into it, asked someone else to help move the stuff. The fact that Bear wasn't keen to hang around said it all, really.' He gave her an apologetic smile. 'Sorry.'

Her heart twisted for him. She had no idea this had been going through his mind. 'Please don't beat yourself up about it. I could just as easily have said no, but my curiosity got the better of me. Actually, nosiness is probably a more apt word.' She gave a light laugh.

'Please take it,' he said imploringly. 'I want you to have it.'

How could she resist the look in those dark brown eyes? 'Okay then. Thank you.' She stood on her tiptoes and kissed his cheek, her nose catching the smell of soap and furniture wax.

'Actually, I've got something for you, but I'll get them after we've eaten.'

'Sounds intriguing.'

'Crystals,' she said, by way of explanation. 'Powerful ones.'

'Ah.'

'For the next time you go to Crayke's Cottage. Come to mention it, have you decided when that's going to be? I know you're keen you get Mr Thurston's key back to him.'

'It'll be early next week. I'm going to try and get hold of him, see if he can meet me there seeing as though I don't know where he lives. I can hand him his key back once I've had a last check round. You're welcome to join me – no pressure.' He raised his palms. 'Though I'll understand if you'd rather not. I know it's not your favourite place after all the weird goings on last time. And, for the record, I didn't give you the box to guilt trip you into keeping me company there.'

'I didn't think that for a second,' Lark said and meant it. 'I'm okay to give you a hand. And don't forget I performed a cleansing ritual last time we were there, and there's nothing to stop me doing another one.' It somehow didn't feel right letting him go there on his own when he looked so drained and had a backlog of work to contend with. If two people hunted around for any hidden cupboards or doors, then it would take half the time. She'd be sure to replace the malachite crystals in her pockets before they set off for the cottage – and make sure Nate had some in his – and take her sage stick just in case.

'You sure you don't mind?' he said, looking pleased at the prospect.

'Not at all. The sooner we get it done, the sooner you can get the house key back to Mr Thurston and the one from the case to Louisa.' Lark still wasn't keen on Nate hanging on to something from the smaller case after the weird vibes it had contained. She couldn't shake the feeling he was absorbing some of its negative energy.

'True. And hopefully, there'll be no peacocks on the roof sending spooky messages down the chimney this time.'

'Ugh! Don't,' she said, pulling a face of faux horror.

'That was amazing and sure beats the ham sandwich I was going to have. I've got loads of delicious flavours running around my mouth now.' Nate smacked his lips together and rubbed his hand over his stomach. 'Your dad missed out big-time there. I sincerely hope the food he's having at Oscar's is tasty. Mind, I don't think I'll be able to eat for at least a week.'

'Yeah, I feel stuffed too. I'm glad you enjoyed it though.'

They'd finished their meal and migrated through to the living room which looked inviting and cosy. The table lamps cast their soft light around the room, added to by the warm glow of the wood burner. An abundance of fairy lights twinkled from the Christmas tree to the others that were strung around the room all year long. Lark plonked herself on the sofa while Nate negotiated the tangle of Bobby and Luna as he went to throw another log on the wood burner. That done, he flopped on the sofa beside her, stretching his arm out along the back.

'I wonder how your dad and Louisa are getting on?'

Nate's question triggered an unexpected flutter of nerves in her stomach. The way her dad had spruced himself up, including a spritz of woody cologne, clearly had some significance. Louisa, too. She'd looked lovely at the reading on Thursday night, but she'd clearly made an extra effort this evening. And now Lark thought about it, tonight had all the hallmarks of a first date.

The nerves jiggled about some more. *Oh my days!*

'I hope they're both having a wonderful time.' She wondered how it would be when she picked them up from the restaurant. Not that she wanted to dwell on it too much, but would her dad and Louisa maybe want to finish their evening with a kiss? *Yikes!* And if so, how was that going to happen if she was dropping Louisa off at her house before bringing her dad back here? The prospect of playing gooseberry on her dad's date was not at all appealing. Ordering a taxi for them crossed her mind, but she dismissed that thought quickly, knowing the taxi company wouldn't be impressed at such a small fare.

She kept her concerns to herself; if she mentioned it to Nate, he'd offer to collect them and bring them back, and she didn't want to put him out. Plus, though it wouldn't be as bad, it would put him in an awkward situation too. And she didn't want to push the problem onto him. She'd just leave things as they were and deal with the situation when it arose. *If* it arose.

An hour and a half later, Nate yawned and stretched his arms above his head. 'Ah, man, it's so warm and cosy in here and I'm so full of food, if I don't heave my backside off this sofa, I'm in serious danger of falling asleep.'

Lark gave a relaxed sigh. 'I know what you mean. That walk along the beach fettled me, all that cold air. There's no wonder Bobby's shattered – he must've run miles today.'

'He had a whale of a time.' He peered down at the Labrador and Luna, baking themselves in front of the stove. Bobby was now laid flat on his back, his legs splayed and head thrown back. 'And have you seen the state of him? Talk about making yourself at home.'

Lark followed Nate's line of sight, laughing at the image that greeted her. 'He's certainly got bags of character.'

'Aye, he has that all right.'

'I've heard it means a dog feels safe or content when they sleep like that,' said Lark. 'Something about not having to worry about protecting their delicate organs, which is what they're doing when they curl up. It's left over from when they lived in the wild and had to keep themselves safe when they were sleeping.'

'Well, I think it's time I took Bobby and his delicate organs home,' Nate said dryly.

Walking to the door, Nate stopped and turned. He looked down at Lark, his eyes like pools of chocolate in the dim light. Resting his hands on the top of her arms made her heart skip a beat. 'Tonight's been great. In fact, despite all the stuff with Crayke's Cottage, the rest of the week's been great, too. I've enjoyed the time we've spent together.'

Unable to speak, Lark felt her heart thudding as his gaze drifted to her mouth. Before she knew what was happening his lips were on hers, soft and warm and delicious. She closed her eyes and allowed herself to be swept up by the waves of emotion that washed over her. Her stomach flipped and her knees threatened to buckle at any minute as what felt like a riot of explosions went off inside her. Lark had never experienced a kiss with such intensity before. Never knew they could make her feel this way.

Bobby barked, breaking the spell in an instant. Lark stepped back, looking at Nate in disbelief. She clapped her hands to her face. 'Oh no! What have we done?'

Nate looked crestfallen. 'What do you mean? I thought... I mean, it felt perfect to me.'

'We shouldn't have done it, Nate. It was a mistake. I don't feel that way about you. We can't be anything more than friends. Sorry.'

'Oh, right.' Nate looked stunned, as if he'd been slapped across the face.

'I'm sorry if I gave you the wrong impression.'

'No, no. I'm the one who should be sorry. I got it wrong. But we can just forget it, act like it's never happened.' He reached for his coat and clicked his tongue for Bobby.

'Nate—'

'I'll see you later, Lark. Like I said, thanks for the food.' With that he headed through the door, leaving Lark feeling utterly wretched.

Lark pulled up outside Louisa's house as her father's text had instructed her to do. She couldn't decide whether to knock on the door or simply text her dad and let him know she was there – if she did the former, would it mean they'd still have the problem with "the goodnight kiss" or would it seem unfriendly if she did the latter? Blimey, this was tricky.

As if she didn't have enough on her plate with Nate and what had happened before he'd left Seashell Cottage. She clapped her hands to her face and groaned loudly at the memory, just as her dad headed through Louisa's front gate.

'Hi, Dad.' She fixed a smile to her face as he climbed in beside her.

'Hello, sweetheart, thanks for this.'

'No problem. How was your evening?'

He turned to her and smiled. 'It was quite wonderful actually.'

'Oh, Dad, I'm so happy for you.'

'I know it's going to sound like a corny old cliché, but it feels like I've known Louisa for years. She feels the same too, says we're kindred spirits.' He gave an embarrassed laugh.

Lark could have done a happy dance on the spot. Instead, she fired up the ignition and pulled out into the road.

'I'm over the moon for you.'

'Thank you, sweetheart. And how's your evening been?' he asked, blissfully unaware of how loaded his question was.

THIRTY-ONE
SUNDAY 7TH DECEMBER

After dropping her father off at Nate's workshop, Lark had headed straight to her shop. She hadn't called in to say hello to her friend – if she could still call him that; he might not think of her that way any longer – as she normally would. After what had happened last night, it would've felt too strange, and she didn't want her dad to pick up on any weirdness between her and Nate. It would only lead to him asking questions, and the last thing she needed was to have to navigate those first thing on a Sunday morning. She hadn't even got her head around it all herself without having to explain whatever it was to her dad. It was bad enough trying to think of a way to get him to come round to Lark's Vintage Bazaar rather than her pick him up at Nate's workshop without him asking questions. They'd agreed to finish whatever they were working on at twelve o'clock, which would give them enough time to get home and get changed before heading to the Jolly for the Sunday dinner she'd promised her dad. As a rule, she wouldn't think twice about picking him up from Nate's, and her dad would know that too. But today, Nate was the last person she wanted to see, which wasn't an ideal situation since Nate and Louisa were supposed to be joining them for the meal.

She puffed out her cheeks as she parked her car in a space a few doors down from her shop. 'How have you even got yourself into this mess?' she asked herself out loud. She didn't know where things were going to go from here. How could they ever be the same? And as for that dratted feeling that just wouldn't go away. Jeez, if anything was outstaying its welcome, it was that! It was all such a crazy mix in her head and she didn't know what to do about it.

She swept her gaze around the square through the car window, taking in all the festive displays and halting at The Happy Hartes Bookshop, which was a delicious Christmas confection. Everywhere was cheerfully oblivious to the turmoil that was raging inside her.

Heaving herself out of the car, she made her way to the shop, avoiding the icy patches that had managed to dodge the salt. She'd just put her key in the door when she heard a voice calling her from further up the square.

She turned her head to see Ando Taylor in his usual garb of ripped jeans, battered leather jacket, the latest trainers favoured by students and baseball cap turned back-to-front. His hair was hanging down his back like over-bleached rats' tails. No matter what the season, or how inclement the weather, Ando always wore exactly the same. Today, he must be freezing, thought Lark.

''Ow do,' he said, giving a familiar Yorkshire greeting and a lopsided smile. His eyes were bleary, and he looked somewhat worse for wear. She wondered if he was hungover from indulging in the home brew he regularly spoke of. Gut Rot, he called it. He seemed to have an endless supply and had regularly tried to tempt Jasmine back to his digs with the promise of a glass or two to help wash down his out-of-date pickled eggs. Despite the fact Jasmine had never taken him up on his offer, he'd persisted until she'd started dating Max. Which was when he'd turned his attentions to Lark.

Lark massaged her brow with her fingertips. She didn't want to hurt Ando's feelings, but she'd hardly slept a wink last night, fretting about what had happened with her and Nate. And she could really do without Ando's clumsy, ill-advised advances right now.

'Morning, Ando.' She busied herself with opening the door, hoping he'd get the message that she didn't want to talk.

'That's a couple of fit birds you've got there.' He nodded towards the mannequins in the shop's window display. 'Just my type, they are an' all.' He gave a leery smirk that made her instantly picture Stella wiping the floor with him for his inappropriate comment.

Not knowing how to answer his rather odd statement, she said, 'I'll see you later, Ando, I've got lots to do today.'

'What? On a Sunday? Who works on a Sunday?'

Ando didn't seem to work on any day. As far as anyone knew, he spent his time with the skateboarders at the local park.

'Thought you might fancy grabbing a bag of chips and some scraps from the chippy and having a wander down to the skate-board park.'

Jasmine popped into her mind this time. Lark could picture what her friend would have to say about that. It would definitely feature something about it being her idea of hell.

'I don't know what on earth gave you the idea I'd like that, Ando, but it's a no, thank you. See you later.' With that, she left him, mouth agape, standing on the pavement, as she pushed the door open, stepped inside and quickly closed it behind her.

Inside, with the door bolted, she clutched her hands to her chest, guilt flooding through her and making her face burn. What had made her speak to Ando so coldly? It wasn't like her at all. And he was a harmless soul really. A bit lost, maybe, but he didn't deserve her being so dismissive of him. What had happened with Nate wasn't Ando's fault and it wasn't fair that she took her bad mood out on him. She had to fight to stop herself from going out there and apologising. But the rational side of her told her to do that would be a mistake. He'd only take it as encouragement, and she didn't need to add Ando to her list of problems right now.

Lark spent the morning arranging the clothes rails and setting up a new display of vintage evening bags. That particular task had been a welcome distraction, not least because the items were so exquisite. Using artfully arranged tree branches she'd sprayed silver and stood in a hammered silver bowl, she'd created a display from which to hang the items. Amongst them was a nineteen-fifties clutch covered in ruby-red sequins with a faux ruby clasp. Next to that she'd hung an electric-blue satin affair from the seventies, trimmed with zigzags in silver leather. But her favourite was the nineteen-thirties pouch-style bag in silver chainmail that she'd found at the bottom of a mixed box of goods she'd picked up at a vintage fair in Harrogate. Though the metal of the bag had tarnished, it was still a thing of great beauty and she'd had to think hard about whether or not she could part with it.

She was still tweaking the display when there was a knock at the door, making her start. 'Oh no, who's this?' she grumbled to herself. Her first thought was Ando. And just as she was considering whether or not to ignore it, she heard her dad's voice calling her name as he knocked again. Her next thought was to check the time. Was it midday already? She was surprised to find it was only eleven thirty.

'Hi, Dad,' she said, as she opened the door to him. 'You're early.'

'Nate said he had to be somewhere unexpectedly, so we finished up earlier than planned. I offered to stay and carry on with sanding the units, but he wouldn't entertain it, said it was fine, that I should get myself home.'

'Oh, right.' Though she could feel herself squirming inside, she tried to act casual. 'Maybe he had something to pick up. He occasionally gets calls from people wanting to get rid of stuff there and then. You'd be surprised how many folk expect you to just drop everything. I get it with stuff for the shop, too.'

'I'm not sure that was the reason. The lad didn't seem himself at all today – he's been quiet all morning. I did wonder if he wasn't feeling well, or coming down with something. The shadows under his eyes were much more pronounced today. He looked pale, too.

When I asked him if he was all right, he muttered something about how he'd been better. I didn't like to push after that, thought if he wanted to tell me he would in his own time.'

Lark felt her father scrutinise her face. 'Well, I s'pose there's a lot going around at the moment, and he has been under a lot of pressure to get those units finished.' There was no way she was going to share with her dad what had happened between her and Nate last night. Though she had a feeling it wouldn't be long before he started digging with a vengeance.

And though she couldn't help but feel relieved when her father told her that Nate wouldn't be joining them for Sunday dinner, a big part of her was consumed by guilt at the thought of him being on his own when he could've been spending time with them.

THIRTY-TWO

Sunday dinner with her father and Louisa would've been perfect if it hadn't been for Nate not being there. And not just because Lark was missing him, or wanted to see him. But his absence was definitely felt, not least because of the numerous reminders of him from her dad and Louisa, who both held him in high esteem.

Though she'd felt uncomfortable, she'd done her best to hide it, not wanting to spoil her dad's time with her and Louisa. Luckily, the meal had been as excellent as Lark had promised them it would be, and she'd done what she could to manage questions about Nate's whereabouts and what reasons he could possibly have to avoid such a delicious meal. Lark had tried to steer the conversation towards the heritage centre and the new exhibitions Louisa had planned. She'd mentioned how her father had found a relative of Betty's apparently living there in Micklewick Bay, which had sent Louisa into raptures, saying how she had access to local records and would check them first thing tomorrow. Despite being keen to use the topic as a distraction, Lark had been genuinely keen to discuss it. And of course it had been heartwarming to see her dad looking so happy in Louisa's company. There was definitely a romance blossoming there and she expected it wouldn't be long before he was back in Micklewick Bay.

But by the end of the meal, with the topic of conversation turning back to Nate and his whereabouts once more, Lark was beginning to feel exhausted. It wasn't her style at all to try to manipulate a conversation or dodge questions. She much preferred to be honest and open.

By the time they left the Jolly, her head was spinning with it all.

'Let me know when you get back, okay, Dad?' Lark watched as he threw his overnight bag into the boot of his four-wheel drive.

''Course, sweetheart.'

They were in the private car park for locals not far from Seashell Cottage and her dad's brief visit had come to an end. The blue skies of yesterday had been replaced with dark, brooding clouds, the occasional snowflake floating down lazily.

She threw her arms around him, squeezing him tight. Her hug was returned with equal enthusiasm. 'It's been great having you here.' Her voice was muffled by his jacket.

'It's been great to be here. I'm just sorry I waited so long before I paid you a decent visit.'

'That's okay, you weren't ready.'

Silas released her from his embrace and stepped back, keeping his hands resting on her shoulders. Lark was thrilled to see the change in him from when he'd first arrived last Thursday. Even the lines around his eyes seem to have filled out.

'I would say it's been great to see you, but that would be a fib since I've hardly seen you at all. You seem to have developed an interest in local history and, in particular, the heritage centre. I'm beginning to think there must be a new attraction there.' She flashed him a mischievous grin.

Silas took her teasing in good spirits and laughed. 'I'm sorry, I hope you don't feel I've abandoned you.' His smile faltered briefly.

'Don't be daft! I'm thirty-four years old, nearly thirty-five, I'm hardly a baby. It's been great to see you getting along so well with

Louisa, she seems a genuinely lovely person and it's obvious you're well suited.'

Her reassurances made him smile. 'You're right, Louisa is a genuinely lovely person. In fact, I was going to ask you something – and I'll totally understand if you'd rather not – it's just I was wondering about Christmas, and how you'd feel about Louisa joining us for the day? She's got no close relatives nearby and has actually gone into work the last few Christmases since her husband died, which seems rather sad.'

'It does.' The thought of anyone going into work on Christmas Day because they had no one to spend the day with nearly undid her. Lark didn't need to think twice. 'And I'd be thrilled if Louisa joined us, the more the merrier.'

His face broke out into a smile. 'Thank you, sweetheart. Am I okay to do the inviting, or would you like to?'

'I'll leave that entirely up to you.' Snowflakes started swirling around them. Lark raised her eyes to the sky to see the clouds had darkened. 'Looks like we're in for another covering. Might be a good idea to make a move before it gets too bad.'

'You're right. But before I go, I'd just like to say that whatever it is that's going on with you and Nate, you will try to sort it out, won't you? Don't think I haven't noticed you've been out of sorts today as well as him.' He pinned her with a knowing look. 'He's a decent lad with a good heart, and he cares for you. And what's more, I think you care for him.'

Lark didn't know how to answer that.

'Bye, sweetheart.' Her dad kissed her brow and went to climb into his car.

'Bye, Dad.'

As she watched him drive away, his words hit their target. Her throat tightened and her eyes blurred with tears.

What had she done?

She turned to walk back home, tears streaming down her cheeks.

It was too late. Too much had been said. And it was all her fault.

THIRTY-THREE

'Lark, flower, what's up?'

Lark picked her gaze up from where it was fixed to the cobbles to see Maggie's kind, brown eyes looking back at her, full of sympathy.

'Oh, Mags, I've been such an idiot.' Tears were tumbling down her cheeks and dripping off her chin.

'Why? What's happened?' Maggie reached out and rested her hand on Lark's arm.

Lark shook her head. How could she even tell her friend what she'd done? She felt too ashamed.

'Come on, lovey, you're shivering. Let's get you back home and out of the cold.' Maggie took charge, wrapping her arm around Lark and steering her back to Seashell Cottage.

Inside, she'd sat Lark down in the kitchen and made a pot of tea, Luna observing them curiously from the doorway.

'Right then, come on, tell all. You'll feel a hundred times better when you've got it off your chest, you know I'm right.' After placing a box of tissues in front of Lark, she poured tea into two mugs, sliding one across the table to her friend. 'There you go, flower.'

'Thanks, Mags.'

Maggie sat herself down in the seat opposite, waiting for Lark to begin.

But where *did* she begin? How could she tell her friend what she'd said? What she'd *done*? It was so unlike her, even she found it hard to believe it now she was thinking about it. It was all so awful. What she'd give to be able to turn the clock back. Poor Nate.

Mustering every ounce of courage and with a rapidly thudding heart, Lark said, 'Nate and I kissed.' Now it was out there she couldn't backtrack. Her mind bounced between relief and regret and back again.

A beat passed, Maggie clearly processing this unexpected piece of information. And now Lark's overriding feeling was regret. Regret for so many things.

'And you're crying because...?' Maggie looked at her in disbelief.

'Because it was a mistake.'

'A mistake? Are you sure about that? I mean, are you sure that's what you really think?'

'Of course. You know my stance on having a relationship with Nate.'

'So you're having a relationship with him?'

'No, nothing like that.'

'Okay, so, it was a one-off?'

'Yes, but I don't think Nate thought it would be. It was totally out of the blue. It just happened. A moment of craziness. One minute we were chatting, the next we were kissing.' She gave a shrug, disliking herself for attempting to appear dismissive. Nate was worth more than that. She felt her face burn.

But it wasn't really like that at all. In her explanation she was missing out how wonderful it had felt to have Nate's lips against hers, the feel of his strong arms around her, and how that very first kiss had triggered an explosion of emotion that had sent shockwaves rippling right through her. How it had all felt so tender and loving and special. And how she'd never experienced anything like it before.

'I had a moment of craziness once,' Maggie said matter-of-factly. 'Ended up married to it.'

They both spluttered a laugh at that. Maggie and Bear were known for their rock-solid marriage. They'd been through thick and thin together, their marriage growing stronger by the year.

'So, what's happened that's got you in floods of tears?' asked Maggie.

Lark covered her face with her hands. 'I was horrible to him, Mags. I feel so mean and cruel. His face when I told him it was a mistake.' She shook her head as if shaking the memory from her mind. The hurt in his eyes was too much to bear. 'I handled it so badly and ended up hurting him.'

'I should imagine his ego's bruised a bit, but more than that, Lark, flower, I think it's his heart that'll be hurting the most. The lad's in love with you. Proper head over heels in love. Surely you can see that? The rest of us can.'

Lark scooped up her mug, cradling it in her hands.

'Don't tell me you genuinely didn't know?'

Lark shook her head. 'I was aware he had feelings for me, as I have for him, but I had no idea they ran so deep. We've been spending a bit more time together recently, what with the Crayke's Cottage clearance and the heritage centre, and I suppose we've been growing closer.'

'So how're things between you now? Do you think your friendship can recover from it? I know that was one of your fears about getting romantically involved with Nate.'

Lark cast her mind back to last night. Nate had leant in tentatively, his eyes searching hers as if seeking her approval before kissing her. Everything about what had followed had been perfect, until Lark had decided it wasn't. The hurt on his face would stay with her for a long time.

'I don't know what to do to make things right between us again. I want to talk to him, but I don't know what to say. There's only so many ways you can describe something as a mistake.'

'Harsh,' said Maggie. 'And not at all like you. Whoever's got my friend Lark, can you please bring her back and take this one away?'

'I know! I don't feel like me. I feel like the biggest cowpat in the world.'

'That's probably cos right at this minute, you are. Or, rather, right when you told Nate he was a mistake, that's when you were.'

'You do know you're not helping, don't you?'

Maggie inhaled deeply. 'I want to help, but I kind of get the feeling there's something you're not telling me, that you're holding something back. I mean, I know you've explained the strange energy you've been sensing around Nate, but I don't think that's it. I reckon that would've had the opposite effect.'

Lark felt her stomach turn over. Maggie was on to her. 'I do love him, Mags. More than I could ever put into words. But I'm scared. Really scared.'

'Scared of what?'

'I'm scared of losing him.'

'I very much doubt you're going to lose him, flower. He adores you.'

'It's not that.' Lark felt her emotions building. 'I've been having these weird feelings, you know how I get them about some people?'

'Yes. So what's the problem? You get feelings about loads of people.'

A plump tear spilled onto Lark's lashes and rolled down her cheek. 'The last time I had a feeling like this, it was... It was with Greer.'

Maggie's mouth fell open. 'Oh, Lark, c'mere.' Before she knew what was happening, she was enveloped in a warm hug, Maggie uttering soothing words and smoothing her hand over Lark's hair as her friend sobbed into her neck. 'It's okay, flower, I promise. Everything's going to be okay.'

Lark sat back, her face tearstained. 'That's what I keep telling myself; I really want to believe it,' she said, a sob jarring her words. 'I couldn't bear the thought of it being another situation like Greer. It's almost as if I'd blame myself, as if I'd jinxed him.' Lark knew her logic sounded ridiculous, but it was a fear that had really begun to take hold over the last few days.

She was aware of Maggie looking back at her, absorbing her words, trying to formulate a reply.

'This isn't like you at all, lovey. Is there anything he can do to stop you from worrying? Like make an appointment with his doctor? Not that I think he needs to, but I admit, he is looking a bit under the weather at the moment. It's probably cos he's been working too hard. I mean, we've all had a time when we've felt rundown.'

'I honestly don't know what it is, Mags.' Lark wiped her eyes with the back of her hands. 'I've tried to think rationally about it, told myself it's because he's absorbed energy from the stuff he buys and sells, and the stuff at Crayke's Cottage. And just when I've convinced myself of this, something happens to make me doubt it, and the warning feeling returns.'

'I can see why it gets you so upset, but I honestly think you need to talk to him. You can't just leave him wondering what he's done wrong. And maybe, if you do have a chat with him, you'll get the chance to encourage him to make an appointment with his GP; put your mind at rest. You don't need to tell him about the feelings you've been getting, just say he's looking under the weather, which is true.' Maggie tipped her head, peering into Lark's eyes. 'You need to call him. Today. Then you can move forward from this awkward situation.'

Lark knew Maggie was right, but for the first time she could remember, she didn't have the first clue of how to start a conversation with Nate. Assuming he was still speaking to her, of course.

THIRTY-FOUR
MONDAY 8TH DECEMBER

There'd been no stopping the snow once it had started properly on Sunday evening. And now the whole town was once again muffled under a thick eiderdown of white.

Bear had kindly given Lark a lift to the square in the Land Rover that morning, since he was on his way to a decorating job in town. As she'd sat beside him, catching up on what they'd done at the weekend, he'd spoken about Lucy's latest antics, his face glowing with pride. He was a besotted father if ever there was one. Lark wondered if Maggie had told him about their conversation and her awkward situation with Nate. She guessed she probably had and hoped he didn't judge her badly for it.

Despite texting and calling Nate's number, she hadn't managed to get hold of him and he hadn't returned any of her calls. That was a first and it made her all the more determined to put things right between them. So she made up her mind to close the shop for an hour at lunch time and walk round to his workshop. Lark was sure she'd find him there, especially with him having such a backlog of work to catch up with.

The beautiful wooden box he'd given her on that fateful night had caught her eye from its new home on her dressing table as she'd been getting dressed that morning. The sight of it had triggered an ache in her heart. It was a thoughtful gift. Typically Nate. And he'd been right to think she'd like it. As for the necklace with the amethyst pendant, that spoke for itself. He'd have chosen it simply because of her love of crystals. And he'd listened to her rabbiting on about their individual uses and properties for him to have absorbed at least some information. She wondered if he was aware that amethysts represented trust. She felt a pang of guilt, wondering if he'd lost his trust in her. Amethyst also helped alleviate anxiety. She was wearing the necklace now in the hope that it would help ease the tension that currently had her in its clutches. She'd also worn it in the hope that Nate would see it, that it would send a message to him that she valued his gift.

Though she wasn't so sure how she was going to get him to see that she valued him if she couldn't get hold of him.

But there was more than that. The past couple of days had given her time to think and clear her head. And she realised there was something she needed to say to Nate.

Wrapped up well and with her wellies on, Lark crunched her way over the snow-covered path down the square and onto Endeavour Street. The town had been quiet, and the lunchtime traffic was taking it steady thanks to the wintry conditions.

Arriving at the workshop, she was a mix of surprised and disappointed to find everything was locked up, including the small shopfront. She knocked on the door, telling herself if Nate was there then Bobby would probably bark, giving him away if he was ignoring callers to the door. But she was met with a wall of silence. She knocked again, just in case, but the response was the same. She made her way round to the front of the shop and peered in through the window but was disappointed to find the shop floor in darkness.

Admitting defeat, Lark plodded back to the square where she

headed over to the bookshop. The bell jangled noisily above as she poked her head round the door. 'Am I okay to come in with my wellies on?' she asked Florrie, who looked up from where she was busy adding more books to the Christmas table display. She spotted Leah serving a customer at the counter. Gerty looked up from her bed and was now ambling towards her.

'Only if you can levitate,' came Florrie's speedy reply, her face straight.

'Only if I can lev—'

'I'm just joshing, 'course you can.' She grinned. 'Come on in. If I turned away everyone who was wearing wellies at the moment, we'd have zero customers, which isn't what we want.'

'Thanks.' Lark noted the woman Leah was currently serving was also wearing wellies. She headed in, pushing the door shut on the chilly weather outside. 'I was wondering if you'd seen Nate around and about recently? I've just been round to his workshop but there's no sign of him and there were no recent footprints outside. I know it's been snowing, but I don't think it's enough to have completely covered them.'

'I agree about the snow. And as far as Nate's concerned, I'm sure Ed mentioned something about him having to drop some furniture off somewhere today. So he could be doing that before the weather gets any worse.'

'Oh, okay. That would make sense.' Lark wondered if it was the units for the pushy couple from Lingthorpe. She could understand why he'd want to get them off his back as soon as possible, and her dad had said between them they'd made good progress on the units yesterday. The thought offered her a modicum of relief.

'Have you made any progress with the stolen books?' she asked quietly as Leah served a customer.

Florrie rolled her eyes wearily. 'Well, the cameras did capture someone stealing them, which was good news, but whoever it was they evidently knew what they were doing and managed to keep their face hidden from view.'

'Oh, I'm sorry to hear that. I know you were hopeful it would help identify the thief.'

'Ed's sure it's connected to Dodgy Dick still having sour grapes about us not selling him this place. Ed's heard a rumour Dodgy Dick and Wendy had been hounding the Coopers who have the gift shop round the corner, sending thugs round to wreak havoc on their behalf. D'you remember, they'd had a window smashed six months ago?'

'I do actually.'

'And the hanging baskets they had outside the shop this summer were stolen. They were found in a nearby street with all the plants ripped out. Mindless stuff.' Florrie shook her head. 'Ed said the Coopers apparently threatened them with legal action if they didn't stop making a nuisance of themselves. And we all know how Dodgy Dick and that disreputable company he's frontman for don't like mention of the police.'

'Good point.' Lark had heard about the trouble the Coopers had been having earlier in the year but hadn't realised it was at the hands of Dodgy Dick.

Dick Swales originally had a reputation for being a bit of a wheeler-dealer who only just kept himself on the right side of the law. He'd been a likeable character until he joined the payroll of a shady company from out of the area. It appeared to have brought out a menacing side to him, one he was putting to use with increasing regularity. Dodgy Dick relished his role as their frontman for the town, keeping his eyes and ears open for any suitable properties for the group. Their strategy was to buy businesses at a knockdown price assisted by Dodgy Dick who enlisted the help of his equally disreputable extended family. They used force and bullying tactics to get the owners to agree to a sale. The properties would then be sold on for a hefty profit.

'Well, if the stolen books are to do with Dodgy Dick and his cronies, I hope they don't give you any more trouble.' Lark knew how upset her friend had become when Dodgy Dick had turned his attentions onto the bookshop last year. But he and Wendy hadn't been acting on behalf of the company he worked for, they'd wanted the business purely for themselves. Florrie had told her she wasn't sure what was worse.

A shadow crossed Florrie's face. 'You're not the only one. I just wish they'd leave us alone once and for all.'

THIRTY-FIVE
THURSDAY 11TH DECEMBER

Lark was unpacking a delivery of crystals at the shop when her phone rang. She was surprised to see Louisa's number.

'Hey, Louisa, how's things?'

'Hi, Lark. I'm good, thanks, how about you?' Lark picked up on the happy note in the curator's voice. She wondered if it had anything to do with her new friendship with her father.

'I'm good, too.' Lark held back from sharing how her heart was aching and her soul was filled with sadness. Or that she was layered up with crystals in various guises, from beaded bracelets, necklaces and earrings to chunks in the pockets of her dungarees, hoping they'd help rid her of the disconsolate feeling that had hung over her since Nate had left her house last Saturday.

'So, the reason I'm calling is because my friend, the one I mentioned who's an expert on old documents, has had a look at the ledger you found in the Crayke's Cottage suitcase.' Louisa's excitement was building by the second.

'Did she manage to get it opened okay?'

'She did, and it's... well. Oh, my goodness, Lark. I think you and Nate should really come and take a look for yourselves. It's utterly amazing! It's even better than we expected and it's full of so much fascinating information, including names – actually, quite a few familiar local surnames feature. You can call around after work tonight, if you like? I don't mind hanging back.'

Lark's stomach lilted at the thought of taking a look at the ancient book. She was desperate to see it. 'If you're sure you don't mind, I'd love to take you up on your offer. I'll head to the heritage centre straight after I've closed the shop.'

'Wonderful! Can I leave it to you to contact Nate? I assume you'll be calling here together.'

Lark's heart sank and she hesitated a moment before she answered. 'I'll do my best. He's been hard to get hold of for the last few days. He's bogged down with work, so it might just be me. If I can't track him down, or if he can't make it, I'll get the bus that leaves here at five-fifteen and passes Old Micklewick – a friend gave me a lift here this morning.'

'Yes, of course, that's fine. Looking forward to seeing you then.'

With the call ended, Lark wondered if her father had discussed hers and Nate's friendship with Louisa. Her dad was a private person, so she very much doubted he'd go into detail, other than to say they were good friends. And she'd be amazed if he'd mentioned anything about sensing that things weren't right between them.

With nothing to lose, Lark called Nate's number. It didn't come as a surprise when it rang out and the voicemail message kicked in, but it left her heart feeling heavy. All the same, she knew he'd be keen to see the ledger, so she decided she'd send him a text, keep her tone breezy, and just mention Louisa's call, see if that would generate a reply from him.

> Hi Nate, hope you're okay. Just heard from Louisa. She says the expert has managed to open the leather ledger. L says it's full of fascinating stuff! She thought we'd like to see it so has asked if we want to call at the HC tonight after we shut up shop. I'm heading down just after 5pm. Maybe see you there? Lxx

Her heart rate took off as she pressed send. How had her friendship with one of the best people she'd ever met come to this?

Her hand went to the amethyst crystal pendant he'd given her, her eyes misting with tears. The idea that had been circling around her mind gradually took centre stage.

Maybe her mum's suggestion of going to stay with her and Elfie over in Koh Samui for a while wasn't such a bad idea after all. At least if she was there, Nate wouldn't have to hide himself away in order to avoid her, which seemed to be what he was doing right now. In Lark's mind, she was the one who'd caused this situation, so it was only right she should make herself scarce and leave Nate to get on with his life. He was always saying how happy he was living in Micklewick Bay.

The idea of holding meditation classes on a beach with the sun warming her back was suddenly rather appealing, especially with the weather being so bitterly cold in the UK, and likely to remain so for quite some time if the forecasts were to be believed. She could do a refresher course, bring her Reiki skills up to date. Help out with the well-being classes her mum and Elfie ran. It would be positive vibes all the way. Which she thought would be rather nice after all the weird energy she'd been bombarded with recently. She still didn't feel fully recovered from it. In theory, relocating to Thailand and working at the well-being retreat couldn't have sounded more perfect for her.

'That's all well and good, Lark, but what about your dad?' she said aloud, just as a customer walked in and gave her a questioning look. She was what Lark would describe as a typical customer in her outfit of vintage clothing, with makeup and a hairstyle to match, and clearly favoured the nineteen-fifties era.

'Just talking to myself,' Lark joked.

'Oh, I do that all the time, not that I talk much sense, mind,' the young woman chuckled.

'I know the feeling.' Lark gave a light laugh. 'Just shout up if there's anything in particular you're looking for.'

'Will do.' The customer smiled as she made a beeline for the rail of fifties-style evening dresses.

Lark got back to her thoughts as she distractedly checked through her crystals order.

In practice, relocating to Thailand would mean closing Lark's Vintage Bazaar and not seeing her dad for ages. And not just that, she worried how it would impact on his budding relationship with Louisa. Where would he stay until he'd bought somewhere to live in the town and moved there permanently? She was pretty sure Elfie would want to put a long-term tenant in Seashell Cottage if Lark was with them in Koh Samui. That would leave her dad high and dry, unless he booked into a B&B, or rented Seashell Cottage until a more permanent tenant was found. A thought struck her like a lightning bolt. He'd stay with Louisa! Of course! If their relationship developed then it was only natural he'd do that – not that she wanted to dwell on the reasons why, that would be way too weird!

And could she really go to Thailand knowing her dad was only just shaking off his grief? Lark couldn't bear to think of him having a bad day when she was so many miles away. Would it be selfish of her to go?

She knew her dad would encourage her all the way, saying she was a young woman with a life to lead. That she should take opportunities by the horns and go for it. He'd add the proviso that it had to be what *she* wanted and not what anyone else *thought* she wanted. And she'd know it was her mum he was referring to. They both knew that when Serena got an idea into her head, there was no stopping her. As Lark was proof.

Lark scrubbed her face with her hands, her bracelets chiming away with the motion. *Ugh!* It was all so confusing. And it was all her fault.

'If you don't mind me saying, you look like you're torturing yourself over something.' A voice cut into her thoughts. Lark looked up to see the young woman in the nineteen-fifties clothes standing at the counter, a garment in her hands. She had kind green eyes and her lips were pushed into a sympathetic smile.

Lark blew her hair off her face. 'I don't mind at all, and I am.'

'I always find that if something's really bothering me, you can't beat a talk with good friends for getting whatever it is off my chest. Someone else's perspective always helps, while bottling it up and agonising over it never does.'

The young woman's words struck a chord. 'You're right. Thank you, I appreciate your advice.'

Once she'd taken payment, she wrapped the midnight-blue dress with the sequinned bodice and full tulle skirt in plenty of tissue before sliding it into a Lark's Vintage Bazaar paper bag.

Though she'd sworn Maggie to secrecy when she'd confided in her about Nate, Lark knew it was time to share everything with her friends. The thought sent a mix of anxiety and relief racing through her.

With the customer gone, Lark checked her phone to see the message she'd sent to Nate hadn't been delivered. He must be somewhere out of range. It offered a glimmer of relief that the reason he hadn't replied was because he hadn't received her messages rather than him ignoring her.

By the time five o'clock arrived and Lark was locking up the shop, she still hadn't heard from Nate, though she'd noted that the text had finally been delivered. She wondered if he'd go directly to the heritage centre, rather than reply to her? Or maybe he wouldn't be there at all. Maybe he'd choose to go when she wasn't there. That thought saddened her.

Stuffing her keys into her floral backpack, she made her way to the bus stop around the corner, fairy lights and Christmas trees twinkling in the dark, their cheerfulness at odds with her unsettled mood.

'Come in, Lark.' Louisa greeted her with a broad smile. It didn't escape Lark's notice that she peered over her shoulder as if looking for someone else.

'S'just me, I'm afraid. I sent Nate a text, but I haven't heard anything back so I'm guessing he's rushed off his feet.'

'That's absolutely fine, come through to the back,' Louisa said in her usual jolly tone.

If she'd guessed things weren't right between her and Nate, then Lark was grateful she wasn't letting on. She'd feel too uncomfortable mentioning anything.

'Right then, if you just want to put your bag and coat over there, then pop these gloves on – we wear them to protect special documents.'

'Yes, of course.' The lighting was dim, much softer than it had been when Lark and Nate had called round before. She slipped her fingers into the gloves and followed the curator over to the table where the ledger was set out.

'So, here it is,' Louisa said in a reverential tone. 'And I'm beyond thrilled to say it's in remarkably good condition considering its age. We've taken copies, but I thought you'd like to see the original.'

'Ooh, I'd love to.'

Louisa took a step sideways, making room for Lark.

Lark instantly noticed the energy emanating from the pages. It was still hard to define, a confusing mix of so many things. Crayke's Cottage flashed through her mind, sending a prickle of discomfort running over her skin. She pushed it away, intent on seeing through whatever the energy was trying to tell her and focusing her full attention on the book.

She took a moment to take it all in.

'Oh, wow!' Looking back at Lark was what appeared to be a list of names, occupations, items, monetary amounts and street names. There was also a list of what Lark assumed to be the names of ships. And though the ink had now faded, it was still clear to see that everything was written in a strong, clear hand. The author was evidently educated and bold.

'This is incredible,' Lark whispered in awe.

'And have you noticed anything about the names?'

'Um...' Lark peered closer, her eyes running down the carefully drawn up list, spotting a handful of Crayke's, including one Jacob. 'Oh, my goodness!' She clapped her hand to her mouth and laughed. 'Denton, Harker – that's both sides of my family, my mum's going to be devastated. And there's a couple, no, three Marsays, that's Bear's family, Maggie's going to have a whale of a time teasing him about that. Ooh, and Ingilby and Appleton are Jasmine and Florrie's forebears.' Lark hooted with laughter. 'Looks like loads of us have a dash of smuggler DNA. Ooh, and I've just spotted a few Hartes, so Ed from the bookshop is included, too.'

'There are a couple of Pearsons, too, and Roberts. I wonder if they could be related to our Betty? Her married name was Roberts.'

'I'm sure they are.'

'Speaking of which, I managed to track down Betty's great-granddaughter. You might know her, actually. She's called Bethany – her name's still Roberts – and I'd say she's a similar age to you. She's lived in Micklewick Bay all her life – maybe you were at school together?'

Lark twisted her head to Louisa. 'I know a Bethany Roberts! She wasn't in my year at school – I think she was a couple of years above – but our paths definitely crossed a fair bit. I haven't seen her for ages. I wonder if she'd like to hear about the suitcase and her great-grandmother's clothes?'

'There's only one way to find out.' Louisa beamed at her.

'Oh my days, this is so incredible.'

'It is, and I'm so grateful to you and Nate for donating the ledger and other items to the heritage centre. We're going to have a replica made to put on display, give people a proper idea of what it's like. I think it's going to be part of an exhibition in the cottage. Maybe have it set out on an old desk with an inkpot, a character sitting at it with a quill in his hand and the replica leather ledger in front of him.'

Lark could see it in her mind's eye. 'What a wonderful idea, that would really capture a feel of the time.'

'I've printed off a copy of the ledger for you to have for your own records.' Louisa passed her an A4-sized envelope.

'Thank you.'

'And as for the pistol, I've locked that away in the safe until my friend can get here. We'll need to get it decommissioned before it can go on display. But as soon as I have any further information about it, I'll let you know.'

'Thanks, Louisa, I appreciate that.'

'You're welcome. Now, after all that excitement, can I get you a cup of tea?'

'Actually, how would you feel about having a cuppa back at my place? There's something else I'd like to show you.'

'That would be lovely, and I have to say, after the last lot of stuff you had to show me, I'm more than a little intrigued.'

'I think you'll like what it is, but I won't say anything more. I don't want to spoil the surprise.'

'The plot thickens.' Louisa grinned. 'I'll just fetch my coat.'

Moments later Louisa was back, shrugging her bag on her shoulder. 'Is there any point me driving to your house?'

Lark explained how there was no direct parking but that she could use the small parking area for locals which was closer to Seashell Cottage than the heritage centre, though not by much.

'But my logic is the less time spent in that savage wind, the better,' said Lark. Louisa readily agreed.

'Oh, this is so cosy!' Louisa stood in the living room of Seashell Cottage as Lark headed over to the wood burner and opened the spin wheels to let more air into the firepit. Then, she threw on a handful of sticks followed by a couple of eco-logs. In a matter of seconds, flames were leaping around behind the glass.

'It's usually a lot toastier but with me being out most of the day, the fire's died down a bit. It'll warm up quickly though.'

'It's a good deal warmer than my house at the moment. I think the boiler's on the blink so I'll have to get it looked at or replaced.

How typical that it starts to act up just before Christmas.' Louisa gave a resigned shrug.

'I'll make us a cup of tea in a minute, but there's something I'd like to show you first. Make yourself comfy, I'll just be a tick.'

Lark was back in a flash, a large leather suitcase in her hand. 'Here's what I wanted to show you.' She eased the coffee table out of the way and set the suitcase down on the rug. 'It's Betty's suitcase.' She flicked open the clasps and lifted the lid.

'Oh, how wonderful!' Louisa said, pressing her hands together as she peered in at the items Lark had replaced with care.

After the two women had finished poring over the garments, Louisa sat back and said, 'That's a snapshot of Micklewick Bay history captured in a suitcase. It's incredibly rare to have so many items of clothing kept together from the same era. And as for that wedding dress, I'd say it's definitely made of parachute silk.'

'Which is why I'd like to donate them to the museum. It struck me the other day that it didn't feel right to sell them in my shop. They've been together all these years, and they should still be kept together.'

'I don't know what to say. You and Nate have already been so generous.'

'It's not about being generous. It's more that if it helps resurrect Betty's memory, and gives visitors a proper idea of a real person from the town at a particular time in history, with her actual clothes, then I'm more than happy.'

'Are you sure?'

'I'm positive.'

'Goodness, it'll be quite a draw and increase our footfall. Thank you so much, Lark. I can see why your father is so proud of you.'

The two women drank their tea, chatting about Micklewick Bay, Lark's Vintage Bazaar, and the museum Louisa had worked at before the heritage centre. Lark kept mention of her father to a minimum, not wanting Louisa to think she was being interrogated.

When she'd gone, with Betty's suitcase in hand, Lark acknowledged to herself that the more she got to know Louisa, the more she liked her. And more than that, she was struck by the feeling that her father and Louisa were destined to have a long relationship. She got a sense of marriage, and contented days with their matching laid-back and genial personalities.

The understanding that her dad was in a pair of kind and caring hands, meant Lark was free to head to Thailand with a clear conscience and without worrying she was leaving her dad on his own.

THIRTY-SIX
FRIDAY 12TH DECEMBER

It had been snowing on and off all day, but it didn't stop the regulars from turning out at the Jolly on a Friday evening. Though it was only seven thirty, it was already busy.

Lark was the first to arrive, which was hardly surprising considering she lived just around the corner. She'd organised the wine and five glasses and was busy checking her phone when Maggie arrived.

'Now then, flower. I'm glad I've caught you before the others arrive. How've you been doing since our chat? I know we've been texting, but to be honest, you don't reveal much about how you're really feeling.' Maggie's words tumbled out in a torrent, presumably so she could get the conversation over with quickly in case Lark hadn't shared any of it with the others.

Before she had a chance to answer, Jasmine arrived along with Florrie, Stella a few minutes after.

With them all settled in their seats, glasses of wine in hand, Stella said, 'So, lasses, have we all had a good week?'

Maggie's eyes flicked to Lark. Lark lowered her gaze to the table and cleared her throat.

'Ey up, do I detect something's been going on that you two

know about?' Stella was regularly described as having eyes like a hawk and a nose like a bloodhound. 'Come on, share what you know.'

Maggie raised her palms. 'I'm saying nowt.'

All eyes turned to Lark.

'So that leaves you, missus,' said Jasmine, her copper eyebrows raised in interest.

Lark closed her eyes and drew in a fortifying breath. She wasn't so sure sharing what she'd done with Nate was going to be such a good idea, especially with the way her friends were all looking at her and holding their breath in expectation.

'I've donated Betty's suitcase to the heritage centre.'

There was a collective sagging of shoulders and exhaling of breath.

Maggie's eyebrows twitched.

Lark felt the weight of four pairs of eyes scrutinising her.

'Talk about an anticlimax,' said Jasmine. 'Not that I mean it's not a good thing about you donating the clothes, but—'

'But, with respect, we thought you were going to give us something a little juicier than that,' Stella interjected.

'Yeah, way juicier,' said Maggie, sotto voce, but apparently not "sotto voce" enough.

'What was that, Mags?' Stella's head whipped round.

Lark shot Maggie a pointed look.

'What's been going on?' asked Florrie, looking totally baffled.

'Come on, spill the tea,' said Stella in an authoritative tone Lark didn't like to ignore.

What made me think this would be a good idea?

She inhaled slowly once more, her hand reaching for the amethyst pendant at her neck.

Just say it. Just rip the plaster off and get the words out.

'I kissed Nate.' She spoke as quietly as she could, keeping her eyes trained firmly on the table, bracing herself for the wave of reactions.

'What did Lark just say?' Jasmine looked at Stella who had a smile inching across her face.

Florrie nudged her glasses up her nose and blinked in apparent disbelief.

'Oh, this calls for a celebration,' said Stella, before leaning in to Jasmine. 'She's just fessed up to having a snog with Nate. Praise the Lord.'

'Woohoo! About bloomin' time, woman!' Jasmine danced a jig in her seat, causing heads to turn at nearby tables.

Lark willed the ground to open up and gulp her down in one.

'This is exactly why I didn't want to tell you. I knew you'd all get carried away with yourselves.'

'I'll bet Nate's floating around on cloud nine now.' Stella started easing herself out of the settle. 'Don't say another word till I get back. I'm just going to grab us a bottle of fizz.'

'Fizz?' Lark clapped her hands to her face. 'Why fizz?'

'To mark the occasion, that's why. It needs to be celebrated.'

'Have you any idea how bonkers that sounds, Stells? Please don't,' Lark pleaded.

'Leave it, Stells,' said Maggie. Lark sent a grateful look her way.

Stella gave a throaty giggle. 'Don't get your knickers in a knot, I'm only teasing. I'd never do anything like that.'

Relief washed over Lark as she watched Stella sit back down.

'Am I right in thinking the reason you've shared this with us is because what you feared would happen if you got closer to Nate has actually happened, and you realise you like him more than as a friend?' asked Florrie.

Lark nodded. 'It has, and it's my fault.'

'And how d'you work that one out?' asked Jasmine, scratching her head in puzzlement.

Four eager faces looked back at Lark as she raked her hair off her face and filled them in on the details and how Nate wasn't speaking to her.

When she'd finished, they all sat looking at her wearing crestfallen expressions. She felt the weight of their disappointment sitting on her shoulders.

'I always told you it would be a bad idea, that I'd end up losing his friendship, which is exactly what's happened,' she said with a shrug. 'And, like I've said, now he's ignoring me.'

'But what I don't get is why you thought it was a mistake?' Stella was looking at her as if she was crazy.

'Pot, kettle and all that,' Florrie chipped in. 'Sorry, Stells, but you were finding all sorts of excuses to keep Alex at arm's length.'

'That's different. I hadn't known Alex for long, whereas Lark's known Nate for years. *He* knows they're meant to be together, and *we* know they're meant to be together. It's only Miss Fussy-Pants here who keeps telling herself they're not.'

'And you're absolutely sure it's a mistake, Lark?' Florrie asked.

Lark nodded. 'It's this feeling I keep getting and can't shake off. It's odd and I've never experienced anything like it before, but I get this really strong sense of something about him.' It made her feel sad to put these feelings about Nate into words.

'But you clearly didn't feel them for however long it took to play tonsil tennis with him on Saturday night. How did that happen, then?' asked Jasmine.

'I honestly don't know. I guess I must've pushed them to one side or ignored them. I have no explanation for it.' She wasn't going to say all she was conscious of then was the way Nate's kiss had made her feel. 'I've always followed my gut, my senses, whatever you want to call them, and they've never let me down. It's why I can't ignore this.'

'Oh, flower, that must be hard.' Florrie pulled a sympathetic face.

'Well, it's actually worse than you think.' She swallowed down the lump of emotion that had formed in her throat. 'And the reason it's worse is because...' *Oh jeez, this is hard.* 'It's because I love him.' A sob escaped her mouth and her friends all reached for her, squeezing her hands or wrapping their arms around her. Lark fought the tears that were threatening to spill over.

'I'm sorry I made fun of you,' said Stella. 'I wouldn't have done it if I'd known how you felt.'

'I know, Stells, it's okay.' Lark sniffed.

'So what happens now?' asked Florrie as they all sat back in their seats.

'I've been thinking about Thailand.'

'*Thailand?*' they all chorused in disbelief.

Before she had a chance to explain, Lobster Harry cleared his throat and burst into song, filling the pub with a tuneless rendition of a local sea shanty. It wasn't just the notes that sounded dodgy, some of the lyrics did, too. Everyone looked on in morbid fascination as the old fisherman belted the song out at the top of his lungs, one hand over his ear as if he were a seasoned folk singer, the other clutching a half-full pint of Micklewick Mischief that sloshed around precariously as he waved his arm.

A lively round of applause broke out when he was done, but it was more an acknowledgement of the entertainment value than any talent he'd displayed.

'Thank you very much.' Lobster Harry gave a gap-toothed smile. 'If any of you would like to show your appreciation, I'll be taking pints at the bar.' He cleared his throat once more then opened his mouth, where he proceeded to produce a painfully long, whining note. Snorts of laughter followed before a springer spaniel threw its head back and started howling. Everyone in the pub collapsed into fits of laughter. The fisherman was quickly guided back to the bar by Mandy the landlady. Moments later, the local folk band struck up, filling the air with a jaunty tune, much to everyone's relief.

Though Lark was laughing too, she was glad of the unexpected interlude, glad the heat and attention was being directed elsewhere for a while.

But it wasn't long before it was back on her and she was forced to explain why going to stay with her mum and Elfie in Thailand was a good idea and not the hare-brained plan they seemed to think it was.

By the end of the night, her friends had helped her see sense and talked her out of leaving Micklewick Bay for Thailand, telling her that she wouldn't be going for the right reasons. It was something she'd had to agree with, even though she still hadn't heard from Nate.

THIRTY-SEVEN
SUNDAY 14TH DECEMBER.

The heady mix of Lark's latest aromatherapy blend she'd created to instil calm and clarity filled the living room at Seashell Cottage as she brought the meditation session with her father to an end.

Silas opened his eyes and released a slow breath. 'Ooh, that was wonderful, sweetheart. I feel light as air now.' He pushed himself up from where they'd been sitting cross-legged on the floor and placed his crystals on the sideboard ready for Lark to cleanse. 'I can see why it's gaining popularity. I've been making time for a session every day and I can really feel the benefits.'

'Glad to hear it, Dad.' She smiled up at him. Lark wished she could say the same for herself. But since her fallout with Nate – for want of a better word – and anxiety had hijacked her thoughts, meditating didn't work the wonders it usually did for her.

'I'm going to introduce Louisa to it, I think it's something she'd embrace.'

'She's very welcome to join us, if you think she'd like to?'

'That's kind. I'll run it past her, see what she thinks.'

The "romance" between Louisa and Silas seemed to be blossoming even more so, much to Lark's delight. He talked about her all the time. 'Louisa this, Louisa that.' It made Lark smile. He'd travelled over from High Nedderton on Friday straight from school and spent the evening at Louisa's where he'd helped her cook their meal – rib-eye steak and fondant potatoes with wilted greens, followed by warmed Bakewell tart from the deli, served with lashings of custard. It had made Lark drool just hearing about it. Last night, Louisa had joined them at Seashell Cottage where they'd dined on a large chilli served with wild rice and soured cream with a garnish of coriander. Simple but tasty. And tonight, the couple were going to the Jolly for some fish and chips. 'I think I'm going to have to take up running as well as meditation if I continue eating this way,' he chuckled when he'd told Lark of his plans.

The radio silence from Nate had continued. If silence could ever be deafening, then this was it. She'd taken the hint and left him alone, waiting for him to contact her when he was ready. She was beginning to think he never would.

Her father had asked a few subtle questions, but never pushed it, for which she was grateful. And she had no idea if Nate had been back to Crayke's Cottage as he'd planned, or what he was going to do with the key from the small suitcase.

'Right then, I think I'll head upstairs and get changed. Louisa and I are going to have a sift through the archives, see what we can find about the families named in the ledger.' His eyes shone at the prospect.

'Sounds like fun.'

'You're welcome to join us. I'm sure Louisa wouldn't mind.' His smile told her he'd like her to tag along, but Lark wasn't really in the mood.

'Thanks for the offer, but I've got a pile of clothes that need fixing for the shop, so I'd better get on with that.'

Her father had been gone for an hour when there was a scraping at the front door, making both Lark and Luna look up. The sound stopped and Lark turned back to her work thinking it was just someone walking by a bit too close to the house, but it soon started up again, this time with increasing urgency, and it was accompanied by a whimpering sound.

'What *is* that?' Lark tucked the needle carefully into the fabric of the skirt she was working on and set it down on the coffee table. The whimpering was growing louder and she opened the door to find a familiar looking black Labrador on the doorstep. He was covered in a light dusting of snow. 'Bobby! What are you doing here?'

Bobby whimpered, his amber eyes looking at her pleadingly. He was agitated and Lark sensed he was trying to communicate something to her.

She crouched down to his level, stroking his head. 'It's okay, Bobby,' she said soothingly. 'Have you got lost, or sneaked out of somewhere?' She recalled his Houdini act at the Millingtons. 'Where's Nate? And does he know where you are?'

Bobby continued to whimper and whine. Pulling himself away from her, he rushed out into the street, circling before coming back, then heading out into the street again, his paw prints churning up the snow. His behaviour was starting to worry her.

Lark knew she had no choice but to call Nate. She rushed back into the cottage and grabbed her phone from the arm of the sofa and hurriedly found his number. She pressed call, her heart pounding as she waited for him to pick up. As usual, it rang out and voicemail kicked in. She left a garbled message before tapping out a quick text to say Bobby was with her. If he wasn't going to listen to a voicemail message, he might at least read a text.

She went back to Bobby who was still whining on the doorstep. As quickly as she could, Lark grabbed her coat and pushed her feet into her wellies, before heading out to find out what had got Bobby so agitated.

He trotted along, looking back as if to make sure she was following him. Lark was struggling to keep up, slipping and sliding in her haste, her breathing ragged, floating before her in puffs of condensation. The cold was biting, and she tugged her gloves from the pockets of her coat, pushing her hands into them, grateful for the warmth. She was glad the snow-covered streets of Old Micklewick were quiet as she hurried along after Bobby.

She'd reached the end of Gabblewick Gate when she realised she'd lost him. 'Bobby! Bobby!' she called. She scanned the snow for paw prints and noticed they turned into Micklemackle Yard. A feeling of foreboding crept over her as she followed Bobby's paw prints and walked towards Crayke's Cottage where the door was standing open.

THIRTY-EIGHT

'Hello?' Lark took a tentative step into Crayke's Cottage, goosebumps pinging up all over her skin. 'Hello?' she called again.

An icy breath whispered over her neck, and she turned sharply, her heart thumping, her ears whooshing, but there was no one there. *It's only a draught, that's all. Nothing more.*

Her chest heaving, she stepped further into the darkness of the room, every fibre of her body on high alert. She had a bad feeling about this. A very bad feeling.

The door slammed shut behind her, making her shriek. 'Oh my God!' Her breathing was jagged, her chest tight.

There was a loud crash from the room at the back and Bobby came hurtling back into the room, his ears flat to his head.

'S'okay, lad.' She reached down and smoothed her hand over his head, the feeling that she was being watched from every quarter making her pulse race even faster.

'Hello?' She headed towards the back room, a draught rushing at her. Another slam had her jumping out of her skin. She felt nausea swirl in her stomach. What was she doing here on her own? She had the urge to leave, but found she was unable to do anything about it. It felt as if the house was drawing her in, tugging at her arms.

In the back room, the door to the yard was standing open. She tiptoed towards it, tentatively peering out to see the snow had been recently disturbed and was covered in an array of footprints. Had Nate been here?

Nate! Was he the reason Bobby had brought her here? Nate must've had the last check around and brought the Labrador with him. Maybe Bobby sneaked off and Nate had gone looking for him.

Lark checked her phone once more, her heart sinking as she saw there'd been no replies from Nate and her text message remained unread.

She closed the back door and slid the bolt across, making sure it was firmly driven home. Bobby started scraping at the floorboards and his whining started up again. He then rushed over to the oak-panelled wall by the stairs, sniffing and whimpering.

'What is it, lad?' She started pressing at the panels frantically, working across them as fast as she could. She was about to give up when a small door popped open, the smell of the sea rushing at them. Bobby nudged it wider with his head before disappearing through it.

Lark would've preferred not to have to venture through a door that led to who knew where when she was on her own and nobody knew she was there, but a groan made her ears prick and she knew she had no choice.

Turning on her phone light she braced herself as she stepped inside, her hand shaking and her heart pounding.

It didn't take long for her to realise she was in a tunnel, the rough, uneven floor sloping downwards. The groan came again, sending fear spiking through her.

'Bobby! Where are you?' She shone the torch around but there was no sign of him. 'Hello? Nate?'

'Lark?' a voice replied weakly.

THIRTY-NINE

Lark's stomach clenched. Though the voice was weak, she knew who it belonged to in an instant.

'Nate!' Panic surged through her. 'Nate! Where are you?'

Her question was met with a groan.

She stumbled her way over the rough ground until the torch light found a figure slumped on the floor. Bobby was standing over it, whimpering. Her heart froze in fear.

'Nate!' Lark rushed forward, falling onto her knee, pain searing through her but she pulled herself up and kept on until she reached him.

'Oh my God, Nate!' She pressed her hand against his forehead and was concerned to find he felt almost icy to the touch.

She took a moment. A deep breath. Fear was causing chaos in her mind; she needed to get her thoughts straight so she could do what needed to be done. Never mind why Nate was down here, she had no idea how long he'd been there but he felt cold so there was every chance he could be suffering from hypothermia. Panic flared again and tears stung her eyes. Then there was the possibility he could have an injury that wasn't obvious to her. She checked her phone for a signal, but there were no bars. Acting quickly, she took off her coat and laid it over Nate, putting her gloves over his hands, making a pillow from her scarf.

'Stay with me, Nate. Bobby's here, but I need to go back into the house to call for an ambulance, okay? Please, *please* hang on,' she said, her voice thick with emotion.

She scrambled back up to the house, panic and fear making her uncoordinated. Racing to the living room, four bars appeared on her phone. She called for an ambulance, doing all she could not to break down in tears as she gave them details and directions. That done, she called her dad's phone, knowing paramedics would need to have someone at the end of the lane to guide them here; Crayke's Cottage would be impossible to find to people who didn't know Old Micklewick.

'Hello, Lark sweetheart.' Her dad's voice was full of cheer, so at odds with the distress that held her in its grip.

'Dad! Dad! It's Nate! I need your help.' She almost crumbled on hearing her father's voice and fought hard to get her words out. She needed to make sure he could understand what she was saying. But the panic in her voice was enough to have both Silas and Louisa scrambling to help.

'Stay calm, my love. We'll be there as fast as we can. You go back to Nate; keep talking to him,' Silas said calmly.

Lark rushed back to the panel, scrabbling down the tunnel, pressing her hand against the cold, damp wall to steady herself. Her torch quickly picked out Nate and Bobby on the floor.

'Nate, it's me, Lark, I'm back. An ambulance is on its way and so are my dad and Louisa. One of them is going to flag the ambulance down at the end of the lane.'

The moan that came from Nate was so weak, Lark only just heard it.

Emotion squeezed in her chest, making it hard for her to breathe. Tears were pouring down her cheeks now. She reached for his hand and pressed her face to his cheek, her hair spilling over him, the chill from his skin making fear her overriding emotion.

'Stay with me, Nate. Please stay with me. The ambulance will be here soon. Please don't go to sleep.'

Bobby whimpered and nudged Nate with his nose.

Thoughts started piling into Lark's mind. What if...? *Don't think that!* She couldn't let Nate think she didn't care for him, that he was nothing more than a mistake.

Realisation hit her like a lightning bolt, her heart thumping harder than ever. This was it! This was what she'd been picking up on for all these years. The warnings telling her she wouldn't have a future with Nate. They were all pointing to this very moment.

But she needed to take control, needed to tell him. Needed to make sure he knew.

'Nate, I love you. I love you with all my heart. And I always have. I'm so sorry I let my stupid senses and premonitions get in the way. But all I know is that I love you. And I want to be with you.' She pressed a soggy kiss to his cheek, his skin cold and yet clammy. 'Please stay strong. Please, Nate. Please.'

Nate gave a barely discernible groan.

The sound of feet thudding on the floorboards above were followed by a shout of, 'Lark!'

'Down here, Dad. It's the wooden panel that's slightly open.'

'Got it.'

Moments later, Silas had joined them, the extra light from his torch showing that Nate had sustained a nasty bump to his head Lark hadn't spotted before.

'Nate, lad, stay strong for us,' Silas said, his voice soothing and yet firm.

In the distance came the faint screeching of an ambulance siren.

FORTY

Nate was propped up on his pillows in the hospital bed, a dressing covering the wound on his head, his right arm in a sling. He was hooked up to a variety of monitors and drips. Despite all of this, Lark was relieved to see he was finally getting some colour back to his cheeks.

She'd been sitting in the chair beside him for the last hour and a half, watching as he slept, his eyelids fluttering, long, dark lashes resting on his cheeks. It had been two days since he'd been admitted to Middleton-le-Moors hospital suffering from hyperthermia and concussion thanks to the bump on his head, along with three broken ribs and a badly bruised arm. The doctors said it was lucky he'd been found when he had. Much longer and it would've been a very different story. Their words had sent an icy shiver running through Lark.

But that wasn't the only diagnosis he'd received. While he was undergoing the great slew of tests to make sure he hadn't sustained any hidden injuries, a mild heart murmur had been detected. The medical team had informed him that it was probably the result of him being anaemic – something else their tests picked up – which had put his heart under pressure, making it work harder. The anaemia also explained why Nate had been so pale and tired.

Lark realised she'd been right to be worried about his health. Granted, what had been making him unwell wasn't as serious as it had been for Greer, but it was these symptoms that had contributed to the increased intensity of the vibes she'd picked up about Nate. They'd been sending her a warning, albeit a confusing one.

But watching him now as he slept, Lark couldn't resist the temptation any longer. She leant over and gently brushed her lips over his. It terrified her how close they'd come to losing him down in that tunnel. The doctor had told her she'd reached him at a crucial time. Any later and he might not have been so lucky. The implications of the doctor's words didn't bear thinking about. Lark would never have forgiven herself if he'd... She scrunched her eyes tight shut, unable to even think about that outcome. He'd never have gone to Crayke's Cottage on his own if it hadn't been for what she'd said to him.

She kissed him again and his eyes pinged open. She felt his mouth pulling into a small smile.

'Hey, you,' she said, nuzzling her nose against his.

'Hey, you back.' Though his smile was weak it still managed to reach his eyes. 'Am I dreaming? Or did you just kiss me?' he asked, his voice hoarse.

'You're not dreaming.' She kissed him again to prove it.

'Cool.' He smiled again before closing his eyes. Lark sat back down on the seat. 'Didn't think I was going to get out.'

'You mean from the cellar at Crayke's Cottage?' She couldn't imagine how that must've felt.

He nodded. 'Felt so cold, everything was so dark. Hearing your voice brought me back. That and Bobby's breath. Man, it's strong.' His mouth quirked into another smile and Lark couldn't help but laugh.

'It was Bobby who alerted me to where you were. He's a little star. Dad's been calling him the hero of the day. He had an extra special bowl of food that afternoon. Went down a treat. Not sure he tasted much of it, he devoured it that fast in typical Labrador fashion.'

'Good old Bobby.' Nate's chuckle was like music to Lark's ears. 'And did you mean what you said when we were in the cellar?' He opened his eyes, fixing them on her.

'You mean when I told you that I love you.'

'Yeah, that.'

'I meant every single word.' She leant forward and kissed him again.

'The things I had to go through to get you to say that.' He rolled his eyes playfully. 'Don't suppose you fancy reminding me, do you?'

Lark didn't have a problem reminding him. In fact, she was so relieved he was okay, she'd be happy to shout it from the rooftops.

'Nate Wilkinson, I love you.'

He heaved a happy sigh. 'And I love you too, Lark. Have done for years. You stole my heart the minute I set eyes on you with all your quirky, hippie, boho stuff.'

'It's good to see you looking brighter.' A smiley-faced nurse arrived at the foot of the bed, a tray of medication in her hand which Lark took as her cue to leave.

Nate told Lark later that he'd gone to Crayke's Cottage, armed with the old key from the suitcase, and with the intention of having a final check around. After what had happened between him and Lark, he hadn't troubled her to accompany him. He didn't realise at the time how grateful he'd be for taking Bobby with him.

He'd patiently checked the walls and cupboards for any likely places that could potentially hide a secret drawer or panel, and was just about to give up when the oak panel had popped open.

Armed with a torch, he entered what he quickly realised was a tunnel and was making his way along when he heard a sound behind him. He turned to see two men wearing balaclavas. They immediately started demanding where the money was, saying if he didn't tell them, then they'd lock him in there and he'd never get out.

They didn't seem to believe that he didn't know where any money was and started pushing him about. They only stopped when a spine-chilling howling sound started echoing all around the tunnel. The thugs had seemed genuinely terrified, yelling that the place was haunted and cursed. They'd made a run for it, knocking Nate over in their panic.

It was while Lark and her dad were with Nate, waiting for the paramedics to arrive, that they realised the strange, haunting sounds both she and Nate had heard there before were nothing more sinister than the wind whistling through the tunnel and into the house. The shrillness of the shrieking increased according to the strength of the wind. No doubt it was where the stories of the house being haunted had originated. Lark could imagine such rumours served the smugglers well, keeping unwelcome visitors and the prying eyes of the customs men away.

FORTY-ONE
THURSDAY 18TH DECEMBER

Wrapping Christmas presents was one of Lark's very favourite things to do. It was something she liked to take her time over and always put in a great deal of effort, matching the trim and the label – which she also made herself – to the recipient, while at the same time, making the parcels look delightfully festive. She trimmed them with a variety of re-purposed items, including vintage ribbons and lace, buttons and beads, and even pieces of fabric she considered suitable. These treasures were stored in a box she kept tucked under the stairs, and it always sent a thrill dancing through her when she lifted the lid.

With her father helping Louisa at the heritage centre and likely to remain there for a good few hours, and with Zara holding the fort at Lark's Vintage Bazaar, Lark decided that her free afternoon would be the perfect opportunity to indulge in a spot of present wrapping. There was no chance Nate would get in the way, since he was snoring contentedly on the sofa, where he'd been stretched out for the last hour, Bobby and Luna snuggled up beside him. So, with a mug of hot chocolate freshly made, she retrieved the box of gift-wrapping goodies, removed the bowl of fruit from the kitchen table and set to work.

She'd just finished writing the label of the gift for her new assistant – a pair of silver hoop earrings finished with tiny shells from the shop's stock that Zara had admired – when the ringing of her mobile broke through her thoughts. Setting the pen down, Lark reached for her phone, her eyebrows dipping as she saw Louisa's number. Her first thought was that her father must be on his way home; she'd have to scrabble his yet-to-be-wrapped gifts together and quickly tuck them out of the way before he returned. Lark tapped on the screen and accepted the call.

'Hi, Louisa.'

'Hello there, Lark lovey, I hope I'm not intruding on your afternoon off work.' Louisa's voice was filled with the familiar warmth Lark had come to associate with her. It sent a smile spreading over her face.

'No, not at all, it's good to hear from you. Is my dad still with you? I'm only asking cos I'm in the middle of a Christmas pressie wrapping session and don't want him to burst in and see Santa's gifts for him,' she said with a chuckle.

Louisa giggled too. 'Ah, well, I can put your mind at rest as far as that's concerned, he's still here.'

'Phew!' Lark said jokingly.

'Actually, there's someone else here, too, and they're the reason I'm calling.'

'Oh?' Lark's mind started whirring but before her thoughts could get very far, Louisa spoke again.

'I'll totally understand if you're too busy, but I don't suppose you could spare some time to pop across to the heritage centre in the next hour, could you? Only, Bethany Roberts is here – *our* Betty's great-granddaughter – and I feel it's only right that you and Nate are here, too, when I show her the case of her great-grandmother's clothes – if Nate's up to it, of course. And it's not just that, Bethany's brought some things I think you'd both be rather keen to see, too.' The thrill in Louisa's voice was unmistakable and sent a burst of excitement rushing through Lark. The present wrapping could wait!

'Ooh, talk about intriguing! Nate's here with me actually, and

I'm sure he'd love to come – he's been having a bit of a grumble about being bored with having to take things easy since his accident.' She looked up as the man himself shuffled into the kitchen, all ruffle-haired and sleepy-eyed. Lark had been watching him like a hawk since his accident, relieved to see an improvement with every day that passed. 'You okay?' she mouthed to him. He gave a heart-melting smile and a thumbs-up. Lark returned his smile and went back to her conversation with Louisa. 'I reckon we could be at the heritage centre in about twenty minutes, if that's okay? I assume Bethany's not in a rush to head off.'

'Fabulous! And Bethany's already told me she's in no hurry to get away, so don't worry about that. Your father's been having a good chat with her about local history; he's in his element,' Louisa said fondly.

'Oh, that I can well believe!' Lark said with a laugh. 'Right then, I'll get these presents and paraphernalia put away and we'll see you soon.'

After relaying her conversation with Louisa, Lark wasn't at all surprised to see Nate's eyes light up. 'What are we waiting for? Get your coat and wellies on, lass, and let's get over there,' he said, his voice brimming with purpose.

'Ooh, come in and get yourselves out of the cold.' Louisa held the door open at the side entrance of the heritage centre, a welcoming smile on her face as she took in the snowflakes that had settled on Lark and Nate.

Once they'd stamped the snow off their boots, the pair stepped into the warmth of the small hallway, relieved to escape the biting cold. 'Ugh, blimey! I'm nithered!' Though the walk from Seashell Cottage to the heritage centre wasn't far, Lark felt chilled to the bone. There was no escaping that winter was baring its teeth, its fury building by the day as it raged across the North Sea towards the little cluster of cottages in the cove.

'No wonder, it's glacial out there!' exclaimed Nate, his nose and cheeks glowing red, making the bruise on his face stand out more than ever. 'That wind's definitely colder than it was first thing.'

'It is – the forecasters had predicted a drop in the temperature today. And apparently there's a good chance we'll have a white Christmas,' said Louisa, looking thrilled at the prospect. Her eyes met Lark's and they exchanged a happy smile.

The pair followed Louisa down to the room where they'd first shown her the suitcases, Louisa asking how Nate was doing and telling him he was looking better which seemed to please him no end. He'd been itching to get back to work, much to Lark's alarm, and she'd lost count of the number of times she'd had to tell him how important it was that he followed the advice of the doctor who'd treated him in hospital.

'Hello, you two.' Silas beamed over at Lark and Nate who returned his cheerful greeting.

'Bethany! I haven't seen you for ages!' Lark rushed over to the dark-haired, petite young woman who was standing at the table in the centre of the room, her eyes quickly glancing at Betty's suitcase that had been placed upon it, alongside a box Lark hadn't seen before.

'Hi, Lark, yes, it's been a while.' Bethany gave her a friendly smile as Lark scooped her into a fragrant hug.

Releasing Bethany from her embrace, Lark kept her hands on the other woman's shoulders, her gaze running over Bethany's features. Lark was instantly struck by the powerful vibes that were emanating from her; they were remarkably similar to the ones she'd picked up from Betty's clothes. It sent a rush of joy through her. 'You know, I'd say from the photos I've seen of her, you bear a remarkable resemblance to your great-grandmother.'

Bethany beamed, apparently thrilled with Lark's assessment. 'You're not the first person to have said that. My Grandad Roberts tells me that all the time; says I have similar mannerisms to her, too.' Hearing that came as no surprise to Lark.

'I agree, you do look like Betty,' said Louisa. 'I think it's pretty striking.'

After a brief catch-up, attention turned to the suitcase, Louisa slowly opening the lid. A gasp escaped Bethany's mouth and she clasped her hand to her chest as, between them, Lark and Louisa lifted out Betty's wedding dress.

'Oh, my goodness, it's stunning!' A tear tumbled down Bethany's cheek as she reached out to touch the delicate silk fabric. 'I can hardly believe I'm seeing it for real.'

'It's an amazing feeling, isn't it?' said Lark, absorbing Betty's upbeat presence all over again.

Bethany nodded, smiling though more tears were rolling down her cheeks. 'I'm not sure how true it is, but there's a story in the family that this dress was made from the parachute that my great-grandfather had been wearing on a secret mission to France. It's described as having played an important part in that mission. The story goes that he brought it back with him and gave it to my great-grandmother so she could make her wedding dress with silk being in short supply, and rationing making it hard to get hold of things. I'm not sure how true it all is, though.' She glanced between the four people listening to her, each wearing an intrigued expression, her eyelashes wet with her tears.

Louisa smiled kindly at Bethany, giving her arm a squeeze. 'I'd say it's an accurate description of what happened, and how lovely that we can add this information to our display.'

After showing Bethany the rest of the contents of her great-grandmother's suitcase, as well as photocopies of the newspaper reports, all attention turned to the box on the table.

'So, after our conversation, Louisa, I spoke to Grandad Roberts who gave me this. He thought you might find the contents interesting.' She pushed the box towards the curator.

Lark watched, her heart pumping with excitement, as Louisa reached inside and carefully lifted out a jewellery box, setting it down on the table and gently easing the lid open. Inside, it was filled with costume jewellery and though the items had dulled with age, they still managed to muster up a sparkle under the bright lights of the room.

'Oh wow!' said Lark, followed by a gasp from Louisa while Nate and Silas looked on with interest.

'Grandad Roberts says his mum wore this jewellery when she was singing on the stage.' After her success when she'd stepped in and come to the rescue of the event at the local dance hall, Betty had been much in demand and performed regularly not only in Micklewick Bay but other towns nearby.

'What a truly wonderful story,' said Silas.

'Aye, isn't it just?' said Nate.

'There are quite a few cuttings from local newspapers in there, too, as well as a couple of posters advertising my great-grandma's events. And there's this.' Bethany reached inside the box and shuffled amongst a collection of paper items before holding out a small square of thick paper, curled at the edges and yellowed with age.

Lark, Nate and Silas peered over at it.

'It's an invitation to your grandparents' wedding. Oh, how wonderful!' Louisa exclaimed. 'Thank you so much for sharing these beautiful treasures with us, Bethany. Please be sure to pass on our thanks to your grandfather.'

'I will.' Bethany beamed. 'And after I told him about your plans for a display for Betty, he said you could keep them. Reckons the heritage centre's the best place for them.'

'That's so very generous of him – and you.' Louisa swallowed, clearly struggling with emotion.

Lark reached over and squeezed her arm before turning to Bethany. 'Louisa's right, it is very generous. And I also agree with your grandad, the heritage centre is the best place for Betty's items. They're treasures and it's wonderful that they'll get to tell your great-grandparents' story all over again, adding even greater depth to it.'

'And not just that' – Silas glanced over at Louisa, as if seeking her approval before he continued – 'Louisa plans to incorporate audio into the biggest displays and she's asked Bethany if she'll be the narrator for Betty's story which is going to have a room dedicated to her and Ralph.'

'And I've accepted,' Bethany said happily.

Lark's throat tightened as tears gathered in the corners of her eyes. 'I can't think of anything more perfect.'

'Me neither,' said Nate, an unmistakable waver in his voice. He sniffed, dashing a tear away from his eye as Lark slid her arm around him.

FORTY-TWO
CHRISTMAS DAY

It was at least a decade since Old Micklewick had been cut off from the main part of town, but thanks to heavy snowfall that started midday on Christmas Eve and continued through the night, that's exactly what had happened on Christmas Day.

The notoriously precipitous Skitey Bank that snaked its way to the newer part of town was impassable, as was Wilbert Hill that climbed out of Old Micklewick and connected the residents to the rest of the world that way. Though not as precipitous as Skitey Bank, the hill was steep enough to make tackling it a treacherous prospect in wintry weather, as plenty of drivers had discovered to their peril.

It had given Lark an almost childlike thrill when she'd thrown open the bedroom curtains to see a snow-covered Smugglers Row glittering under the glow of the streetlights, fluffy snowflakes gently floating down. A proper white Christmas! A smile tipped up the corners of her mouth at the view of the characterful cottages opposite, with their rooftops covered in an impossibly thick layer of snow – they seemed to be huddling together as if to keep warm.

Word had spread quickly the previous evening that the cove would very likely be cut off, which had generated a flurry of excitement, not to mention activity, at Seashell Cottage.

Lark's father had been staying with her since school had broken up – interspersed with the odd overnight stay at Louisa's – and he planned to be in Micklewick Bay until the New Year when he'd need to get back for the new term. And, since his discharge from hospital, Nate – and Bobby – had spent more time at Lark's home than he had his own. She'd been looking after him, keeping a close eye on his recovery and being gently bossy when she thought he'd been doing too much or needed to rest. He was spending Christmas Day at Seashell Cottage, as was Louisa. As soon as they'd heard the alarming weather warnings, Silas had hurried over to the town in his four-wheel drive, gathered Louisa up and brought her to Old Micklewick, delivering her safely to Lark's cottage. He didn't want to risk his new friend spending the day on her own.

Leaving Nate sleeping soundly, Lark tiptoed out of the bedroom, avoiding the creaky floorboards, and padded downstairs. She could hear the now familiar sound of her dad whistling happily in the kitchen, the smell of sizzling bacon greeting her and making her stomach rumble. It had been so good having him around, watching his playful sense of humour come back to life. The transformation had continued at a pace over the last few weeks, and she was glad to see he'd gained weight, his once gaunt face filling out and the colour returning in his cheeks.

Further good news was that he'd put in an offer on a cottage there in Old Micklewick, next door to Jack Playforth and Jenna. It was Jack who'd tipped him off about it before the property had actually gone on the market. Though there was no avoiding the fact it was a renovation project, Pebble Cottage's charm and potential was obvious to Silas. He'd been particularly taken with the garden at the back, planning a new layout in his mind. He'd put in an offer straight away which had been accepted, and had set the ball rolling.

In the kitchen, Lark found her dad busy at the oven. He was being closely observed by Bobby from his bed near the radiator where he was sitting, drooling, with Luna stretched out alongside him – the pair were now inseparable, the days of her swiping at his nose a distant memory.

'Morning, Dad, merry Christmas.'

Silas turned, a smile lighting up his face. 'Merry Christmas, sweetheart.'

She headed over to him and kissed him on the cheek. He wrapped his free arm around her, his smile deepening.

'Smells *so* good,' she said.

'You can't beat a Christmas morning bacon and scrambled egg butty, especially if you'll be braving the elements to take his lordship for a walk,' he said, nodding in Bobby's direction. 'I've put the turkey in, thought we might as well get that under way, and I've peeled some potatoes which I'm currently parboiling along with the carrots and parsnips in readiness for roasting.'

'Wow! You have been busy.' She went to grab a mug from the cupboard. 'Is there anything I can do?'

'Maybe give Nate a shout; this'll be ready in a minute. As far as I'm aware, Louisa's on her way downstairs.'

'Sure.'

With breakfast out of the way, Lark and Nate bundled themselves up and headed outdoors, taking Bobby for a quick walk. The glowering clouds had given way to a blue sky, and though the sun was shining, the air was eye-wateringly cold. The snow was so deep on the way to the beach it almost reached the top of Lark's wellies. It didn't seem to dampen Bobby's spirits though, and he leapt about in a comedic fashion, making Lark and Nate howl with laughter.

But for the sound of the seagulls screeching and the waves crashing on the shore, Old Micklewick was eerily quiet, particularly without the sound of traffic rumbling by. But to Lark's mind, there was something magical about being cut off and cocooned in their own little world down there in the cove. As she and Nate walked across the snow-covered sand, hand in hand, she couldn't remember a time when she'd felt so happy and content. The strange feeling that had plagued her about Nate had vanished and been replaced by a sense of warmth and contentedness, which supported her theory that it was linked to what had happened in the tunnel at Crayke's Cottage.

And, as she'd expected, her friends had been overjoyed when she'd finally confessed that she and Nate were an item – she'd hidden her face in her hands when they'd cheered and whooped in the Jolly, her cheeks blazing hot.

As for Nate's backlog at work, which hadn't been helped by his injured arm and ribs, her father had stepped in with an offer of help, as had Bear, Max, Alex and Ed. Between them, they'd managed to get the units finished, which had got the pushy couple from Lingthorpe off his back, for which he was enormously grateful.

There'd been a bittersweet development in the situation with Bobby. Nate had received a somewhat curt text message from Cyril's son stating that his father had passed away and Bobby now belonged to Nate as they'd agreed. They'd been saddened to hear of Cyril's passing, but Lark could see that Nate was relieved to think Bobby would be staying with him. And looking at the Labrador's glossy coat and the way he gazed so adoringly at Nate, it was clear to her that Bobby was more than happy with that arrangement. He'd particularly enjoyed the attention he'd received after he'd led Lark to Nate at Crayke's Cottage, and was now often referred to as a "little hero". The dog treats that accompanied such praise were enthusiastically devoured.

In developments of a different kind, the police had called round to Seashell Cottage and informed Nate that the men he'd had the misfortune to encounter in the tunnel at Crayke's Cottage were none other than Dodgy Dick and an equally dodgy colleague by the name of Ronnie Plews. It transpired that the people Dodgy Dick and Wendy had joined at the bookshop's tearoom had overheard Lark and Florrie's conversation about the rumoured hidden chest of gold. They'd shared this with Dodgy Dick and Wendy, who'd organised the theft of the local history books at the bookshop, hoping to glean information as to its alluded whereabouts. Having cottoned on to Nate's involvement with Crayke's Cottage, they'd decided that would be the best place to start. Which was why they were there when Nate had unexpectedly turned up.

Dodgy Dick and Ronnie Plews were now in police custody for their trouble, the pair complaining bitterly that the rumours about Crayke's Cottage being cursed and bringing bad luck to people were true. But the local police force, who'd been trying to pin something on the duo for years, couldn't have disagreed more.

'I'd like to propose a toast,' said Silas, holding his glass of wine aloft as they were sitting at the table having devoured their Christmas dinner. 'To new beginnings.' He caught Louisa's eye, the pair exchanging a not-so-secret smile.

'To new beginnings,' the others chorused, clinking glasses.

Later that evening, when Lark and Nate were alone in the living room, the Christmas tree casting its festive glow around the room, while soothing Christmas music murmured in the background, Lark found herself suddenly overcome with emotion. She'd been fighting her feelings for Nate for so long, she hadn't realised how exhausting it had been. But now she was allowed to be honest with herself, she was overwhelmed by the level of happiness she felt that they were finally together.

A sob escaped her mouth, causing him to turn.

'Lark, what's up?' He tilted her face to him, concern in his eyes as he rubbed a tear from her cheek with his thumb. 'Why are you crying?'

'It's cos I'm happy.' She sniffed and gave a watery smile as more tears tumbled down her cheeks.

'You sure about that?' he asked, an amused note in his voice.

'Yes.' She nodded. 'Very.'

'And I'm happy too.' He grinned before kissing her tears away. 'This has been the best Christmas ever.'

A LETTER FROM THE AUTHOR

Huge thanks for choosing to pick up *A Snowy Seaside Christmas*. I hope you enjoyed this instalment of the Micklewick Bay series and getting to know Lark and Nate, and all their seaside friends – not forgetting Luna and Bobby! If you'd like to join other readers in hearing all about my new releases and bonus content, you can sign up for my newsletter!

www.stormpublishing.co/eliza-j-scott

We won't share your email address, and you can unsubscribe any time.

If you enjoyed this book and could spare a few moments to leave a review that would be hugely appreciated. It doesn't have to be long, just a few words would do, but for us authors it can make all the difference in encouraging a reader to discover our books for the first time. Thank you so much.

I always enjoy returning to Micklewick Bay and hunkering down to write a new book, and I was thrilled to finally be able to tell Lark's story. She's a kind and gentle soul who lives her life on an even keel, and I really enjoyed developing her relationship with Nate – if ever a couple are meant to be together it's those two! It felt great to give them their happy-ever-after, even if it had taken years for them to get there. But I suppose good things are always worth waiting for!

Lark grew up in a laidback environment – some would describe it as "hippyish" – where alternative therapies and crystal healing were considered the norm and her sixth sense was regarded as nothing out of the ordinary by her mother and grandmother. She's a person who's comfortable in her own skin and is slow to judge others. It's fair to say, if Lark doesn't like someone, it's a decision she hasn't arrived at lightly.

I also enjoyed developing the relationship Lark has with her father. They're very similar, not only personality-wise, but they also share the same core values. Indeed, Silas is where Lark gets her innate sense of what's right as well as her empathetic qualities. She also inherited his trait of being self-contained at times, not wanting to burden other people with their worries. Hopefully, Silas's stay at Seashell Cottage helped alleviate that for both of them and made them realise it's okay to open up a little more. And though they believe in trying to see the good in everyone, they both struggle to find even the tiniest grain of goodness in Dodgy Dick and his cronies, which is hardly surprising! Boy, did it feel great to knock that particular character off his perch for a while. Will he make an appearance in the next – and final – book in the Micklewick Bay series? Watch this space...

I appreciate a lot of people are sceptical about the healing power of crystals but they're something I view with an open mind and enjoyed learning about from a friend who swears by them. I have a few crystals dotted around my home – rose quartz and amethyst are favourites – as having them near gives me comfort. The same goes for aromatherapy oils in their various guises. I have a diffuser in my writing room, pumping out a variety of calming or soothing fragrances (the current one is Nourish by The White Company – it's lovely!). And I'm no stranger to a pulse point! They're not my only similarities with Lark, but I'm not going to elaborate on that for now. I'll save it for the first book in my new series with Storm: *The Secrets of Inkwell Cottage*. Let's just say, I've had a couple of experiences that have helped inspire that particular story.

KEEP IN TOUCH WITH THE AUTHOR

- facebook.com/elizajscottauthor
- instagram.com/elizajscott
- bookbub.com/authors/eliza-j-scott
- bsky.app/profile/elizajscott.bsky.social

ACKNOWLEDGMENTS

I've reached the part where I get to thank all the people who've played a part in getting *A Snowy Seaside Christmas* ready for publication day and beyond.

As ever, I'm going to start with my utterly fabulous editor, Kate Smith. I'm loving every minute of our journey through Micklewick Bay, Kate! I owe you a massive thank you for believing in my writing and for all your kindness, encouragement and words of support, and not forgetting your insightful edits that make my stories so much stronger. Thank you! Oh, and an extra thank you for deciding on the title for this book after much to-ing and fro-ing! I love what we settled on!

Next up, big thanks go to the captain of the Storm Publishing ship, Oliver Rhodes, for setting up such a wonderful publishing house and gathering together a crew of the kindest people. Storm's tech wizard, Chris Lucraft, deserves a mention for all he's done in getting my books into the hands of readers – as well as all the other behind-the-scenes work he does that my non-techie brain doesn't understand. Thank you, Chris! I must also mention Alexandra Begley for her continued patience and skill in preparing this book for publication day, ably assisted by Naomi Knox and the newest member of the Storm editorial operations team, Maheen Mehmood. Thank you all so much! Many thanks also to head of marketing, Elke Desanghere, for her wonderful marketing campaigns, and to publicity manager, Anna McKerrow, for her fab posts on social media. Copyeditor Shirly Khan and proofreader Amanda Raybould also need a mention for their eagle eyes and giving this book the final polish before it gets into the hands of readers. Book cover designer extraordinaire, Rose Cooper, gets a huge thank you for yet another stunning Micklewick Bay cover.

Rachel of Rachel's Random Resources gets a huge thank you for setting up yet another amazing blog tour for one of my books. I know I've mentioned this before, but I'm in complete awe of Rachel's organisational skills. Rachel was juggling a whole host of things while I was booking this blog tour, but still managed to get everything done calmly. And while we're on the subject of blog tours, many thanks also to the awesome book bloggers who signed up for yet another blog tour. It's always a treat so see so many familiar names as well as those that are new.

I also owe a mahoosive thank you to my fabulous friends, Jessica Redland and Sharon Booth, for their continued support and kindness. Writing can be a solitary occupation, which I don't mind too much as I'm generally content to be in my own company, but Jessica and Sharon definitely make the job less isolating and I always look forward to our catchups over cheese scones, tea (for me) and cake.

I must mention two Facebook groups I'm so happy to be a member of. The Friendly Book Community and Riveting Reads and Vintage Finds are two places filled with kindness and friendly fellow bookworms. I might not post there much, but I always enjoy popping by. Thank you so much, Sarah Kingsnorth and Sue Baker – and all the wonderful admins – for all you do in running these wonderful groups.

As ever, I'm indebted to my family for their unwavering support and cups of tea – I know I say it every time, but if you knew just how *many* cups of Yorkshire Tea it takes for me to write a book, you'd understand why I owe them such a debt of gratitude! I haven't quite reached the stage where I slosh when I walk, but I fear it's not far off! And I've stopped keeping count of how many ginger biscuits have met their end being dunked in one of the afore-mentioned cups of tea, but it's a *lot*!

My final – but by no means least – thank you goes to you, the reader. I can't put into words how grateful and humbled I am that you've chosen to pick up my book and read it. Thank you from the bottom of my heart.

Until next time...

Much love,

Eliza xxx

www.ingramcontent.com/pod-product-compliance
Lightning Source LLC
LaVergne TN
LVHW031537060526
838200LV00056B/4537